THE CHOSEN ONE

Praise for
Black Girl Unlimited:
The Remarkable Story of a Teenage Wizard

A William C. Morris Award Finalist
An *SLJ* Best Book of the Year
A NYPL Best Book of the Year
Rise: A Feminist Book Project List Selection
A YALSA Best Fiction for Young Adults Selection
A BCCB Blue Ribbon Title
A Bank Street College of Education Best Book of the Year

★ "With the nods to Langston Hughes, Maya Angelou, Malcolm X, and Alice Walker.... This revelatory YA book deserves space on shelves for its healing power for all readers to break the chains of intergenerational pain and trauma."
—*SLJ*, starred review

"A guidebook of survival and wonder."
—*The New York Times*

"Just brilliant."   —*Kirkus Reviews*

"This story marks the arrival of a bold new literary imagination."   —*Esquire*

"This is a story of Black girl magic, trauma and healing, learning to save oneself, connection and forgiveness, and given and chosen family."   —*Book Riot*

ECHO BROWN

THE CHOSEN ONE

A First-Generation
Ivy League Odyssey

Christy Ottaviano Books

LITTLE, BROWN AND COMPANY
New York Boston

Christy Ottaviano Books
Hachette Book Group
1290 Avenue of the Americas, New York, NY 10104
Visit us at LBYR.com

First Edition: January 2022

Christy Ottaviano Books is an imprint of Little, Brown and Company. The Christy Ottaviano Books name and logo are trademarks of Hachette Book Group, Inc.

The publisher is not responsible for websites (or their content) that are not owned by the publisher.

Library of Congress Cataloging-in-Publication Data
Names: Brown, Echo, author.
Title: The chosen one : a first-generation odyssey / Echo Brown.
Description: First edition. | New York : Little, Brown and Company, 2022. | Audience: Ages 14 & up. | Summary: "A YA coming-of-age novel about a first-year, first-generation Black student at Dartmouth College"— Provided by publisher.
Identifiers: LCCN 2021010558 | ISBN 9780316310666 (hardcover) | ISBN 9780316310833 (ebook)
Subjects: LCSH: African Americans—Juvenile fiction. | CYAC: African Americans—Fiction. | Universities and colleges—Fiction.
Classification: LCC PZ7.1.B794 Ch 2022 | DDC [Fic]—dc23
LC record available at https://lccn.loc.gov/2021010558

ISBNs: 978-0-316-31066-6 (hardcover),
978-0-316-31083-3 (ebook)

Printed in the United States of America

LSC-C

Printing 1, 2021

For the Jedi of Chosen Ones

*And the day came when the
risk to remain tight in a bud
was more painful than the
risk it took to blossom.*

———————◆◆———————

—ANAÏS NIN

PART I

The Joker

He rises from a horizon of chaos. An eternal conflicting force disrupting the balance of things. The God of Opposition, a cosmic Darth Vader dressed as a clown to prevent you from seeing the true darkness of his antics. A trickster—look at the wicked smile on his face—mocking, unsettling. He knows. He thrives off disorienting the living. His purpose is to destroy from the inside out until pain rolls down like water.

He's the ultimate test for Luke and the Jedi of Chosen Ones. He wants to know what their souls are made of, to test whether they have the strength to answer the call, survive his madness, and complete the mission.

CHAPTER ONE

Someone is watching me. It's not my mother's Jesus, who hangs in blissful peace above the desk in my dorm room, or my roommate, Amanda, aka Mandy, aka Manda Panda, which her closest friends have painfully named her. There are many watchers and they are always white. My mother warned me about "lookin' ass white people" that follow you in stores and stare at you on the sidewalk when you're in the wrong neighborhood, attempting to control your entire existence with their eyes. I've learned from *Children of the Corn, The Hills Have Eyes*, and Jason Voorhees from the *Friday the 13th* movies that white people are always watching, especially when they are about to kill you. I don't think anyone's trying to murder me, but I am concerned.

Dartmouth has more white people than I've ever seen in my life. Sometimes I just walk around campus marveling at how many there are. Prior to being here, I thought most of the world was Black, like my neighborhood in Cleveland. I was wrong. *The real world is white and they are all watching me.* Dean Harrison, the dean for first-year students, who also happens to be Black and talks in riddles and quotes, says everything happens for a reason, but she wasn't in math class with me last week when I caught a group of students blatantly *staring* at me. The only possible reason for that is intimidation.

I am sitting in class looking down at the blank piece of paper in front of me, pretending to study, but I'm really doodling, which I regularly do in this class since I never know what Professor Cartwright is talking about. Math is a foreign language. Even though I can speak and comprehend a few phrases, I am nowhere near fluent. I feel so stupid in this class. The stupidest. Professor Cartwright is world-renowned, yet he is a terrible teacher. He lectures like he is bored or can't be bothered with the words coming out of his mouth. His "simplified" explanations are always complicated and confusing. What's the point of all that brilliance if you can't transmit anything to others?

Instead of listening, I draw long curvy lines across the length of the page. On this particular day, I am doodling cheerfully when I feel the familiar chill of watching eyes. I glance up at the clock and notice a group of classmates to my right staring. Their hands are folded on the table in front of them. Their eyes, piercing and calm, land decisively on me. They don't blink. I look around the room to see if anyone else notices, but everyone is focused on Professor Cartwright. I turn back toward them and shrug my head aggressively in frustration, at which point they look away one by one. I feel like I'm in the Twilight Zone. I wonder if this is a bullying tactic against students of color? A way to make us feel unwelcome and out of place? I heard about stuff like that happening from juniors and seniors, but I'm not going to stand for it.

Class ends. I stomp over to the culprits and confront them. "Your intimidation won't work on me," I say, inflamed.

"What are you talking about? I don't even know you," a long-blond-haired girl responds. They each shuffle out of the room confusedly, whispering among themselves. The resoluteness of her response makes me question myself. Maybe they *were* looking at something else in my direction. Regardless, it's strange that they would all be staring at the same time.

A week later, I'm still bothered. I grab a large bag of Lays potato chips from the secret stash at the bottom of my closet while replaying the incident in my mind. I hope they aren't all sitting together again today, which makes their group staring more terrifying. I open the chips, inhaling the salty goodness, then, like a character on a soap opera, I emerge from my dorm room, fake smiling for the imaginary camera. I pose dramatically in the doorway before beginning my walk to math class. I take the long route to delay the inevitable.

"The Young, Black, and Restless at Dartmouth College," I say, giggling. I've learned to entertain myself here in the backwoods of New Hampshire. I stop in front of Baker Tower, which is attached to the main library and is prominently featured in all the new student material.

Those brochures made many promises they could not keep. The biggest one being an abundance of rainbow-colored minority students, who are actually very hard to find on campus. We are few and far between, and there definitely was no mention of threatening watchers who intimidate with their eyes. But the white clock tower, stacked on manicured red bricks—a staple of Ivy League architecture—has remained true to its collegiate mythology and is even more stunning in person. I imagined what it would be like to stand before this tower for months, despite my high school guidance counselor Mr. Walsh's repeated attempts to dissuade me from attending a top ten school. I still remember sitting in his office senior year reading the posters on the wall.

"IF YOU BELIEVE IT, YOU CAN ACHIEVE IT."

"REACH FOR THE STARS."

"NO DREAM IS TOO BIG."

"Why Dartmouth?" he asks.

"It looks nice in the brochure."

"Well, you know, you really shouldn't choose colleges based on the pictures in the brochure."

He reaches into his desk drawer and pulls out several pamphlets: Ohio State, Kenyon College, and Oberlin College. "All great schools. All local. Perhaps you should consider one of these. I would hate for you to . . ."

He hesitates. I know what the silence

◆

between Professor Cartwright's words mean. "Well, this really isn't a good way to start the semester," he continues. He hands me the paper, which has a large red F circled at the top. "I mean, these quizzes won't be a big percentage of your grade, but . . . I don't want you to fall further behind. Why don't you stop by the student center and get a tutor? This kind of math is complex. You really needed to start establishing a solid mathematical foundation in high school, which I bet you didn't. Real shame so many come here unprepared for the vigor of academic life." He assumes he knows my story, subtly suggesting I'm not capable given my background. I thought getting into Dartmouth was enough to escape low expectations, but he builds another cage of limitation around me. As if the one Mr. Walsh built wasn't enough

◆

to make me rethink my entire path in life. "Take some time to mull it over," Mr. Walsh continues. "I want you to be realistic and clear about the odds. That's my only goal." I stare up at the posters on his wall again and then back at him, trying to mend the gap. Why did he bother hanging them at all?

7

"Fools," I say while continuing to take in the beauty of the clock tower and munch my chips. "How dare they try and dash the dreams of a savant"—a word I recently learned in Comp Lit—"from the inner city. We are already a rare and endangered species." *I'll show Professor Cartwright*, I say to myself triumphantly before shaking my head in disgust. I often engage in deep conversations with this tower, which briefly makes me feel like I belong here, even though I don't really feel that way inside and the watching doesn't help. I hilariously name the tower Matthew McConaughey to further amuse myself and distract from the deep discomfort churning in my core. I chose the whitest and cutest actor I could think of to channel the experience of being on a mostly white campus. I'm trying not to focus so much on race, but it's hard when I feel so Black and out of place.

"You know what?" I ask Matthew defiantly. "I'm gonna ace all my classes, confront them both, and fling my transcript in their faces. I can't wait to watch their shocked reactions." I speak passionately, convincingly, but deep down I wonder if Professor Cartwright and Mr. Walsh are right. It's still early in the semester, but I'm also struggling in other classes. "Crap," I say, careening backward down a rabbit hole of self-pity. Will I be among the thirty percent of first-generation college students who flunk out? Why are the voices of the naysayers always the loudest? Why do I never feel good enough no matter how much I achieve? I sulk as students scurry to class all around me, unconcerned about my growing self-doubt and probably consumed by their own.

What the hell am I doing? This place is going to eat me alive. I concede my defeat. Then, Hark! The Defiance emerges. I knew they would come. They always show up when I doubt myself or am about to make a bad decision. They are my inner voice manifested as dramatic one-dimensional characters, reminding me of my own greatness. They are called the Defiance because they oppose all the negative messaging that has been programmed into my mind. Every Black girl needs a team of inner cheerleaders who can lift her spirits when the world tries to come for her.

There are three of them: Shaquanda, who wears dark blond wigs and looks like Lil' Kim; Damon, who is bald and wears glasses and blue jean overalls with tan Timberland boots; and Terrell, who is suave and cool and sounds like the fourth member of Boyz II Men who talks but doesn't sing. Shaquanda always punctuates her statements with "bitch" and claps when she speaks, for emphasis. Sometimes she claps so hard her electric-pink press-on nails come flying off. Damon usually pulls out a microphone as if he is about to give a speech to a large audience and finishes all his sentences with "you feel me." Terrell sounds like a Black preacher with his deep baritone voice and his constant "hah" between words.

When they finally reach me, I tell Matthew to prepare for a show. They form a circle around me and all speak at once, their voices a chorus of validation: *Do you know who the hell you are, bitch?!—You da best dat ever did it! Don't let small minds dim ya light, you feel me? Mr. Walsh and Professor Cartwright cannot see you. How dey gon' know what you capable of, you feel me? Bitch, you ain't neva met an obstacle you couldn't overcome. Fuck da bullshit! Yo mother's God, hah, is sittin' right over dere on dat big-ass mountain, hah, waitin' to pounce on dese hatin' nonbelievers, hah. You gon' win, my nigga, you feel me? All we do is win, bitch, despite the challenges. Keep ya head up, ma.*

I cheer quietly to myself, but loud enough for others in my immediate vicinity to hear, while pumping my fists. "That's right! I'm gon' win! They don't know me. Who gon' stop me, haah?!"

I continue hyping myself up with the Defiance until I hear someone behind me interrupt, "What in the Boyz-N-Da-Hood is going on here? Have you forgotten where you are, Negro Brown? Talking to yourself like that in the middle of this snow-white campus? Now I've seen it all." I know who it is, but I don't turn around. Instead, I roll my eyes and take a deep breath in preparation for dealing with the force of life that is Earnell Jackson. When I finally find the strength to face him, I see that he's with Kelicia, Keli for short, another close friend. Earnell is a "loud, animated negro" (we playfully call each other *negroes* to remember our roots) from Atlanta, and Keli is a short, brown-skinned negro from Chicago. We all have similar backgrounds: poor and the first in their family to go to college. We met during first-year orientation. The entire incoming class can probably recognize Earnell's outrageous laugh, which rang out boisterously across the auditorium as various speakers told jokes while welcoming us. Numerous heads around the room pivoted angrily in our direction—watching—while Earnell unapologetically waved as if he were the president driving down Pennsylvania Avenue on Inauguration Day.

Earnell's lively spirit is infectious. Keli has more of a brooding nature, similar to mine, but Earnell is always positive, upbeat, and outgoing despite the many obstacles in front of us. If you didn't know him well you might never be able to tell that he comes from such impoverished and bleak conditions. Keli, Earnell, and I were all-stars in high school but are struggling to catch up here at Dartmouth. Earnell and I were both valedictorians and Keli was third in her class, which Earnell relentlessly teases her about. "We can't all be number one," he says, after out-arguing her over something unimportant.

Our high school ranks don't matter here, however. Now all of our classes are "introductory preparation" courses, which is just a fancy term for remedial. We are competing against students who come from schools with unlimited resources. Catching up is not easy. I'm taking Introductory Calculus, Comprehensive Literature (Comp Lit), Sociology, and American Government as well as a History of Film class.

"I call them the dream team," Earnell says about the roster of tutors and study groups he uses. "Helping negroes advance since America decided nothing will ever be truly just and equal. I'm not ashamed in the least and you shouldn't be either. The system that failed us created this situation. Do you really think we'd be behind if we had grown up next door to Becky and Ken?" Earnell shakes his head in disapproval. "I think you should call Baker Tower Jim Crow instead of Matthew McConaughey. It's a better fit," he says. Earnell's focus on race is next level. He is deeply suspicious of white people after having grown up in a racist town in the South and he lets it be known now that he's in the "free North."

"And another thing," Earnell continues, "I really think you should liberate yourself from the toxic myth of minority exceptionalism. We are only an endangered species, as you say, because of extraordinary oppression. Not because there aren't literally thousands of people just like us out there in the trenches unable to excel due to systematic obstacles. Sorry to break it to you, but you ain't that special, dear, and you shouldn't turn away from all the resources at our disposal here. It's foolish."

Earnell doesn't want to see me fail, so he is always hard on me. He and Keli are less stubborn about asking for help. Maybe they don't have a Mr. Walsh they are trying to prove wrong. Maybe their egos aren't easily bruised like mine. I don't know why, but they see our predicaments much differently than me. I'm too embarrassed to get a tutor, but Earnell and Keli have completely thrown the lid off the "do it yourself" mentality that got us here, while my pride keeps me suffering in isolation.

"Earnell's a straight-up fool," Keli says, "but he's right. This shit is not a game. I'm headed to meet my tutor now. Tryin' to get these grades locked down. We're not in Compton anymore. You can't soar here without *their* help."

"But you're from Chicago," Earnell interjects. "And we're"—pointing dramatically to him and me—"not from Cali either so do better with your idioms. Again, we can't all be—"

"Shut up, fool," Keli responds. "You know what I meant. I gotta run. I'll catch y'all on the flipside." Keli sprints off, leaving me to reconsider my entire approach since I'm definitely not soaring in Matthew McConaughey's paradise.

"Don't look now," Earnell says, suddenly stiffening and blocking me with his body, "but that Christian white boy you like is walking this way. Alert, alert. Nazarene is approaching." The good thing about a small campus is that if you stand in the middle long enough, you'll run into everyone you know. My body freezes as Bryson Parker, a junior I met during orientation week, walks toward us. Bryce, which is what everyone calls him, is a tall, soft-spoken, curly-haired white boy with the jawline of a superhero. He's so good-looking, I can barely meet his eyes for more than a few seconds. He's devoutly Christian, regularly attending the Servants for Jesus prayer group, and he also participates in some of the diversity programs the college offers. "Sooner or later, he's going to figure out you're actually a pagan and leave you by the side of the road with the rest of us sinners," Earnell whispers into my ear just as Bryce joins us.

"Do you know when it was built?" Bryce asks, referring to Matthew. Earnell rolls his eyes and I respond, "No clue."

Bryce smiles with the radiance of a thousand suns. "Me neither. I just know it was before 1928 since that's when it opened. Pretty cool, huh?"

"What's cool about that?" Earnell snarks.

"This is my friend Earnell," I say, before he has a chance to further interrogate Bryce.

"I've heard a lot about you," Bryce says enthusiastically while extending his hand.

"Super rad to finally meet you." Earnell stares at Bryce's hand for several seconds until I smack him on the shoulder. He reluctantly reaches his arm forward and simply responds "hmph" while sizing him up and awkwardly shaking his hand.

"So *this* is—"

"The guy that does diversity stuff," I say, cutting off Earnell before he has a chance to do more damage.

"Hmph," Earnell says again, unimpressed. "Can you explain to me your interest in helping negroes and other people of color? Now that's something I'm very curious about." I choke on my potato chips. Bryce chokes on air.

"I know," Earnell continues woefully, "the tension is thick when the descendants of slaves and slave owners have difficult conversations in liberal bastions of freedom such as this." He spins around like Mary Poppins. "Well, guess I better get going. Don't want to be late for class."

Bryce and I watch as Earnell sprints off, leaving us to

climb the mountain of discomfort he has erected. *Just like Earnell to stir the pot and then book it.* I shake my head in shame.

"He—" I start, unable to finish.

"I—" Bryce begins, also unable to find more words.

"Are you going to see the hypnotist tonight?" Bryce asks after several seconds of silence.

"No, I'm not interested in mind games."

"It's actually really amazing. And trust me, you won't ever forget seeing some of your peers doing absolutely ridiculous things. One of my friends, Connor Raskins, got hypnotized our freshman year and will still cluck like a chicken if you clap your hands quickly three times. Hypnotist Jerry has been coming for fifteen years and it's always an amazing show."

When I don't respond, Bryce playfully nudges me with his elbow. His gentle touch, however slight, awakens something in me and now I'm the one smiling with the radiance of a thousand suns.

"OK," I reply finally. "I'll go. What time are you getting there?"

" 'Round seven," he says. "Cool. It's a date."

CHAPTER TWO

But it's not actually a date. Bryce shows up with three friends, two men and one woman. All white. I can't believe I'm stuck with him and three of his descendent-from-slave-owner (probably) friends. I find it interesting that Bryce participates in so many diversity initiatives, but I only ever see him with other white people in settings outside of the program. I want to ask him about it, but I don't want to embarrass him like Earnell did earlier. It's a bit strange and hypocritical, but otherwise Bryce is perfect.

"Hi, I'm Connor," one of Bryce's friends says, stepping forward to introduce himself. "I run a lot of the first-year hiking trips. Bryce's told me a little about you. Nice to finally put a face to the name. I actually think you might be on one of my upcoming trips. Unless there's another first-year named Echo. That'd be hilarious," he says while laughing to himself.

I channel Earnell for a brief moment: "Why would that be funny?"

Before he has a chance to answer, one of Bryce's other friends suddenly claps three times and Connor starts clucking like a chicken.

"Damnit, Brad!" Connor exclaims angrily. "Cut it out!" Connor turns to me and says, "That's why I'm here. To get Hypnotist Jerry to reverse this. I was on a trip last year when he came, but I'm gonna corner him and force him to un-hypnotize me."

"And I'm gonna convince him not to," Brad says while playfully rubbing the top of Connor's head with his fists. Connor wiggles away while shouting, "I told you to stop doing that, man. My scalp is super fragile since part of my skull is inverted. And you know that. This isn't kindergarten."

"It isn't?" Brad snarks dismissively before clapping again, which prompts Connor to start clucking once more. "Damnit, dude!" Connor yells before charging Brad, who is buckled over in laughter. They wrestle until Bryce pulls them apart.

These are not the kind of friends I imagined Bryce would have. Connor is a tall, lanky, brown-haired boy with such a goofy demeanor, it's hard to take anything he says seriously. Brad is a beefy blond jock who looks like he eats protein bars for breakfast and chugs beer in dingy frat basements on the weekends. I wonder if Bryce's third friend is his girlfriend.

"Hi, I'm Jess," she says softly when introducing herself. "Don't mind them. They're always like that." She's also blond and wears glasses. When we finally walk into the venue, she playfully pats Bryce on the back, as if he belongs to her. Maybe he does. I sink at the thought of it, sulking as I search for a seat.

"What's wrong?" Bryce asks. "You seem down all of a sudden. I know my friends are a bit much, but they're really good people. Do you want anything? A snack or something to drink?" Bryce's compassion lifts my malaise. I want to lose myself in his stunning light green eyes. I've never met someone as nice as him. *A kiss* is what I want to say, but I just smile and shake my head no. He rubs my back softly, like Jess did earlier, and I wonder if white people just walk around gently patting each other on the back. If that's a thing they all do? No one ever touched me on the back in Cleveland and I definitely don't do that with my friends here, most of whom are Black. It's a mystery I'll have to unravel later.

The lights dim and a hush crawls over the audience. A man in a white lab coat walks onto the stage. I guess this must be Hypnotist Jerry.

"For centuries, we have been trying to understand the human mind," he begins speaking. "Tonight, you will witness its marvels. Remember, no one can hypnotize you if you reject it. Hypnotization is really about surrendering. So decide now if you are ready to let go." He flings his arms dramatically above his head as he says this and looks out into the audience without speaking for at least a minute. A long, drawn-out, awkward minute. People begin to shift nervously in their seats under the weight of his intimidating stares. I remain perfectly calm, however, as I'm starting to get used to white people and their watching. I smirk knowingly while everyone else shutters.

Hypnotist Jerry starts randomly pointing to people in the crowd and beckons them to the stage. He scans the audience with his finger, peering intensely beneath his furrowed brow, before stopping on an unsuspecting victim and motioning for them to join him. I am surprised at how willing everyone has been so far, bouncing up out of their chairs and running eagerly in his direction. *Maybe he has already started his hypnotizing,* I think to myself.

"I need one more participant," he says. "A special someone." I settle comfortably in my seat, determined for it not to be me. I watch his finger slowly move toward us and I grow uneasy. His arm continues its journey across the auditorium, landing decisively in the middle of my forehead. Connor juts in front of me, wildly raising his hand trying to get Hypnotist Jerry's attention, but he adjusts his finger so it is on me again. I move my head to the left and right several times, which doesn't stop Hypnotist Jerry from following me. He doesn't speak. He just points and stares.

"It's you," Bryce whispers in my ear. "You're the one he wants. He won't give up. Just go up there. Promise it will be fun."

I begrudgingly drag myself up to the stage. Once we are all standing next to Hypnotist Jerry, he begins speaking to the audience as if we aren't there.

"Who you are is evident in everything you do. The way you walk and talk. How you respond to life's challenges.

Few of us know how to access the treasures buried inside. We are strangers unto ourselves, blind to the truth of what we came here to do. What a shame." He shakes his head in disappointment. "Tonight is about digging deep...Let us begin, then."

Hypnotist Jerry turns his attention back to us, the scapegoats he has volunteered to be hypnotized in front of a live audience. "One of you used to love to dance. You imitated performers you saw on TV, especially Selena. She was your favorite. You were always moving until your eighth-grade dance teacher said you lacked grace and that 'no company would hire you.' She couldn't see what I see. When I snap my fingers, you will show us your seven-year-old dance routine. They," he says, pointing to the audience, "shall call you the Dancer, honoring your true purpose."

The audience begins to clap and chant, "Dancer! Dancer!" Hypnotist Jerry snaps and Gina, the short, dark-haired Latina woman standing next to me, begins dancing innocently like a child. Her movements are simple, sweet, and slightly uncoordinated, like she's just learning what it's like to have a body. "Yes," Hypnotist Jerry growls, "that's it. Dance for us! Remember why you came." Gina's dancing matures right before our eyes. Her choreography becomes sharper and more complex, until it looks like she has been dancing professionally all her life. She spins, pirouettes, and even lands a backflip. Everyone in the room erupts into applause. I am stunned. Gina takes a bow as Hypnotist Jerry moves on to the next person, whom I pray is not me.

"One of you," he continues, "wants to find a buried treasure. You've gone several times to Carson City, Nevada, with your uncle to search for missing gold. You dreamed of being an archaeologist until your father told you to pursue a 'real' career. Look down in front of you, Billy. History awaits. Your rightful path unfolds before you! Dig for your life and they shall call you the Explorer!"

The audience claps and shouts, "Ex-plo-rer!" as Billy, who is standing the closest to Hypnotist Jerry, begins feverishly digging through a box of sand in front of him. "I think I got something. Look!" he shouts. "Holy shit! Ancient bones...and...and...gold. So much gold!" Billy lifts the sand with closed fists, afraid to drop his precious booty.

"Now don't be greedy, Billy. Share your gold!" Billy begins picking actual gold coins from the sandbox and throwing them into the audience. I am astonished. This can't be happening. I want to run over and claw away as much of the gold as I can for myself, but I manage to stay calm in front of all these spectators. A million thoughts begin running through my head: *How much is gold worth? Where can you sell it? How much is in there? Will there be some left when we finish?* Frustration at missing out on all that treasure grows as I watch the audience scramble to grab the coins Billy is throwing. I stare at them with envy until I notice people peeling away gold wrappers, revealing chocolate underneath. I breathe a sigh of greedy relief.

Hypnotist Jerry snaps his fingers and Billy stops

digging. He stands, baffled, and looks out at the crowd, while everyone claps and eats chocolate in glee.

"The greatest show on Earth," Jerry proclaims while flinging his arms above his head again to receive the applause ringing around the room. He makes a sweeping motion with his hands and everyone stops clapping at the same time, as if on cue. I am terrified that I will be next and try to will my body to walk off the stage, but my legs won't move. I try to scream instead, to beg Bryce and his friends to come rescue me, but my mouth won't open. *What kind of sorcery is this?* I wonder fearfully to myself. *And what is he going to do to me?*

"Next," the showman continues. "We have the one who wanted to leave the planet altogether and investigate outer space, but decided on law instead to make Mommy and Daddy happy. You're not a lawyer!" Hypnotist Jerry yells with impassioned, performative rage. "You're the astronaut! Charles, are you ready for liftoff?" Charles shakes his head enthusiastically. "Well then, strap in, sonny boy!"

Hypnotist Jerry pretends to be talking on a walkie-talkie. "*Saturn V AS-506*, this is *Apollo 11* and we're ready for launch. Here we go...three, two, one. Blastoff!" Charles braces himself as if he's on an actual space shuttle. He grips imaginary straps while shaking from side to side as the audience cheers, "As-tro-naut!"

"Whoa!" he says after several seconds. "It's beautiful up here."

"That's right," Hypnotist Jerry responds. He turns to the

audience with fake curiosity and asks, "Is someone approaching? Is someone coming?" Jerry's back is toward me, Charles, and the other participants. He directs his energy into the side audience, even though he is talking to Charles.

"They're almost here!" Charles cries out in astonishment. "They're coming for you!" I am shocked as Charles points at me, but I still can't get my body to move. "They will help you defeat Darth and his army of wicked creatures."

"Who?!" Hypnotist Jerry demands. "Who's coming?!"

"The Keepers." As soon as Charles says this, he collapses onto the stage. Billy and Gina follow suit and everyone in the audience freezes. Their bodies are stiff, but the sound of their cheers and clapping somehow continues to echo. The cloud of noise rises like mist over a bay while the spectators remain unmoving in their seats as some unseen presence laughs maniacally. I am confused and disoriented. I can't make sense of it.

"Do you know who you are?" Hypnotist Jerry asks from his still-turned position. I can't see his face or mouth, but his words land on me like smart missiles programmed to find their target. "Do you know what they will call you?" he continues, whipping his head in my direction. He hurries across the stage, stopping right in front of me. His eyes are moving, spinning counterclockwise. They are portals to another dimension. I am transfixed. I feel as if I am being swallowed by a force much bigger than me. A deep peace descends and I stop trying to understand. I accept the power he has over me.

"They will call you," he whispers in a barely audible voice before shouting into the auditorium of unmoving people, "the Chosen One!"

The cloud of sound shatters and the audience of frozen people erupts, jumping up in delight. Gina, Charles, and Billy return to their feet. Hypnotist Jerry stands with his arms extended at his sides, receiving the raucous applause. He blows kisses. He theatrically places his hand over his heart and says, "No, you're too kind." The audience is relentless in their praise.

"Cho-sen One!" they chant as the lights finally dim, bringing the thrilling, unbelievable performance to a close.

CHAPTER THREE

Another portal—iridescent and mesmerizing—appears in my dorm room the night of the show. It spins counterclockwise on the wall next to my desk, just like Hypnotist Jerry's eyes. I stand in front of it staring for an hour—maybe longer—until a faint image begins to materialize: me, throwing up on a dinner table while everyone watches in shock. Red wine that looks like blood runs down the sides of the table. Bright flashes light up the sky outside the windows.

I don't know what it means. I squint my eyes, trying to see more clearly, but when I hear my roommate's keys jingling outside the door, I quickly hang my mother's Jesus, which she gave to me before I left home, over the portal and try to look normal. When I realize it's my neighbor going into the room next door, I exhale with relief. I grab Manda Panda's Polaroid camera from the bottom of her closet and snap a picture of the portal. After the picture develops, only the blank wall appears. *How is this happening?* I take another picture. Still no portal, but this time I see the word "He." Not on the wall, but in the fibers of the picture, as if someone took their finger and smeared the ink.

"This is nuts," I say out loud to no one. "Is this some hypnotic poltergeist?" I take more pictures. Four additional words emerge before the camera begins shooting blanks again. I arrange and rearrange the pictures until a coherent sentence is formed: "He Rises, Brace for Impact." I'm trying to figure out what it means when I hear Manda Panda's keys, for real this time. I quickly return her camera, toss the pictures in my drawer, and hang my mother's Jesus back over the portal. I shriek when the door swings open, hitting the wall. Manda Panda comes prancing in, as usual, like the whole world is her stage. I, on the other hand, tiptoe everywhere like an uninvited houseguest.

"What are you doing?" she says. "Why are you standing there awkwardly like Pennywise the clown or something?"

"No reason," I say unconvincingly, afraid to move and praying the picture of Jesus does not fall off the wall.

"I swear, you're so stiff, girl," she says. "You need to learn how to relax. College is meant to be fun. All you do is study and lurk around. Look, I got this bottle of Tanqueray for the weekend." She smiles wickedly and shakes the alcohol enticingly in front of me. "Snoop Dogg's 'Gin and Juice.' 'I got my mind on my money and my money on my mind.' God, he's so hard-core. A bunch of us are gonna hang out at Trevor's place on Saturday. You can totally join

26

if you want." I smile unenthusiastically and watch as she throws a few items in her bookbag before prancing back out of the room. "Smoocha later. K, byeee." It's late so I have no idea where she's going, but she comes and goes so frequently, I'm used to her disappearing.

I stare blankly at the ceiling for several seconds trying to process the night's events: the frozen people, the disconnecting sound cloud, the demonic laughter, Hypnotist Jerry's spinning eyes, the Polaroids, and the portal to another dimension oozing out of my wall.

"I don't know what the heck is going on here," I say to myself, "but I'm going to get to the bottom of it."

Affinity Week—the quintessential first-semester college extravaganza showcasing various clubs, frats, sororities, and shared-interest housing—arrives with a blast of unusually cold arctic air. It's twenty below the normal fifty-five degrees it should be this time of year. Seniors have noted the strange weather patterns since summer ended. Lightning storms, violent winds, and sideways rain.

"It's the Gods of White Supremacy punishing the college for admitting the most 'diverse' class in the school's history," Earnell says sarcastically. "Calm your fury, Zeus. We'll be gone soon enough," he purrs, nostalgic for a future that hasn't happened yet.

Now it's the last week of September, but already feels

like December. The week starts with a bang of controversy. First, the Party for Reparations—a political activist group made up of students from different racial backgrounds that tries to raise awareness about why Black people deserve restitution from the United States government—sponsors a pop-up slave play in the cafeteria. Every single person in Collis Cafe watches in stunned awe as Black students pick cotton balls off the floor while wearing dingy cloth attire and gloomily singing "Wade in the Water," as several white overseers stand by with long black whips. *Actual whips.* When one student accidentally drops her basket, spilling her day's harvest on the floor, one of the white masters walks over and says, "We cain't have these kind'a mistakes, Carol Ann. You know what comes next. Assume the position!"

The woman begs on her knees, "Please, Massa! I's sorry! I promise I won't do it again!" Massa spins Carol Ann around and pretends to whip her as the other "slaves" shriek dramatically in fear. Carol Ann screams with such pain you'd think she was actually being hit. Her cries are deeply disturbing and make me wonder how the ancestors survived it.

After the whipping, Carol Ann gets up and addresses the shocked crowd of onlookers. "What if your ancestors were treated like this for centuries? Would you think they deserved some kind of penance? At least an apology? The United States government should pay for its evil sins." She returns to her knees, back in scene, and screams at the top of her lungs, "No more, Massa! No more!"

When the play finishes, all of the actors stand and bow to a totally quiet and unmoving audience, which is definitely not a Hypnotist Jerry illusion. We look at each other with wide, blinking eyes as the entire scene disbands. "Welcome to college," says someone standing next to me who must know I'm a freshman. "One antic after another for four years straight," he concludes before walking away in disgust.

The slave play is followed by a Mexican-themed frat party where several white people paint their skin brown, wear sombreros, and drink margaritas. Salsa music rings out as drunk people shout random phrases with offensive mock accents, none of which have anything to do with Mexican culture: "Arrivederci!" "Say hello to my little friend!" "Show me the money, Carlos!"

The college administration suspends the frat for several months, barring it from holding any social gatherings at the risk of being permanently closed. The *Dartmouth Beacon*, the most conservative newspaper on campus, writes a scathing editorial asking why the Party for Reparations, "whose egregious slave play, which was equally shameful and appalling, didn't receive the same punishment." The op-ed was published three days ago. College officials are yet to respond. If and when they do, I will be sure to grab a bag of popcorn to watch the Racism Olympics unfold.

I didn't expect Dartmouth to be so racially charged, but everywhere I turn, there seems to be another hot-button debate or event bubbling to the surface. Affirmative action, which is being contested around the nation, seems to be the most divisive issue of all. I've watched people's eyes bulge with rage, their tongues spewing impassioned, angry arguments for why "anything other than a merit-based system is cruel and unfair." I wonder if the people now arguing for blind admissions, absent racial considerations, would have wanted the same thing when the government was enacting Jim Crow laws or when it was giving advantages to only white soldiers returning from war in the GI Bill. Did they argue for a merit-based system then? *The hypocrisy of it all.*

No one is more obstinately against affirmative action than Stephen Clark, whose squirmy face I can barely stand to look at whenever he opens his mouth. Every time he raises his hand in my Introduction to American Government class, I prepare to have my entire existence invalidated. He spews his rage-filled, big-word comments all over the classroom. I pull out my dictionary to keep up as he speaks.

"Affirmative action has made the debate over college admissions litigious, rightfully so, and contentious." *Litigious: suitable to become the subject of a lawsuit.*

"Look," he continues, "let every man and woman stand in the arena on his or her own accord. Those that are truly intelligent, regardless of race, will rise to the top. They always do. I agree that in the past, things were pretty fucked up. Even I can admit that, but we don't live in the past. We live in the present where a lot of work has been done to balance the scales. Furthermore, you can't punish *mostly* white and Asian students for the sins of the past. It's not fair. I just want everyone to have an equal shot. That's all."

The class is silent, but I am exploding inside. Does he really not realize how much unchecked privilege got him to where he is? *Not merit.* I look around and read the expressions on other students' faces. Some burn with rage, just like me. Others, like Daniel McCullum, a Black student from Detroit, smile with righteous indignation as if their leader has just silenced the critics. "Might I add," Daniel chimes in, "that you can't fix a broken system by creating another broken system. Affirmative action is just as wrong as slavery or segregation in my opinion. Let the test scores speak for themselves."

Back home, when someone says something that is too outrageous to be taken seriously, you might turn to your equally shocked friend and say, *"This nigga."* Which is short for "this nigga has lost his mind." I want to turn to the Black person next to me and commiserate, but I remember where I am. I never use the N-word, not even in Cleveland, but if ever there were a moment that called for it, it's now. No shade to people who do use it, because I firmly believe that a person is allowed to reclaim derogatory word missiles that have been aimed at them in the past.

Professor Alexander-Grant, who is usually neutral, offering perspective on both sides of a debate, stands up with an expression on her face I've never seen. It's a mix

31

of anger that she is trying hard not to show, disappointment, and befuddlement, another Comp Lit word. I'm very curious to see how she responds, since she is also white. I expect her to soothe his angst and massage his very wrong opinions, which is a phenomenon I see repeatedly in contentious debates: the rush to alleviate the suffering of white students.

I have watched so many of my professors (all white) do this, which is why I don't trust any of them. Not only do they placate white students, but I know they can't see my true potential and don't really believe in me like Professor Cartwright. I can tell they don't see a student of promise, but instead a stereotype—another one of the many students of color they've known who have dropped out. They can't imagine what pushes anyone to leave school: not having financial or emotional support from your family, not understanding this white new world with its different social cues and customs, and most importantly, the exhaustion of constantly being underestimated and questioned even though you know you've had to work twice as hard to get there. These professors don't comprehend how much worse everything can be. So I sit back and wait to be disappointed by Professor Alexander-Grant's response.

"Stephen," she begins, "your argument is based on two deeply incorrect assumptions. First, that we live in a perfect world absent of influence from past injustices. Let's start with that one. Do you really think the past does not ripple into the present like a wave across the ocean? Do you believe we exist in a sort of atemporal vacuum? Society is an aggregate"—I quickly consult the dictionary—"of various living realities. The past, the elements that went into making the systems of those societies, are alive today and must be considered in the rendering of equality and justice. This is really a conversation about atonement. We have a problem with not wanting to take responsibility for past grievances in this country. It's called social amnesia.

"Second, the United States has never operated on merit. It wasn't merit that yielded white leaders across every professional and political field, it was violence and forced inequality. It was the massacre of Black Wall Street in Tulsa, Oklahoma, a thriving community of Black people who had built up wealth and prosperity amongst themselves despite the barriers. It was 'Separate but Equal,' which legalized racial disparity in access and opportunity. It was redlining in urban communities across the nation, systematically denying Black citizens access to resources. The result of those policies and practices granted tremendous privilege to white people. The call 'for merit,' in my opinion, is often used to further disenfranchise the disadvantaged by painting a present that conveniently erases key historical elements. It's inaccurate and unjust. I really hope you come to understand that this is all more nuanced and complex than you are making it out to be."

I want to applaud. I want to stand up and shout from the mountaintops the rightness of what this woman has said. A white lady professor that actually gets it?! Wait till

I tell Earnell and Keli. I close my dictionary in quiet satisfaction. The class is silent. Just breathing bodies with no words. This is why I refuse to get a tutor. I can't let Stephen, his conservative cronies, and Mr. Walsh win. I deserve to be here and am just as smart as them, even though I'm in remedial classes and have to use a dictionary to decode what is being discussed. They can't be right. They can't win again. I have to figure this out on my own to prove that I'm so brilliant, I can catch up from generations behind. To prove that there are some people who can't be stopped. No matter the injustice.

———— • ◆ • ————

I am still brimming with joyful contentment remembering Professor Alexander-Grant's speech as I make my way to the Servants of Jesus prayer group, which is my last affinity activity of the week. So far, I've been to events hosted by the Little Club of Africa, where we wore dashikis and ate traditional African food; the Victorian Tea Club, where we drank tea with our pinkies turned up; the Bitchy Feminist Reading Group, where we discussed works by Nikki Giovanni and Gloria Steinem; and a lunch thrown by Kappa Gamma. I have no interest in joining a sorority, but I went for the free food.

There is so much to eat and drink at Dartmouth. Unlike in Cleveland, there is no struggle for sustenance. A cornucopia of nourishment awaits at every table, café, professor's house, and dining hall. In fact, there is such an abundance of food, each incoming freshman class gets an all-you-can-eat lobster dinner the second week of the semester. Initially, I was hesitant since I'd never had fancy seafood before. I inspected the red hard shell, poking and prodding at it until Manda Panda showed me how to crack it. I removed the tender white meat and dipped it in the lemon butter sauce. It was love at first bite. What joy. What a delectable delight. It's the best thing I've ever eaten at Dartmouth. I returned so many times, the cafeteria worker remarked disgustedly, "You again," as she plopped another onto my plate. By the end of the dinner, I was comatose. I laid my head on the table in agony and deep satisfaction. "The Freshman Fifteen is definitely coming for you," Manda Panda whispered knowingly into my ear. I smiled, not caring. Now, four weeks later, my jeans betray me, bursting at the seams. "Find your ability to stretch," I implore them jokingly.

I remember the joy of that lobster as I head toward the prayer group to which Bryce has invited me. He has promised fresh-baked cookies, which draw me forward like the Eye of Mordor from *Lord of the Rings*. "My precious cookies," I say, imitating Gollum as he pines for the ring. I stop in front of Matthew and tell him where I'm going in case the Christians kidnap me and cut out my beating, pagan heart. "Send help if you don't hear from me by tomorrow," I chuckle to myself. "K, byeee, smoocha later," I say, imitating Manda Panda.

As soon as I arrive, I head straight toward the snack table only to find there are no cookies. *Damnit.* I am preparing to sit through a two-hour prayer session without any treats when someone emerges from the kitchen carrying a tray of freshly baked peanut butter cookies. I am so happy, I begin clapping proudly until the person carrying the platter stares me down, confused. "Save those claps for Jesus, young lady," she says haughtily.

I grab the large black Bible on the table and pretend to read, which gives me an excuse to remain standing near the cookies. I nod my head knowingly, as if I'm absorbing something profound while chewing rambunctiously. I'm just about to grab another treat when I notice the words in the book start to crumble and break apart. At first, I think it must be crumbs. I try to wipe them away, but the letters slide down, somersaulting over the edge of the book until only a few letters remain, with gaping white spaces between them on the almost-empty page. They spell out, "Not the call and not your mother's God."

"I hear that's a good read," someone says from behind me. I slam the book closed and almost choke on the unchewed cookie still in my mouth. When I see that it's Bryce, I swallow hard and try to form a cohesive sentence, despite what I've just seen.

"Excited," I say finally. "I mean, seems like everyone's super excited to be here. I've never seen so many happy people in one place." Bryce tells me it's because they have a special musical guest from a famous church in California.

"It's going to be totally awesome," he says. "Oh, there he is. Jim! Buddy! How are you? We can't wait to hear you sing later, man." Jim is a tall white boy with blond hair and blue eyes who literally looks like the picture of Jesus hanging over my desk.

"Bryce, my man," Jim responds. "How was your summer? Tell your dad I'll be touring on the West Coast for the rest of the year, so hopefully we can head to the lake and bait some hooks. Would be amazing to see him."

"Dude, you should hit up the ocean too. The tide will be killer this time of year." They talk like the people in all of the white movies and TV shows I've ever seen. Later, when I get back to my dorm room, I practice adding "dude," "killer," and "rad" to random sentences. *Dude, this fried chicken is totally killer. No way, that's so rad.* I stand in front of the mirror watching my African lips fold awkwardly around these foreign words. I feel different talking like this. Freer, more carefree. *The caucasity*, I think to myself.

"Oh hey, let me introduce you to Echo," Bryce finally says after catching up with his "bro." "She's a first-year and still figuring things out." Jim turns to me, smiling so hard I wonder if his face is going to tear apart.

"Welcome," he says, "we need as many warriors of the light as we can get." I smile plastically, but warmly.

"Well, they're about to start," I say. "I better go find a seat. Nice to meet you." He smiles intensely again. I wonder what's the point of smiling that hard? If it's truly from the soul, like Earnell's laugh, shouldn't it feel easy? In Cleveland, people only smile like this when they're trying to hide something.

I make my way to the bloodred chair in the front of the room. *This can't be a good sign,* I think to myself when I notice it's the only one of its color. Rebellious paganism compels me to sit anyways. Others start filtering in wearing their forced smiles and chatting along the way. When most people are seated, Bryce walks up to the front and introduces Jim, who I learn is an old friend of his family's. Bryce beams with pride recalling precious memories. The lights dim and Jim begins his performance.

I've been to many churches in Cleveland, but I've never heard singing like this before. "He's our saviorrrr," Jim sings. "He walks with us," he continues. It's the whitest music I've ever witnessed in my life. In our churches, everyone gets to shouting and *a*-clapping and *a*-catching the Holy Ghost like it's a festival in New Orleans. Beads of sweat roll angrily down the pastor's dark brown face, landing in his handkerchief, which is already soaked from hours of prayer. The pastor gyrates and moans into the microphone, "Well, I wanna tell ya'll something tonight. Can I tell you something? The lawwwd gave his only begotten son so that we may live out our lives on this good earth. And the lawwwd is the only saving grace in this world of sin. Can I get a hallelujah? Can I get an amen?"

Jim doesn't say lawwwd. He says Lord, perfectly pronouncing all of the consonants. Everyone is enthralled.

Many of them place their palms over their heart or raise a hand high in the air, moved by his angelic singing. I close my eyes and try to sense something inside as he sings, but I only feel hunger pangs for more cookies. When Jim finishes, the crowd gives him a standing ovation. They clap like they just witnessed Jesus turn water into wine. I stand in front of the bloodred devil chair, plastering on a smile to hide my lack of enthusiasm. I don't know how Jim does it. I feel ridiculous trying to fake joy. My face drops. A woman standing across from me on the side of the room suddenly whips her head in my direction. She claps wildly, her mouth turned up in the hardest dragon smile I've seen all night. Then, several people around her stare also, just like in math class, except this time they all nod their heads in my direction while their eyes glare disturbingly at me. One of them mouths something to me. I only catch the word "coming" and have no idea what she means. They clap harder before flinging their arms to the sky like Hypnotist Jerry. They each return their eyes to me, not blinking until everyone returns to their seats and the room fills with the quiet hum of anticipation again. *Am I imagining all this?* Surely, random people I don't know would have no reason to stare at me. I think the pressure of being around so many non-Black people is getting to me.

An older white woman with sandy-brown hair stands to take the microphone after Jim leaves the stage. I can tell she has a lot to say by the way she hustles to the front of the room. She holds the microphone dramatically in silence while locking eyes with several people in the audience. A few people look away to avoid her searing gaze.

I look down at my shoes, which are old and worn out. I really need another pair, but I can't afford it. I glance around at others' well-manicured shoes. Everyone seems to have such nice things around here. I try to slide my feet under the chair so no one else notices.

The woman, who I later learn is named Carla, starts speaking very slowly. "Can I share my testimony? Can I tell you about the obstacles God has moved for me?" As soon as she says the word "obstacle," I am reminded of all the barriers I overcame to get to Dartmouth. The violence, drug addiction, mental illness, and lack of money. I never talk about it, not even with Earnell or Keli. Whenever I think about everything I went through to get here, emotion starts crawling up my throat, like it is right now. I shift uneasily in my chair and try to suck my tears back in, but a few still manage to escape down my cheeks. *Maybe I'm self-sabotaging by not getting help and not talking about my problems*, I think to myself.

"I was self-sabotaging," Carla croons into the microphone. I look up in shock. She seems to be echoing my inner thoughts. "Deep down, I knew what I needed to do, but I felt like I wasn't good enough. And I wasn't. You know why?"

I stare at Carla, mesmerized. How can this white woman with pearls and boat shoes be channeling my exact thoughts?

She continues, looking directly into my eyes, as if she knows me. For a moment, I swear her pupils spin like Hypnotist Jerry's. I look away, trying not to get sucked in. "I wasn't good enough because I didn't have the Lord in my life. There is only one way you can survive this journey," she whispers into the mic. "You must answer the call." I am dumbfounded thinking about the somersaulting letters from earlier that seemed to be referencing this moment. "Answering the call of our Lord and Savior Jesus Christ has saved my life and it can save yours too," she says, pointing at me.

Bryce is thrilled I'm the focus of Carla's attention. He grins gleefully, pats his heart supportively, and then points up at the sky, less intensely than the watchers from earlier, signifying the presence of his all-consonants-pronounced Lord. The dorkiness of his gesture makes me want to throw up in my mouth. I nod my head affirmatively, as if we are on the same page, and then release myself from the pressure of his expectant gaze.

Carla finishes her sermon and then asks for new members to identify themselves. I sit peacefully in my red devil chair knowing "new member" does not apply to me as I only came for the cookies and Bryce. Before I can get away, Bryce draws Carla's attention to me. The thirst in Carla's face erupts. All thirty-two of her pearly white teeth are visible through her Moses-parted lips. Her eyes soften and she leans toward me while speaking into the microphone. She looks like a cult leader preparing to slather me in Christian snake oil. I want to lower my head in silent shame, but everyone is looking at me now—for real this time. Beads of sweat start gathering on the periphery of my forehead. The sweat doesn't roll. It holds, right on the line, like soldiers waiting for an order from their commander.

"Now, Echo," she pours her voice demandingly in my direction. "I'm not a gambling woman, but I'm gonna bet that there must be something in your heart that brought you here." *Yea, the cookies.* Carla lifts her hand to the sky and says, "The Almighty must have called you to us." Everyone in the congregation raises their hands in my direction.

"Oh dear God," I say out loud.

"That's right," Carla responds. "*Our* dear God. Come on up here and answer the call."

I don't move. Carla's eyes grow dark like thunderstorms. "Bring her up here," she speaks out into the crowd. Suddenly, I feel myself and the red *this-can't-be-a-good-sign* chair beneath me being lifted up off the ground, my worn-out shoes visible for all to see. Embarrassment swallows me whole. I claw the arms of the chair for dear life while they march me up to the stage. They set me down in the front, facing the audience, with Carla standing next to me. The commander gives the order, and the sweat starts to roll. I am too shocked to wipe it, so my Black face drips, displayed for this sea of white faces.

I plead to the three other people of color in the crowd to please come save me, but they turn away in shame. They know this debacle will reflect poorly on them too. We are all representatives of each other here, a pressure white people don't have or understand. When a white person does something wrong, it's just one individual's perpetration, but when one of us does something wrong, it reflects negatively on all of us. I can handle my own shame at being singled out like this, but I can't handle the pressure of having it projected onto the other Black and brown bodies in the room.

"This young woman is lost," Carla says, still speaking low in dark growling tones. "She doesn't know who she is, that she is here to serve our Lord. THAT SHE IS A SERVANT OF THE LIGHT! PRAY FOR HER!" Carla starts shouting in a shrill tone. She is possessed, seemingly overtaken by the spirit of her Lord. "Pray she finds clarity," Carla hisses into the microphone. "Pray she finds the right path. HIS way!" Suddenly several people move to the front of the room, extending their arms out toward me. Their faces are wrinkled in fiery concern. They are praying as if their prayers can save me. I grow increasingly angry. Enraged at these white people trying to force their white Lord upon me. Have they learned nothing from their own history? This is yet another conquest, but they have targeted a breaker of chains who cannot be conquered.

"Stop it!" I recoil in shock at the force of my own words. "Stop it! I don't need you to pray for my soul. You know who I need you to pray for is my brother who just got out of prison. And my other brother, who's schizophrenic. And my dad, who's still drinking himself to death. And all the people I know who will never be able to realize their dreams no matter how hard they try because the system trampled them. Where was your God when all of that shit was happening? Why don't you pray for the dismantling of systematic oppression—then we can talk about the state of my soul."

I turn my head toward the staring group from earlier, who seem just as shocked as the math class watchers, and I shout, "And why the hell are you people always staring? It's invasive and rude. Knock it off!"

I rush out into the brisk fall air toward the Big Green where Matthew and a thousand broken promises lay scattered: the promise that I could catch up, that I could fit in, that I belonged here. The decaying flesh of those promises sinks back down into the earth and disappears. It all becomes clear in this moment how unevenly the scales are tipped, how gravely wrong Stephen Clark is about everything, and how far behind I am—generations behind. I was naïve to think I could gamble against the house of oppression and win. Negro Brown and her ancestors never stood a chance against these kinds of odds.

CHAPTER FOUR

I may not have privilege, but I will have Prince Charming, who is white, like the men I see in all the romantic comedies and superhero movies. My attraction to white boys has ballooned since arriving at Dartmouth, and it is squarely at odds with my prolific critiques of whiteness. I never expected to be attracted to white men and I don't fully understand it myself.

Prior to being here, I thought I would find a good-looking, but troubled, brown-skinned boy who definitely needed me to save him with my love. We would be unified in the struggle against oppression and grow closer untangling our past traumas and problematic patterns of behavior in relationships, since so few people ever loved us right. Regardless, we would emerge on the other side healed and risen. Two Black, Ivy League–educated phoenixes, deeply in love and soaring high above it all.

The Black men here barely look my way, however, except Earnell, who's more like a brother to me. Rejection from your own kind feels treacherous, like betrayal. If they won't have me, who will? It's not that the Black men here don't date Black women. Many do. They just don't date Black women who look like me: dark-skinned, nappy-headed, glasses-wearing, and tomboyish. They go after girls with long pretty hair who are brown- to fair-skinned, and who "beat their face for the gods," as RuPaul would say, meaning they wear a lot of makeup, even though we are in the middle of the woods. I tried to put on lipstick once, imagining it might finally get them to see me, but I felt ridiculous and wiped it off.

Something in me turns away from my fantasy of the rising Black phoenix after I meet Bryce. I still don't know if he's attracted to me romantically, if he has a girlfriend, or if he's just interested in making sure I get to heaven, but he looks at me like he can see inside me, like I matter. That's the look I think I'm chasing in my pursuit of white Prince Charming, and it's what I've never had from a Black man who wasn't related to me, or like a family member in Earnell's case. I was searching for it in Black men when I first arrived, for some evidence that I was important and visible. Now, Bryce has me looking for affirmation in white men.

I'm ashamed to admit that I'm trying to find some value in myself through the love of the "oppressor." I compare myself to the white girls on campus, looking at my Black face in the mirror, dark and disfigured, like all the other unworthy things in the world, and wonder why white Prince Charming would ever pick me? *Why weren't you born a privileged prancer, like Manda Panda?* I ask my reflection. I plead desperately, but she doesn't answer. She never does.

The complexity of trying to untangle my new desire for white men burns in my psyche. A range of feelings and considerations—guilt, betrayal of Black men, shame, fear of judgment, and confusion—wash over me every time I think about white men romantically. The hardest part is feeling like I can't talk to anyone about it, definitely not Earnell and Keli, who are both super pro-Black. Keli constantly proclaims she "can't wait to find her Black king and make Black-ass babies." They have both picked up on my attraction to white guys through Bryce, and Earnell constantly jokes that he knows I'm "going to end up in an 'ice cream sandwich' partnership," but I don't feel comfortable discussing it further with them.

Despite the challenges, I'm on the hunt. Good-looking white boys are everywhere and any one of them could be my Prince Charming. So I keep my eyes peeled: at the gym while pretending to work out on machines that I actually hate; in the cafeteria; and right now, behind a bush next to the math building. I carefully bend the leaves backward and peek as this super-hot boy-man—*boy-man: a young fellow who is no longer a child, but is also not a full-blown adult yet*—sits on the stairs scanning through a textbook. *He must be so smart*, I think to myself. *I bet he's a great kisser.*

I am deep in fantasyland when I feel hot breath on my ear. "What are you doing?" someone whispers. I shriek and fall forward out of the bush, right in front of Prince Charming. "Whoa, that's gnarly," he says. "Were you in the bushes?" Prince Charming and Earnell, who is the surprise bush whisperer, pull me up off the ground. I am too busy staring into Prince Charming's green eyes to talk. I smile, awkwardly, mesmerized by being so close. *Finally, sooo close.*

"Hello!?" Earnell says while snapping and clapping his hands right next to my ear. "What's wrong wit you, girl? I thought you liked Nazarene? I told you these white boys are going to be the end of you. Have you learned nothing from the past four hundred years?"

Prince Charming looks bewildered like a deer caught in headlights.

"My great-grandparents were abolitionists, for what it's worth. And my parents voted for Jimmy Carter, Bill Clinton, and even Al Gore. So yea. Well, uh, I should probably get going. Hope you're OK and stay out of the bushes. There could be ticks in there." Prince Charming shuffles up the sidewalk, taking all his liberal declarations with him. I turn to Earnell in playful rage and smack him several times on the arms.

"Earnell! Stop ruining my life!" Earnell laughs diabolically, then jets up the sidewalk yelling after Prince Charming, "Wait, come back, Massa! Carol Ann done went and fell in love wit ya. I swear all these negroes have Stockholm syndrome."

———— • ◆ • ————

There are two and a half weeks left until midterms and my grades, like the melting early October ice outside my window, keep sliding. The search for Prince Charming is a welcome distraction, but I know at some point I'm going to have to face the music, which is screeching, whether I'm listening or not. I still can't bring myself to get a tutor, but I've agreed to see a therapist to help me better adjust, untangle some of my past, and deal with the magical delusions I seem to be experiencing. I don't actually want to do therapy either, but Earnell and Keli suggested it when I told them I was "seeing things." I'm confident I can fix my grades alone, but I'm not sure I can fix my mind. I know what kind of tricks it plays, the chaos it can cause, especially when I feel ungrounded and out of place. Hopefully after therapy, I'll finally be normal.

Dean Harrison also recommended therapy. "One day it just might become one of your greatest assets," she says decidedly.

"I highly doubt that," I rebuff. She then stares at me entirely too long with blank eyes before pouring me a cup of tea. She's always offering me herbal beverages. "We don't drink this in Cleveland," I tell her. "And we're not in the United Kingdom so there's no need for all this tea. Hey, this is how they drink tea at the Victorian Tea Club," I say, laughing and prissily extending my pinky finger. I sip delicately as if I'm the wealthiest person in the world. Is this how Bill Gates drinks his tea also? Why do rich people always have to be so measured? There's no need for this kind of pomp and circumstance in the trenches.

"Some say tea is a portal to another dimension," Dean Harrison blurts out randomly.

"Who? Who says that?"

"Some."

"Some who?"

"The who that are some."

She gets weirder every time we meet.

I expect today to be no different. I'm headed to my weekly check-in with her now. I'm ten minutes late, per usual, and sprinting across campus. I've never met a Black person so totally out of the box. Dean Harrison has a short bowl cut, wears custom-tailored cream or light orange dresses (*only* those two colors), and doesn't understand Black colloquial speech or humor. One time while leaving her office I said, "I'll holla at you later." She looked at me confusedly and said, "It is not necessary to yell at me or anyone else now or later. Balanced audible tones are more than suitable."

While standing outside her office I finally realize who Dean Harrison reminds me of. This entire time I have felt I've seen her likeness and mannerisms somewhere, but couldn't place it till now. *Mr. Spock from Star Trek!* I feel relieved, satisfied.

Just as I'm about to knock, her door comes swinging open. "Echo," she says, "late as always. Please come in." I sit and she walks directly to the kettle. I shake my head amusedly while my eyes roam around her office, trying to piece this peculiar person together. The space is barren except for a framed quote by Yoda on the mantel that reads "Luminous beings are we, not this crude matter." *I guess she must be a Star Wars fan too.* That's the only thing I can surmise from her decor. I want to ask why she doesn't have any family pictures or fancy award plaques like the other deans, but I know that wouldn't be polite.

She returns and sets a white mug of steaming tea in front of me before sitting on the other side of the desk. She taps the sides of her mug with a small silver spoon, while smiling awkwardly at me and staring. I meekly look back before returning my gaze to the cup. I am shocked to see the light brown beverage spinning counterclockwise. "Huh," I say quietly. "That's strange."

"What?" Dean Harrison asks. "Are you still in the room?"

"What do you mean? Why would you ask something like that? I'm sitting right here. Are you blind?"

⬥

I say hostilely to the therapist, Jennifer.

"Look at me. I'm a Black woman in the middle of nowhere. Of course I'm uncomfortable here. Wouldn't you be if the tables were turned?"

I hate when people ask obvious questions: *Do you feel uncomfortable in a place like this?*

Like, *Is water wet?* Duh.

Her office smells like roses and lavender. *If I was a white woman, my office would probably have a similar perfume,* I think sarcastically to myself. *What an easy life.*

"I didn't mean it like that," she says, more gently this

time. "It's just hard to get a sense of how you are doing here since you don't share much."

"I'm doing fine."

"Well, can I ask why you came to see me? What brought you in?"

"My friends said I should come."

I don't understand why I am acting like this. I am mostly disarmed in her presence, despite the soft background chime of my "Reading White People" sensor—or RWP, as Earnell, Keli, and I call the inner tool we use to assess the intentions of melanin-deficient people. Her office is so cozy, her light pink couch like a cloud beneath me. I want to tell her my entire life story, pour it all out, but I can't. It's like there is a door between us that I can't open.

"Well, weird things have been happening lately," I say finally. "Unexplainable stuff. I mean I'm sure there must be an explanation, but I just can't figure it out…" My voice trails off. "And a lot of hard shit happened to me back in Cleveland. I can't remember most of it," I say quickly, trying to mask my inflamed vulnerability. "The stuff I do remember, I wish I could forget."

She scribbles

notes on the blank sheet of paper in front of her.

"What are you writing?" I ask.

Dean Harrison holds up her paper and says, "Nothing, just doodling."

"I do the same thing in math class."

"I know."

Slightly confused about how she could "know," I keep talking. "It helps soothe my mind."

"So your mind is turbulent?"

"I didn't say that."

"What are you saying, then? And how do you feel right now? Near or far?"

I don't even ask her what she means. I give up trying to understand her riddles and quotes. I stare back at her, but again can't hold the intensity of her gaze for long. She smiles at my discomfort and stands to pour more

◆

tea into the green mug, which also spins counterclockwise, just like in Dean Harrison's office. "Do you want some chocolate or biscuits?" Jennifer asks.

I shake my head no. She takes more notes, then begins speaking.

"Based on everything you've told me," Jennifer says, "I think I have a preliminary diagnosis of what's going on with you. It looks like complex PTSD."

"What's that?"

"It stands for Post-Traumatic Stress Disorder. It just means you've suffered a lot of trauma in your life that you need to heal from. There was a study a while back that said PTSD rates in inner-city Chicago were higher than among soldiers returning home from war. Astounding. I imagine Cleveland must be similar."

"Yea."

"Are you open to trying an exercise? It's called EMDR, which is short for Eye Movement Desensitization and Reprocessing. It's a type of therapy that has done wonders for people suffering from this condition."

"OK," I respond. "What do I have to do?"

"Well, the first step is to get comfortable. Take a deep breath. Next, I would like you to tap the tops of both of your thighs while following my finger back and forth with your eyes. These techniques help stimulate the deeper parts of the brain we have locked away. It's simple, but transformative."

It sounds silly to me, but I try. I follow her finger and tap my legs.

"Now close your eyes," she says, "and tell me if anything rises."

As soon as I close my eyes, I feel like I'm falling into a vacuous, dark space inside myself. Jennifer is speaking, but I can't hear her. It suddenly comes rushing back—the ten-year-old memory I keep trying to bury. *He smelled like whiskey. Cockroaches crawling around the bed. The TV blaring in the background. I pray like my mother told me—"Our Father who art in heaven, hallowed be thy name"—but God doesn't come save me. I search for a place to hide, at the bottom of his clothes hamper, but he finds me. It takes two weeks for anyone to figure out what happened. Then the hospital room. They can't find a gown small enough for me. I cry for my mother, who is nowhere to be found. Where is she? Does she not love me enough to be here? I shouldn't have been a bad little girl.*

My eyes fling open, glazed with sadness. Jennifer observes and doesn't speak. I grab my jacket and race toward the door.

"Wait!" she says suddenly. "Will you come back for another session? I feel confident I can help you."

"I don't know," I say, escaping into the freedom of the outside world where I can forget again in peace.

———— •◆• ————

The first glass of wine takes me by storm. I chug it all in one gulp. I've never finished a glass of alcohol in my life, but tonight I'm determined to get drunk. The Defiance, who have been banging on the windows trying to get through to me, shout angrily: *This is not the way, you feel me? Bitch, put that glass down. Baby girl, hah, don't do this.* I raise my glass, my third, and tell them they can't stop me tonight. I swallow the dark red liquid in one breath. A jolt of electricity courses through me, causing a headache, but I keep going. "Throw the damn tea into the harbor where it belongs!" I shout with a mock British accent, referencing the Boston Tea Party, which no one at the table is discussing.

Professor Alexander-Grant has invited me to a special

dinner with an award-winning *New York Times* journalist. This is definitely not the right place to be wasted, but I don't care. I'm still trying to rebury what rose up in therapy today. "Don't you remember we talked about the tea taxes earlier today in class?" I say to Professor Alexander-Grant. She smiles uncomfortably before continuing her side conversation with another student.

There is a burning feeling in the center of my chest. I had forgotten how much pain there was here in the middle. How deep the despair runs, way down in my bones, beyond me, back to the first ones forced to wade in the water. A thread of sorrow, linking all of my lineage, now struggles to find its release through me. I won't let it come out; it hurts too much. The wound grows more infected. I drink until the pain surrenders to my will, the captain of this vessel.

"Cheers," I say in drunken stupor, raising my glass. "I wish everyone success and good tidings"—I burp—"for the upcoming midterms. How is it October fourth already? Are we in some kind of time warp? 'Cause time seems to be flying. Am I right or am I right?" I guzzle the drink. My fifth.

Stephen Clark and Connor are at the dinner. Both white men, neither one my Prince Charming so I hardly pay them any attention. There are also other students whom I've never met, so I don't focus on them either. Professor Alexander-Grant invited students from varying backgrounds with different political views in the hopes of having a "lively, dynamic discussion."

"Where are you all from?" the *Times* journalist asks. "All over, I'm sure."

"Well, I'm actually from Wisconsin, believe it or not," Stephen says. "My parents are both very liberal, which is unfortunate, but hey, no one's perfect."

Our guest of honor, who must be conservative also, laughs along with Stephen.

"That's not funny," I say before burping again. "Liberalism is some people's only hope for freedom. People like me," I say, pointing to myself. "Stephen, I had no idea you came from a liberal family." My words are slurred and clearly annoy him. I cradle my chin in my hands with both my elbows on the table. "If your parents are lefties, then why are you like this? Are you hiding something? Are you secretly gay?" I say, whispering loudly. "I hear a lot of conservatives are in the closet. You can tell me. Don't be afraid."

Everyone gasps in shock. Professor Alexander-Grant scolds me and tells me I'm being inappropriate and that she's shocked to see me like this. "So am I," I respond, unphased. "Life is a joke. It's all so funny, isn't it?" I laugh uproariously, slapping my hand against the table several times.

"Conservatism for me," Stephen continues, totally ignoring my outburst, "is really about keeping the balance of society. I think you need both, the left and the right. My parents went so far left, they won't vote for anyone in the Republican party and their views have become quite extreme. I definitely think that's influenced me leaning more to the right. For God's sake, they're vegans. No one in their right mind should be a vegan. It biologically makes no sense."

"I'm with you there, buddy," I say, raising my glass of water. "I'll never give up bacon. Hey, we actually agree on something. Cheers to that!" I chug the water down in one swallow and then burp again. I try to cover my mouth, but the belch comes out too quickly.

"It's funny to hear you say that," Connor chimes in, also ignoring me, "because my family is just the opposite. My parents are both conservative and I'm as liberal as they come. I'm from Vermont, but they're originally from Montana and still have a ranch there. I'm an only child and spent a lot of time alone in the woods growing up. Nature has a way of teaching you about life. Everything you could ever want to learn is there: the importance of balance, the interconnectedness of everything, and the value of all living things. It's all precious, a miracle of existence. That's why I'm a big believer in a colorblind society. I truly believe we're all equal."

"Pfff," I respond sarcastically. When everyone looks at me in disappointment, I apologize and say I was just clearing my throat. I drink more water and then stick out my tongue and say, "Look, I swallowed all the bullshit from tonight. All gone." I chuckle loudly to myself. "Oh hey, want to see something cool?" I continue. "Watch this!" I clap my hands three times and Connor starts clucking. I keel over in laughter.

"Damnit, Echo!" Connor exclaims. "I was hypnotized freshman year. This is still a side effect," he says, shaking his head in dismay. "I've seen other hypnotists to try and get rid of it, but no luck."

"Echo," Professor Alexander-Grant cuts in, "why don't you tell our guest a little about yourself."

"Yes." The journalist nods affirmatively. "Where are you from and where do you think your political beliefs came from?"

I am offended by the question. It presses on the pain button in the center of my chest I'm trying to drink away.

"How dare you ask me such a question," I respond. "Where am I from? I'm from the sky, bitch. From way up. Ever been there? In fact, I'm a Chosen One, a rare and endangered species."

As soon as I say "Chosen One," the room grows cold and quiet, underwater quiet. All of the eyes in framed pictures around the room stare, intensely, as if they are suddenly alive and focused entirely on me. The room rotates on its axis. The wall that was in front of me with the staring eyes moves to the right. Now they watch from the side. "Look!" I yell in distress. "The room is spinning! And the people on the wall are watching me."

All conversation at the table halts. Several people sip from their cups nervously, not knowing what else to do. "I think you've had too much to drink," Professor Alexander-Grant says with earnest concern.

"Can't you all see that something strange is happening here?! Something's wrong!" I plead, desperately looking around the table for help. Unlike the pictures on the wall, no one except Professor Alexander-Grant makes eye contact with me. Stephen whispers under his breath, but loud enough for me to hear, "This is ridiculous," while pushing the remaining food around his plate.

I grow inflamed with fury. *You're ridiculous!* is what I want to yell, but the words, like the sweat at Bible study, post up, refusing to march out of my mouth. I feel a wetness dripping from my right nostril. My nose is bleeding, but the blood is not dark red or maroon, it is black and thick like tar. Several drops of the black blood fall into the palm of my hand before dripping down the side of the table. Connor jumps from the table, runs to the kitchen, and grabs some paper towels. He gently places his hand on my shoulder and hands them to me.

Then the whispering starts. The whispering that sounds like a shrill, high-pitched whistle. Broken syllables of incoherent phrases fade in and out like a radio station with too much static. I cover my ears in distress, the blood from my hand now dripping down my ear. I try to scream and force the now fully formed phrases out of their barracks. "They're here," I say softly at first before yelling at the top of my lungs. *"They're here! 2411 Mitchell Lane: Brace for impact!"*

"Why are you shouting the professor's address? Who's here?" the *Times* journalist asks.

My body turns slowly in his direction, as if possessed by an unseen force. I lock eyes with him. He is alarmed by my unwavering gaze, smiling awkwardly from discomfort.

"The Keepers," I say, not knowing what it means. "The Keepers are here."

I thrust my body away from the table, to the shock of everyone who watches without interference. I stumble outside and fall to my knees on the lawn of Professor Alexander-Grant's house. The grass smells sweet. The cold fall air is chilling. "Two and a half weeks until midterms," I say before vomiting up everything in my stomach. "Have to pull it together," I try and convince myself.

There are lights in the sky. Brilliant hues: green, purple, red. I've never seen such a marvelous sight. "What's that?" I ask when I notice my professor kneeling down next to me. "Is it the end of the world?"

She is stunned also. "Wow, this weather has really been insane lately. Now this? That looks like the northern lights, the aurora borealis. It's the result of electrons colliding with the upper reaches of Earth's atmosphere, but they'd never happen here. We're not far enough north."

"They look like the portal in my room," I say in awe.

Professor Alexander-Grant looks at me in confusion, before pointing at the sky again and saying, "Look at that! I think it's a shooting star."

"Wow!" I exclaim in drunken glee, watching the point of light streak across the sky.

"You really see all this too, right?" I ask, after a few minutes of silence, confirming it's not some kind of mind trick like the portals.

"Yes, of course, we can all see. It's magical."

CHAPTER FIVE

Except, there is some magic others can't see. After that night, I am haunted by a series of inexplicable occurrences. Letters, entire word families, jumping over the edge of all my books and papers. What's left on the page, always spelling out the same thing: *He rises, but they're here to help*. Items not found where I left them. My water bottle on Manda Panda's desk instead of in my backpack where I put it after class earlier. "Hey, I poured a little of Snoop's gin and juice in here," she says deviously. "I assume that's why you left it here. I see you, girl. PARTY!" she says, raising the roof remarkably off beat even in the absence of music. My mother's Jesus reborn over the wardrobe on the opposite side of the room. I didn't move him. The portal, spinning clockwise now behind Jesus' celestial figure, and humming as if there is a hive of bees inside.

It doesn't make sense. Time and space seem to be breaking down around me. The watchers are everywhere now, in multiple classes. They stare with wide eyes and always deny their watching. I feel increasingly disoriented and off-center, like I'm losing my mind—the inexplicable occurrences accelerating my descent into madness.

I try to call Hypnotist Jerry and ask him to come back and fix my mind, but his line always goes to voicemail. I email him and report all the strange occurrences. "I must still be under your spell somehow," I write. "Please tell me how to stop this." Now I know how Connor must feel. I meditate and try to re-hypnotize myself back to the life I knew, but there are too many things I have suppressed deep inside so I give up quickly. I ask a quantum physics professor if it's possible for a portal to another dimension that can show the future to just appear out of thin air. "In science fiction movies, yes. In real life, no, not at the macro level of matter, but that should be obvious, Ms. Brown. Are you working on some sort of screenplay or something?" At least in *Harry Potter* there are other wizards who can experience the magic along with you. Here, it's just me and it's getting more outrageous every day.

In Thayer dining hall, right now, a *stunning* sight unfolds. The lunch procession is on the right side of the café instead of the left where it usually is. Just like at Professor Alexander-Grant's house, the entire room rotated on its axis. *This. Is. Not. Possible.* Someone would have had to rebuild overnight, tearing out walls, adding new water and gas lines to make this happen. I know that did not occur. Students shuffle in and out as if they don't notice that the entire configuration of the space has changed. I stop a short, brown-haired woman who looks like she just came off some kind of sports field. Her hair is in a ponytail and she's wearing cleats and white socks that stretch up her calves.

"Hey, has the lunch line always been over there?" I ask.

"Yea," she says flippantly before hurrying on her way.

I sit, dazed, at a table near the back, watching the reactions of everyone who enters. I am baffled that no one seems to notice anything out of the ordinary. I'm waiting to discuss the Bible with Bryce. I regularly study God's word with him. Thanks to my mother, who delivered lines from the Bible to us so often I can practically repeat the entire thing from memory, he is impressed by my knowledge of the divine word. I have continued going to the Servants of Jesus prayer group, basically for him and the cookies. I've somehow managed to forget the Bible he gave me, which is the entire point of our meeting. A wave of fear washes over me at the thought of disappointing Bryce. It is soon replaced by exhilaration when I realize this might mean we have to sit closer together and read from *his* Bible. My face must still be frozen in panic because as soon as Bryce sees me, he asks, "What's going on? You look like you're thinking about something serious. Everything OK?"

"Oh, yea. All good. I'm just bummed that I forgot my Bible."

"No problem. I have an extra. I always carry two in case I come across someone in need of the Word. It's a cold world out there these days."

I know Bryce is one hundred percent serious, so I try my best not to smile at the goodness of his stunning humanity. Ideally, I want Bryce to be my Prince Charming, but I know if he ever finds out that I am just pretending to be a Christian, he probably won't like me anymore. Christianity is his entire life.

Ever since my outburst at the first prayer group, Bryce seems intent on making sure my soul is saved.

"I was sad to hear the hurt in your voice and all the hardship you've been through. I can only imagine what that's like," he says. "But I really feel like God can be an anchor for you. A place of hope and stability."

"Can he?" I ask, questioning Bryce for the first time, annoyed by all this religion talk, but trying to stay connected to him. " 'Cause both my parents are Christians, but that didn't stop them from drinking and drugging." Bryce looks floored by my statement. I suddenly feel guilty for putting him on the spot. "I don't mean to sound harsh—"

"No, it's a good point," he says, cutting me off. "It's something I haven't been able to quite work out myself. Why all this bad stuff still happens when God is omnipotent and all-knowing. It's a paradox."

"Can I ask you something?" I say in a hushed voice. "Has anything bad ever happened to you? I was just wondering because it seems like people here have lived such gilded"—another new word—"lives. I don't understand how my life has been so hard, but there are people in the world who just seem to float along with no problems. I wish it could have been like that for me is all I'm saying. I think a big part of why it was so hard is because I was born poor and Black. If God isn't responsible for that, who is?"

Bryce looks stunned. He doesn't know how to respond. I'm pretty sure I already have the answer to the question, based on what I know about him. He was raised in a mostly white, hippie Christian commune in California where people praised God, smoked cannabis, and hugged trees, and where a lot of bad stuff probably didn't happen. Bryce is open-minded about almost everything, except for his faith, which I think is really a safety blanket that protects him from the harsh realities of the world. If it's all God's plan, the dragon never needs to be faced. Now, I've called the dragon to task and he doesn't know how to confront it.

He nervously thumbs through the pages of his Bible. I decide I've probably ruined any chance of ever dating him. Who wants to be romantic with someone who reminds them of everything that is wrong with the world? He will definitely never look at me like I matter now. He will probably avoid looking at me altogether. I am surprised, when he finally does look up, to see even more compassion in his eyes. I'm so overwhelmed, I glance down at my twiddling thumbs, my place of refuge in moments of discomfort like this.

"I'm just trying to find the right words," he says finally. "To answer your question. No, nothing really 'bad' has happened to me in my life. Wow, I feel super privileged admitting that. Honestly, before I started getting involved in diversity work, I never really thought about race. I didn't even believe it was still a problem. I thought things were pretty good now. I was basing that off my own experience, which is generally easygoing, but I've learned from a lot of students of color that that's definitely not the case for them. I don't know what to do with that. How to make it right, you know?"

He looks to me for a confirmation I cannot provide. I leave him there, wallowing in his privileged guilt. I want to take care of his feelings in this moment, like I always do when people feel uneasy around me, but I'm too busy trying to process my own. Black women are treated like batteries in this society, giving, nurturing, and holding space for everyone but ourselves. Where is the reciprocity when we are despaired, uncomfortable, or drained? Then too we are asked to give more.

I glance over at the inner turbulence stirring in Bryce's eyes. He doesn't know what to say or do. I prepare to help pick him up off the ground when I hear someone yell, "Whose house?!" The question is met by another person calling back just as loudly, "Our house!" The Alphas, an all-Black fraternity, come stomping into the cafeteria wearing their trademark black-and-gold jackets.

There are ten of them putting on an impromptu step show. A few students look disgruntled at their uninvited performance, but several people, especially the group of Black students that followed them in, cheer with delight. Their step routine is impressive, but I'm embarrassed to be sitting across from Bryce while this is happening, especially given our conversation. I don't want Bryce to be reminded even more of my Blackness.

I know I'm supposed to have Black pride, after everything my people have fought for and achieved in America. My entire life is a testament to the sacrifice of those that came before me. I wish I could feel proud and grateful, like the cheering Black crowd surrounding the Alphas, but I feel embarrassed. The shame is buried deep down and tells me I have no value. That I'm too ugly and too Black to ever be loved. Part of my search for white Prince Charming is to erase all that. If white Prince Charming, who is sitting on top of the world, wants me, then surely I must have some worth here. I really hope I haven't ruined my chances with Bryce by asking him challenging questions.

The Alphas continue their show. One of them jumps up on a table and does a solo step routine while shouting, "We're so cold, ice cold, too cold!" The rest of the men follow suit, repeating his moves and words on the floor. I wonder if I should cheer in solidarity with the other Black people in the room. I decide against it and sit quietly with my hand slightly covering my face in embarrassment. This is the real legacy of white supremacy. It means anyone who is not white cannot congregate freely without suspicion and judgment. The power is with the group, so the group is always a threat.

A cafeteria worker comes darting across the dining hall and tells the man on the table to get down. He defiantly does one more choreographed step routine before jumping to the ground and marching out of the room with the rest of his group. Bryce looks across at me, smiling uneasily, and says, "That was pretty cool."

Bryce starts packing his Bible, as if he plans to leave without finishing this important conversation. "I have to run," he says, "but would you be down for grabbing some ice cream after Bible study next Tuesday? I definitely want to think about all this more and discuss it with you."

With you, he says, as if I am his one. As if we can face the world together, despite its challenges. My face lights up.

"Of course," I respond, trying not to sound too eager.

"Great, it's a date," he says, which I now recognize he says every time he makes plans with anyone. I still can't tell if he has romantic feelings for me, but I plan to find out at the ice cream shop.

———————◆·—————————

The closer Bryce and I become, the more I want to be "fixed." I recommit to therapy even though last time I walked away deeply disturbed. Despite the difficulty, it's soothing to have a stranger see inside you and witness your problems. I decide I won't do the EMDR again; it was too triggering, but maybe I can keep talking about the delusions, Bryce, my struggles with Blackness, and the pursuit of Prince Charming. I might even talk about why I can't ask for help, even as my grades continue their free fall, collapsing the window of time I have left to catch up.

Jennifer greets me affectionately, once again disarming my RWP sensor. She is so positive and caring, I find it difficult to activate my defensive mechanisms in her presence.

"How've you've been, honey?"

"Did you move the fountain?" I ask.

"What do you mean?"

"Well, last time, it was over there, wasn't it?"

"No, I haven't moved anything."

"Oh."

"Do you remember it differently? I know last time you said unexplainable stuff was happening. Do you want to talk more about that? Sometimes when someone is overwhelmed, the mind can project inner perplexity onto the outside world. We start to imagine and see things...differently. Does that sound familiar?"

"No," I respond flatly, afraid she will think something is wrong with me. "I'm not imagining anything. I'm fine. I've been fine. Except I got drunk the night I left here last time. I've never been drunk before. The Defiance... I mean, I tried to talk myself out of it, but couldn't stop. I don't know what came over me. It was in front of my professor. I was so embarrassed. I wrote her an apology note."

I sit on the couch, which I'm pretty sure is a darker pink than it was last week, but I don't say anything.

"I actually wanted to talk about that," Jennifer says. "EMDR can be intense. It's probably better if we just talk the first few sessions before attempting that again. So I

70

thought maybe we could start today by you telling me a bit more about your family? Your parents and your brothers?"

I gaze down at my twiddling thumbs, ready to draw back into myself. This nice white lady wants to know about my family and I don't know what to tell her.

"They're good people," I say. "At the core."

I look out the window, fighting the door that is trying to erect itself between us. *Open*, I say gently to myself, knowing I can't keep everything locked away forever.

"My mother, in the summer, she cooks for the whole neighborhood. Everybody calls her Ms. Aprah. And she's so loud, my whole family is. When she talks, she shouts. She's big now. She used to be my size, but she eats away a lot of her problems, I think. It's better than the drugs. I missed her most when she was gone, when she was on drugs. Nobody ever tells you about how the drugs take the soul of a person until you see it yourself, but she's clean now. That's good.

"And my dad, they call him the Mayor of Lorain. He's from the South, Alabama. He grew up in a real poor community where everyone looks out for each other. He still has that mentality. Has to go around pulling people's garbage cans to the curb, playing lottery numbers for folks, and has to wave at everybody. 'All right, how you doin' today?' That's why they call him the Mayor, 'cause he knows everybody. He's not my real father. I mean, he is, but he's not my biological father. He raised me, though. He was in the hospital when I was born. I wonder sometimes where my real father is and why he left me and if he would be proud I'm in a place like this now."

A wave of guilt thinking about my grades crushes me. *Maybe I won't be here much longer,* I think disappointedly to myself. *Then there would be nothing he could be proud of. I'd be the daughter that dropped out of college.*

I plummet into despair.

When I don't say anything for several minutes, Jennifer asks me about my brothers. "Are you close to them?"

"I used to be," I respond. "When we were younger. I thought it would always be like that. Us against the world. The three of us. We were so small, you know. The world was tearing us apart, but at least we had each other."

Tears start to fall from my eyes. Jennifer hands me a box of tissues. I set it on the table, afraid to wipe my tears for fear they might never come again.

"I haven't cried in a long time," I say. "Crying is weakness."

"Who told you that?"

"Nobody had to tell me. I saw it with my own two eyes. If I had stopped and cried about everything that happened to me, I probably would have died. It was so much. I just had to find a way to keep going. And I did. I made it. I'm exceptional, the best that ever did it." I smile weakly, not believing my own words.

"You did and you are," Jennifer says, validating my observations. "Not many make it to a place like this coming from your circumstances, but that doesn't mean you have to continue to do everything on your own. What you have overcome is too much for one person. That kind of trauma will wreck you in the long run if you don't face it and release it."

"I know," I respond. "I've already watched it destroy my humanity. I can't cry or feel anything. I just have to be strong all the time. I can't even be a woman. Being a girl is dangerous so I have to hide my femininity. Not be soft at all.

"And I've already seen it, the pain, eviscerate everyone in my family, including my brothers. That always hits me the hardest. My brothers didn't make it. I don't know how to live with that. I mean, they're alive, but one was recently released from prison and the other is schizophrenic. What kind of lives are those?"

More tears fall.

"Why do you think you're crying right now?" Jennifer asks.

"That's a dumb question," I lash out before immediately apologizing. "I'm sorry. I know you are trying to help. This is just hard. I feel like I'm gonna break apart if I talk about all this."

Jennifer gazes at me understandingly. "Take your time," she says.

"I think I'm crying," I continue, "not because of how sad it is, like the situation itself, but because of everything that's lost. Does that make sense? Like who would I be if I didn't have to be strong all the time and I could just be myself? Who would I be if I had a stable family? What kinds of experiences could I be having with my brothers right now if they weren't sick and struggling? I want those experiences. I feel like it would give me nourishment to have some family I could lean on. I'm mourning the loss of all that. To tell you the truth, I think I've been mourning my whole life. Is that weird?"

Jennifer smiles. Her white-lady eyes water and squint. "Not at all," she says. "It's actually really normal to feel that way."

She glances up at the clock. I know the time is up, but I don't want to leave. I don't want to be forced back into the cold and unforgiving world.

"We're out of time, but can you come back tomorrow?" she asks. "I know it's a bit soon, but I want to make sure you have support as we work through the details of your past. I know these sessions can kick up a lot of inner turmoil."

"Well, I'm leaving for my freshman hiking trip tomorrow. I'll be gone until Sunday. I can come back on Monday."

"Perfect."

I stand up to leave.

"Before you go," she says. "I just want to tell you that this is courageous work, what you're doing. I know it may not seem like it now, but the biggest storm has passed. We're mainly dealing with aftershocks now. Surviving it was the greatest feat of all. Now comes the healing, and with that, a new understanding for who you can be in the world and who you can help as a result. I see tremendous potential in you. One who can rise."

She looks at me as if I'm somebody great. Her compassionate gaze digs new wells of possibility in my soul. I have never known myself outside of internal strife and pain. I wonder what it might feel like to be healed. Me, the girl who builds doors I can shut anytime someone gets too close. The only person I know from my family, from my entire neighborhood, that is sort of healed is my mother, and she is still battling in many ways. What is life if it isn't a battle?

I start to see the quiet streams and brooks she paints for me, flowing nearby. A new sun of hope rising on the horizon, shining a light on the promised land that Jennifer says can be mine. In the distance, wide-open fields of bounty and prosperity bursting forth.

"Many fields," she says, as if she's reading my mind. "Brimming with possibility. I hope you enjoy your trip."

CHAPTER SIX

Everyone says that the first-year hiking trip is one of the highlights of their entire time at Dartmouth. "You really bond and make lifelong friends," a senior tells me during orientation. "The key is to approach it with an open mind and go with the flow." Well, it's already starting off badly because no part of me is excited to spend three days in the woods. Why on earth would anyone choose to be eaten alive by bugs, have no plumbing, and be the potential target of deranged serial killers lurking behind the trees? I don't trust nature, specifically what can happen there when no one is looking. My mother says, "The woods have eyes and ears. They remember our cries." I know what she means. Anytime I'm near a wooded area, I feel it in my blood too. The runaways, the hangings, the hound dogs, the unmarked graves. My body remembers even as my mind longs to forget.

Twelve of us are going on this trip, including Earnell and, suspiciously, mostly other Black people. We are a threat if we congregate on campus, but apparently not if we're deep in the woods where we can easily be picked off one by one like in horror movies. There is a sole Asian American woman, Jia Wang, from Bed-Stuy, Brooklyn, whose slang is so pointed, we anoint her an honorary Black person over the course of the trip. She says things like, "Yo, son, dey be buggin" and "come holla at ya girl." Daniel McCullum from my American Government and Law class is also here. Earnell and I, representing our imaginary Black Delegation of America, secretly trade him for Jia. "He belongs to them now," Earnell says dismissively. "It's a damn shame the self-hate some of us have." I shake my head in agreement but feel guilty remembering my own Black shame at the dining hall with Bryce. I can talk to Earnell about almost anything, but I can't tell him about that. I don't want to lose my closest Black friends in my quest for white Prince Charming.

On the day of the trip, the bus drives for an hour away from Dartmouth and the safety of her liberal campus. Even though racism exists at the college in mostly subtle and complex ways, it's more overt in surrounding New Hampshire towns. I've seen Confederate flags hanging in windows as soon as I wander outside Matthew's purview. I've also heard there are quite a few hate groups popping up here and there. I hope I never run into any of their members.

Stephen Clark and his friends, including Daniel, say we shouldn't be so focused on race. "That's the only way to achieve a truly colorblind society." But Stephen Clark and his lackeys don't know what it's like to live near people that hate you because of the color of your skin. Daniel must know deep down, but he erases it, offering himself instead to the fangs of the status quo.

The worst part is you don't know who is a host carrying the contagion of racism. It could be your doctor or your dentist. The lunch server whose smile disappears just a little too quickly when they see your shining Black face. Or the CVS cashier who just happens to be fixing price tags in all of the aisles where you and your Black friends are shopping. Here, the hills really do have eyes. *Here, I know they are watching.*

I don't want to think about race on this trip, however. I just want to drift like a leaf in the wind for once—not in the direction of any lurking serial killers or racists, of course—carefree and unbothered. I remember my session with Jennifer yesterday, connecting again to the bounty of healing waiting for me. I turn to Earnell, who is bouncing up and down next to me as the bus drives over uneven terrain, and sigh. "You know what we should do," I say. "We should skip through the woods like Goldilocks looking for the three bears just to have a taste of natural freedom. We should ditch the white people and make our own Call Ceremony like Baby Suggs in *Beloved*. You'd make a great Call preacher, Earnell."

Earnell looks at me with the glare of a thousand ancestors and says, "*Nigga*, have you lost your cotton-picking mind?

78

I am not about to engage in a display of Black unity in the woods of fucking New Hampshire! That Christian white boy has confused you and infected you with his blue-eyed savior. Remove that 'messiah' from your wall. Jesus didn't die for you. He died for them. He's a portal to prosperity for them and look at the spoils they have reaped. They are the chosen ones. We, merely lambs to slaughter."

"Jeez, Earnell. Can you be more depressing? We're supposed to be having fun. Besides, you can't be chosen or exceptional if you maimed and killed to get the glory. Righteousness has to be earned righteously. Philippians 3:9."

"Sure, Dr. King," he says dismissively. "Well, my strategy is to be quiet and vigilant at all times during this trip. I'd advise you to do the same."

My eyes squint in skepticism and my lips curl up with doubt just like Gary Coleman in *Diff'rent Strokes* right before he says, "What you talkin' 'bout, Willis?"

"You?! Quiet?! I'll believe it when I see it."

Earnell reaches surreptitiously into his book bag, glances around, and then pulls out a small cotton-stuffed doll with blond hair, red horns, and a red-and-green *Nightmare on Elm Street* sweater. I snatch the doll from him and yell at him as quietly as possible, "Earnell! What is this?! Where on earth did you get this?!"

Earnell lowers his head and whispers in my ear, "I call him Freddy, after Freddy Krueger. It's a voodoo doll that represents white supremacy. My aunt Pearl gave him to me. She said if I ever find myself in trouble 'wit dem honkies,' I can stick needles in it and the ancestral forces will hear my call and come rescue me. Look around, girl, this is a ruse. All these Ivy League negroes conveniently in one place. We've got to be on alert and might end up needing this," he says, pointing at the doll. "Don't worry, I'll tell the ancestors to rescue you and the others also. Everyone except that Uncle Tom, Daniel. We'll leave him with his adopted white tribe."

I am speechless. Earnell has outdone himself. I am cauterized by the ridiculousness of the moment. I hand Freddy back to Earnell and pull a small pillow from my bag. "I can't, Earnell. I literally cantable."

"That's not a wor—"

"Shut up," I say, interrupting his annoying correction. "I'm taking a nap. Wake me up when we get there."

"If we get there," he replies snidely. "Something tells me that this trip is going to be unforgettable in more ways than one."

———————————◆·——————————

The road narrows and we are soon surrounded by thickets of trees. We don't plan it, but we all fall silent as the bus comes to a stop in the middle of the woods. I glance over at Daniel, who also looks unnerved. I wonder if his body remembers now, despite his blind allegiance to the mythology of American equality. "Well, what in the by golly has gotten into you all?" Connor, who was correct about me being on his trip, asks when he notices we've all grown grim and quiet. I don't tell Earnell about the clucking or he will never stop clapping.

"You guys don't have to be afraid. I'm gonna take good care of you. Don't worry, I've wrestled a bear before and won." He chuckles loudly to himself. When he realizes no one is laughing along, he backs down and says, "I mean, OK, not really, but I know my way around. Relax. I've led these trips since I was a sophomore and have never had a problem. Now come on, gang! Let's go find our sleeping quarters. Wait, is *gang* offensive? I'm so sorry if that is offensive in any way. I sincerely apologize. I'm working on being a more aware human in the world. It's hard. Bear with me." Earnell smirks while stroking Freddy through his bag.

We clutch our belongings and follow Connor through the woods. Despite my fear, it feels peaceful and serene like Jennifer's office. I become enamored by the majesty of the trees. I wonder how they do it? Stand so tall and proud after everything they've been through, remaining unbent and unbroken. I feel so damaged inside, I'm not sure I'll ever be fixed. I try to hide it, but it's starting to show. Manda Panda doesn't understand why I sometimes sleep all day, even though I have a million things to do. The pressure to succeed is agonizing. Here, I'm nobody and valedictorians are a dime a dozen just like Mr. Walsh said. I hope Jennifer is able to get me back on the right path.

My biggest fear is letting my family down. I'm the

one that was supposed to make something of myself. I'm expected to graduate, find a good job, and then go home and lift my family out of poverty. When my mother calls and asks how it's going, I tell her it's all great. "Dartmouth is a piece of cake," I say. "I'm A'cing all my classes." She is always so proud.

"I just knew you was gon' be something, girl. I just knew it!" When I ask her for an update on what's happening in Cleveland, she tells me not to worry. "Everythang just fine here. Don't you fret over us. You just focus on dem studies." But I know she is lying. Everything is never just fine there.

At home, the day is just a bookmark between tragedies: another morning finding my father passed out drunk, another visit to the jail where one of my brothers is incarcerated, another empty bank account, no more money, never enough money, and another violent episode somewhere in the neighborhood. Someone bleeding now. Someone's face lumped up now. Another, always another.

I thought I could escape the weight of another at Dartmouth. I had hoped that being six hundred miles away would dissolve the anxiety and pressure, but it didn't. I guess you are the same person no matter where you are, carrying your inside problems everywhere. My eyes are watching God and Jennifer, waiting for the miracle, hoping for some interception that makes these burdens more bearable. Not Bryce's God. I could never depend on white Jesus, for all the reasons Earnell mentioned. My eyes are watching my mother's God, the God of Light. The one that freed the slaves and bends the arc toward justice, despite it never reaching. The one that preserves life even as it is taken by some other wild and opposing force. A cosmic Darth Vader always watching from the shadows waiting to play his next trick, hoping for our eventual fall from grace. *May the God of Light prevail*, I pray to the ether.

I ponder these things as the forest draws us deeper. As soon as we arrive at the cabin, Connor tells us we'll be heading out in ten minutes for an "exciting team-building activity." Everyone releases a collective sigh at the prospect, except Gabrielle Davis, Gabby for short, who is a self-described Black nature girl. She has already hiked the Appalachian and Pacific Coast trails with her dad, who's apparently really into outdoor survival techniques. Gabby knows how to start a fire, fish, climb trees, and pick edible berries. "I feel the spirit of every living thing around me," she said when we exited the bus earlier. She inhales deeply and twirls happily in a circle with her arms stretched up toward the heavens, like Earnell after he embarrassed Bryce on the Green last week. All the Black kids look at her judgmentally, but Connor claps eagerly and says, "Now that's what I'm talking about! Soak it all in. The beauty of nature. She gets it!"

Before coming to Dartmouth, I thought all Black folks were like the people in my neighborhood, but now I see that there are as many different kinds of melanin-rich humans as there are stars in the sky. Some think very differently from me, like Daniel. A few are even rich. Like all cultural and ethnic groups, we are not homogenous. The revelation is unsettling since I want all the Black people to be like me so I can feel more comfortable in this foreign environment.

As we are preparing to leave for the team-building activity, which Connor says is a scavenger hunt to learn more about the traditions and history of Dartmouth, Keli proclaims angrily, "I cain't do no obstacle course. I just got my hair done and I forgot my scarf. They only bring in a Black hairdresser once a month and I paid like eighty dollars for this hairdo so I'm not messing it up."

Keli's hair is pressed straight. In order to achieve this look, the hairdresser blow-dried her hair, applied a hot oil treatment, flat ironed it, and then wrapped it in a silk scarf. Now Keli's hair looks silky smooth and luxurious. I really need to get mine done, so I understand her pain. Jia, who has been complaining about not wanting to hike since we got on the bus, joins Keli's protest. "Yea, I don't want Keli's hair to get messed up either. I'm staying in solidarity with the Black struggle."

"That's exactly why the Black Delegation traded you in," Earnell says with pride.

Connor flips. "But you're Asian?! And your hair, Keli?! Seriously?!" He scoffs. Several of us, including myself, start yelling at him about the differences between Black hair and white hair. Connor is so overwhelmed, he puts his hands up in defeat and says, "OK, OK. Whoa. Calm down."

"Telling people of color to calm down is just an

inconsiderate way to mute our legitimate concerns about injustice."

Connor looks at Earnell in annoyance and continues, "Look, I know the world is full of vast cultural differences, many of which I'll probably never understand—"

"You got that right," Earnell chastises as Connor presses on with his tolerance spiel.

"Keli and Jia, you can both stay here and miss this bonding experience. Your loss. Whatever. Everybody else, here are your groups. Your task is to find all five clues hidden around the forest. Stay on the main trail, which is marked in yellow. Look for your particular labeled, roped-off area. The team that collects all five clues the fastest wins a special nature pin and bragging rights."

"Pfff, well, there goes my motivation to try," Earnell says mockingly.

"Boy, I really don't understand you people," Connor replies. He immediately realizes the implications of what he's just said and starts stumbling over his words. "I mean, not *you people* as in YOU PEOPLE." He laughs uneasily. "I mean like, hey, you very different human beings of varying backgrounds and life experiences."

Earnell strokes Freddy. The rest of us look at Connor in silent scold. Now *we* hold the powerful, watchful gaze. I almost clap my hands as punishment but decide against it. I know that kind of power in Earnell's hands, once he becomes aware, is dangerous. Though we are silently judging Connor, we are not really offended. Our RWP sensor tells us that Connor's heart is in the right place despite his ignorance. That makes all the difference in how we receive his unexamined divulsions. If his pulse burned with hate, we would unleash Freddy and the ancestral forces on him.

Connor snaps his fingers enthusiastically and shouts, "All right, folks! Move out! You have one hour to complete your mission."

Earnell turns toward Connor again and says, "You also shouldn't snap your fingers at mostly Black people—"

"Or Asian," Jia chimes in.

"Like dogs," Earnell continues. "There's a long history of that, which I can tell you about later. Just an FYI," he says before prancing away gleefully with the satisfaction of his chastising.

Connor's round, non-Superman jaw hits the floor. Vermont, a liberal stronghold like California, did not prepare him for woke minorities from Keli's metaphorical Compton. He isn't aware of some of the racial trip wires underlying his comments and actions, but we are happy to teach him. Whether he learns or not will be up to him. I think back to the dinner at Professor Alexander-Grant's house where he proudly proclaimed his color blindness and shake my head.

Earnell, Daniel, Gabby, Elizabeth, and I are all together and have been assigned to zone one, which is partitioned off with white rope. Zone two is enclosed with blue rope. Elizabeth, the only white person in our group, is a blue-eyed, blond, salt-of-the-earth, self-proclaimed "mountain woman" from Colorado. She has packed an assortment of survival tools, including a compass, flashlight, thermos, proper hiking shoes, and protein bars. Elizabeth can tell where we are by reading the direction of the wind. Earnell and I decide that if anything happens, Elizabeth and Gabby will have to save us.

I can tell Daniel is crushing on Elizabeth by the way he lowers the tone of his voice when he speaks to her, laughs at everything she says (even when it's not really funny), and dragon smiles anytime she comes near. He looks at her like I look at my white Prince Charming, a gaze infused with a desire to belong. I guess he's trying to find some worth in this white world also.

We find our first clue in a small envelope taped between two towering trees. Well, the others find it. Earnell and I are busy playing Date, Marry, Kill, pop star edition. "I'd marry Brandy, kill Monica because I secretly think she's a hater, and date all three members of TLC. Polygamy could definitely be in my future," Earnell declares proudly.

"Found the first clue," Elizabeth shouts from a distance. Earnell and I clap like proud parents before continuing our game. "Well, I'm torn between marrying Ginuwine or John Edwards."

"John Edwards?!" Earnell recoils in shock. "You really have been seduced by the white devil in only a few short months." He shakes his head in profound disappointment.

In Cleveland, I would have chosen Ginuwine, not a handsome politician, but I've learned at Dartmouth the importance of status and wealth. I see now that the pie is actually massive, not small like I thought before, and I want a slice.

We all head in the direction of the next clue, which Elizabeth says is a ten- to fifteen-minute walk north, where the river meets the clearing. "Pfff," Earnell says. "I literally have no idea what that means. We'll just follow you."

Midway there, Gabby stops dramatically and stands in front of a large oak tree. She closes her eyes, places one hand over her heart, another on the tree, and breathes deeply. After a few minutes, she starts to cry softly. "There were ancestors in this area," she says. "The blood ran thick here and this tree is still carrying the trauma. I'm sorry," she says with a pained voice. "For what you had to witness." She reaches out and wraps her arms around the trunk. The tree is so big, her arms only reach about halfway.

None of us says a word. Instead, we stand with our mouths open for several seconds beholding her weirdness. "Let's trade her too," Earnell whispers in my ear eventually.

"What?" Gabby says when she's done with her tree healing services. "Don't be surprised. I told you I could hear the spirit of everything. If you get in tune, you'll be able to hear it too. That tree whispered to me. Trees are the keepers of wisdom. They remember all."

When Gabby says "keepers," I suddenly start to hear voices coming from everywhere. I grow cold. I'm shivering now. I look all around me. "You see," Gabby says, pointing at me. "She understands. She can hear the call of nature too. Beautiful!"

Gabby sprints in a direction we assume is north. We follow her after Elizabeth's compass confirms. Earnell turns to me and asks, "Are you all right? You can't let that tree-hugging girl get in your head. Don't start freaking out because of her antics. Freddy is here with us. All is safe." I don't respond.

We make our way through the forest on the yellow trail, in the white roped-off area, collecting clues. Along the way, Daniel and Elizabeth join us in our game of Date, Marry, Kill. Nobody is surprised at Daniel's choice to marry Katie Couric, which he reluctantly shares, not wanting to turn Elizabeth off. We are all surprised, however, at who Elizabeth would wed.

"Well, I'd choose the Rock," Elizabeth remarks.

"The wrestler?!" Earnell blurts out as Daniel smiles slyly.

"So you like a little chocolate in your milk," Earnell teases. "Down with the swirl? Maybe that explains how you ended up on a freshman trip with a bunch of negroes. They must have sensed your propensity for soul people. It's all good. We welcome you."

"I used to watch wrestling with my dad," Elizabeth says. "Always thought he was hot and nice. I like that combination."

"Me too," I say in happy solidarity.

"Well, for me," Gabby chimes in, "I wouldn't kill

anything or anyone because that has serious karmic implications. All life is to be respected. Marriage is an outdated, patriarchal institution that continues to oppress women. And dating is what lower-vibrational beings do when they don't know how to adjust their own internal frequency. When I'm ready for a partner, I'll change the channel on my spiritual radio and my partner will appear. Voilà."

Earnell shakes his head and says, "I cantable, to borrow Echo's nonword. Why are you like this? Who made you this way?"

"Earnell," I interject. "You brought a Freddy Krueger voodoo doll with blond hair in case the whites tried to kidnap us. Why are *you* this way?"

"Shhh," Earnell says. "On'tday elltay ethay othersay ymay ecretsay."

"This nigga is really out here speaking pig Latin," Daniel scolds playfully.

Earnell gasps in shock. "Daniel! You use the N-word?! I thought you were allergic to anything Black," he comments.

"Nigga, I'm from Detroit," Daniel chuckles. "We play spades too. I'm just fiscally conservative and a big believer in individual determinism. We create our own destiny and can't keep blaming white people for slavery that happened four hundred years ago as the reason we aren't advancing. At some point, we have to look in the mirror."

"Wait," Elizabeth interjects, "you think white people are trying to hold you back? I'm just trying to graduate from college. And you thought we were going to kidnap you? Who? Connor and me? Actually, New Hampshire's woods are super safe, except for the ticks. And you call yourselves the N-word? I thought that was offensive. I'm so confused."

Earnell wraps his arm playfully around Elizabeth's shoulders to Daniel's dismay. "Don't worry, kid, we'll teach you the ways of the Africanay Americanay people. By the end, you too will be playing spades."

The final clue is tucked beneath a medium-sized rock right next to the river. I see it first and excitedly rip the envelope open. "It looks like a haiku," I say before reading:

The Keepers of Form
Have Come to Guide You Forward
To Answer the Call

Underwater quiet returns. Everything silent . . . unnaturally still. The river stops flowing. It sits on top of the earth like a blanket on a dirty mattress. I see someone in the woods to the right of me. A figure in the shadows. Then, a smearing fog clouds my mind. "Hey!" I yell in distress. "Are you watching us?" I dart into the woods, trampling the fear that my body remembers. I run at top speed, determined to put an end to this once and for all. The figure, which looks like a little Black girl wearing a hospital gown, moves unnaturally, easily weaving between trees. We approach a cliff with a steep drop-off. *Now I'll definitely catch her,* I think to myself. *She has to stop.* But she doesn't. She leaps right over the edge like a fearless base jumper. I am nearly out of breath by the time I make it to the edge. I peer over the side. No trace of her. *It's not possible.*

Reality comes crashing down on me. My youngest brother, Demetrius, floods my mind. When he first started seeing and hearing things, we thought it would pass. "The imagination of a child," my mother said. We brushed it off, but his hallucinations grew more intense and frightening. One night he woke up and said the devil, dressed in a black cloak and clown clothing, was sitting next to his bed, watching him, asking him to do terrible things. My mother knew something had to be done before he hurt himself or someone else. The doctors said it was the onset of schizophrenia. Said he needed pills, lots of them. Said there was still no guarantee it wouldn't get worse. Said there might be a history of mental illness in the family. "We ain't mentally ill, Doctor," my mother barks. "This ain't nothin' the Lawwwd cain't fix."

"I'm afraid the Lord won't be able to help with this one. Something is wrong in his brain and he needs serious help."

Do I need serious help? I wonder to myself. *Is Jennifer's promised land not possible after all?* I sit with my feet hanging over the edge of the cliff, ruminating. *Maybe this is not the result of Hypnotist Jerry and his spells*, which is the excuse I'd been using to explain all of this to myself, *maybe something is broken in my brain too?* Jennifer said the biggest storm had passed, but this one feels enormous, insurmountable. Sanity has been my anchor in a turbulent world. Who am I without it? Another lost one, nameless, faceless, and irrelevant?

I don't know how I'm supposed to make it through Dartmouth with an impaired brain. I could make it if anything else was broken—a hip, a leg, an arm—all those things get better quickly, but does a broken brain ever heal? I am overwhelmed by the thought, feeling like a judge has just handed me a life sentence. I start sobbing, spiraling loud cries right into nature's belly.

I finally understand. There was no way I would ever make it. Even if the poverty didn't kill me, the violence didn't maim me, the pain of watching the ones I love suffer didn't undo me, mental illness, the highest, most potent card in the deck, would still win. It would be waiting in the woods with consequences far worse than any looming serial killer or hate group. The God of Opposition himself, the supreme joker, the wild card, and, ironically, the only guarantee in the pack, would rise against me, delivering the most brutal knockout of the game. The House of Oppression's kryptonite finally striking Superwoman from the sky.

It's too much to bear. I had renewed hope after my second session with Jennifer, but my old despair comes prancing back just like Manda Panda after a night of partying. All of my accomplishments and exceptionality could not save me from my own broken humanity, my frayed ancestral lineage, or the God of Opposition's wrath. I guess even a Chosen One has to unbury the skeletons eventually.

I decide there is no point in trying anymore if my life will always be like this. I consider jumping, like the shadowy figure, into oblivion.

By the time the rest of the group arrives to find me crying my eyes out, it's almost evening. Snot leaks from my nostrils as I heave in large swaths of air. Earnell comes racing toward me, my very own Black Prince Charming. Then Daniel, looking surprisingly like a Black savior as well. No blond hair or blue eyes in sight, except for the girl who likes a little chocolate in her milk. More irony. They both sit next to me. Earnell wraps his arms around me and says, "I understand. I don't know what it's about, but I understand." His compassion dissolves me further into a puddle of tears and snot. The others bend their knees and sit around me. Nobody says a word. It's the first time I don't feel isolated, despite the silence. I've learned that I don't need words to feel close to people. The fact of another living presence is enough. For once, I'm not crying alone. I thank the God of Light for the miracle of human connection, which somehow makes it survivable. Bearable.

There are no divisions between us now. No conservative Black guy from Detroit, no crunchy granola girl from Colorado, no Black hippie tree hugger from Washington, DC, no sassy Black Prince Charming from Atlanta, and no mentally ill first-generation college student from Cleveland. Just young people lost in a world of chaos where the God of Opposition reigns supreme. Here, at the mouth of the great unknown, our hopes and expectations for how our lives would turn out leap over the edge like the shadowy figure from before.

Then the moment rides on, like a cowboy into the sunset on an old TV western. Our bodies mourn the passing and rise, as if on cue.

"Can you guys please not tell the others," I say with a hoarse voice. "I don't want them to think I'm a freak."

They all smile considerately, Gabby placing a hand on my shoulder, like I'm the trunk of one of her ancient trees. "Don't worry," she says. "We won't tell a soul."

CHAPTER SEVEN

On our last night at the cabin, Connor prepares a feast. Well, a white people's vegan feast. There are green beans, cabbage, tofu, mashed sweet potatoes, and roasted cauliflower. I take a moment to look around the table at the faces that I've grown to love. I am amazed at how quickly strangers become kin in settings like this. I guess that's the point of the trip in the first place, to encourage us to build real community. After everyone has been served, Connor says it's tradition at the last supper (pun intended) to share something personal and deep.

"That's why so many end up staying friends after these trips. We get to see inside each other and not just the masks we all wear. We'll start with lighter topics and get a little deeper as the night goes on. I'll go first. My name is Connor Raskins and my favorite TV show is *Gilmore Girls*. You can laugh, I'm not ashamed. I like long walks on the beach, epic sunsets, anything that has to do with nature, and mayonnaise on my French fries, the European way."

Earnell almost chokes as a green bean goes flying out of his mouth. "Mayo-nnaise?! On French fries? Wow, that's really gross. I think I might throw up in my mouth. I'm going to step outside and get some air 'cause the puke is coming," he says while making vomiting noises and walking dramatically out the door to sit on the porch. I know he's just trying to escape the manufactured vulnerability at hand.

We each go around sharing little quirks and background information about ourselves. Keli goes next. "Well, my name is Kelicia Marie Johnson. My favorite TV show is *Martin*. What's up? What's up? WHAT'S UP?!" she says, imitating the famous opening lines of the show. Most of the people at the table get it, but Connor seems baffled. "That's how the show opens," I lean over and whisper in his ear.

"I like collard greens and cornrows," she continues. "My parents from the South and got accents so thick, it sounds like they have a mouth full of cotton when they talk. I was born in Alabama but raised in Chi-town, where I learned to throw bows, if necessary. Don't let the necessary occur, ya heard? Lastly, I'on think Tupac is dead. He's totally chillin' on an island somewhere in the Caribbean."

Connor raises his hand awkwardly. *He is learning well*, I think to myself. "Can I ask a question? What are cornrows?"

"I guess there's just no Black people in Vermont, huh?" Keli responds teasingly. "They're a type of braid, Connor. I can show you on your hair if you like. It's long enough."

"Yea, that'd be awesome!" he exclaims.

Keli braids four cornrows in the crown of Connor's head. Like a thoughtful teacher, she explains to the other white person, Elizabeth, what she's doing as she works and the importance of braided hairstyles in the Black community.

"Way back in the slavery days, women hid rice in their braids during the Atlantic Passage to feed their children. You should also know that this shit is really important to us. It's one of our main types of expression, like fashion and rap. It would take all night to explain the ways that Black hair has been shamed, politicized, and controlled. These unique styles help us reclaim our heritage."

Keli finishes braiding Connor's hair. "All done." Connor gets up and looks in the mirror next to the couch. "Whoa," he says. "Dude, these are sick!" he yells excitedly from across the room.

Connor leaves the braids in as we prepare to share deeper information about ourselves. His new Black hairstyle makes it hard to take him seriously, but we all do our best.

"All right then, for the last part of the evening, we're gonna do an activity called 'If you really knew me.' All you have to do is answer that question. I'll start again. If you really knew me, you'd know I've really been struggling this year. My grades aren't the best because I'm majoring in something I don't really like. I'm doing it for my dad, who has dreamed of me being a doctor like him since I was young. I'd rather be studying archaeology or even something like architecture, but my dad's an alcoholic asshole. I live in fear of disappointing him so I just do what he says. It's getting harder, though, to comply."

I am shocked by Connor's authenticity. Just like at the cliff, we all sit and witness Connor's openness. He stares down at his plate, pushing leftover food in various directions. He looks like a defeated little boy. I'm so used to seeing white people as oppressors, I never stop to think they might have some of the same problems as me.

"Connor," Gabby says, "I really want to thank you for sharing all that. I'm deeply moved. Ashay, brother." Gabby takes a deep breath. "I guess I can go next."

Earnell comes shuffling back in. "Wait, wait. I heard all that. Wow, man. Wow. Bring it in, bro. Come on." Earnell hugs a reluctant Connor, who is still sitting with his feelings.

"You've really shown me this weekend that we don't always need Freddy," Earnell says.

"Who's Freddy?"

I reach over and touch Connor's arm while shaking my head, assuring him he doesn't want to know.

"Don't ask," I say.

Earnell sits back down at the table as Gabby continues. "Well, if you really knew me, you would know I'm scared. Like all the time. Despite all my spiritual talk, I live in fear of everything. That my parents are going to die before we've had a chance to work out our issues. That deep down I'm not good enough. And that I'm not going to be able to live my life how I want. So many people in my family never got to pursue their dreams. Why should mine come true? It's hard to face."

Cornrowed Connor turns to Gabby and says, "Fuck that. You absolutely have to go after what you want. You only get one life and it's yours to do what you will. I hope all your dreams come true, Gabby."

Keli reaches over and hugs Gabby as she smiles at Connor. Even though Connor was addressing Gabby, we all know he was talking to himself too.

"Well, I don't really have anything to share," Earnell says suddenly. "Things are pretty good for me right now."

I look at Earnell dubiously.

"Really, Earnell? You don't have any struggles or issues you're working through? Have you reached enlightenment?"

"I mean," Earnell responds, "I just try to stay positive about everything. My brother taught me that. He always said, 'You gotta keep ya head up. Keep lookin' for the sunshine. It might be hidden behind clouds, but it's always there.' So that's my mantra. That's what I do. I stay positive."

"But I mean, it has to get hard sometimes, right? You can't be positive all the time. Even I know that," Gabby reflects.

Earnell is very similar to me. For people like us, who have raised ourselves in the lion's den, it takes a lot to show our true emotions. The first sacrifice in the gladiator's pit is your feelings. You can't be soft and survive. I tried to explain that to Jennifer, but I don't know if she truly understands how our very humanity is sacrificed in the arena. We are warriors, Earnell and I, rarely dropping our shields, until things boil over and we can't help it, like what happened to me at the cliff. I can tell Earnell is bubbling inside.

"I mean, what choice do I have?" Earnell says finally. "If I stop and think about everything I'm up against, I would never get out of bed. My brother was my hero. And now he's gone. He was killed by a white cop. We were pulled over. I told him to just hold up his wallet so he knew we didn't mean any harm. It's all my fault. I think about him every day. How proud he would be that I'm at Dartmouth. Maybe he would be here also, three years ahead of me. He was really smart too.... It's all good." Earnell's voice starts to crack. He smiles, trying to bury the dragon.

"I know everything happens for a reason. It's just... I don't know...I would trade anything to have one more day with him. Anything." Earnell coughs, acting as if he is clearing his throat, but I know he is really choking back the tears. If they start flowing, they might never stop. I reach over and grab Earnell's hand.

"It's not your fault. That's too heavy a burden to carry, for anyone." I kiss him on the cheek. I try to give him the tenderness I cannot give myself in such moments. He receives it and then bristles, throwing his shield back up.

"It's all gonna be fine, guys," he says half-heartedly. "It's gonna work out," he tries to reassure himself. We understand, so we nod and let him have his positivity mantras.

Keli tells us about her struggles with impoverished addict parents and siblings. "Everybody's depending on me to save them, but I don't know how to handle that kind of pressure." Daniel speaks about what it's like to be so alienated from the Black community at Dartmouth, even though he comes from an all-Black neighborhood in Detroit. "It feels like I can't be both conservative and Black," he says. "So I choose conservative." Elizabeth talks about her bulimia and body dysmorphia. "No matter what I do," she says, "I hate the way my body feels." Jia shares about the pressure her Chinese immigrant parents put on her. "I can just never please them. So fuck it. I'ma do me."

Jia finishes and then everyone looks at me. I shrink, melting under the attentive gazes of supportive friends. I want to keep the mask on. I open my mouth, but the words stop in my stomach cavity this time, refusing the long walk toward freedom. My mind feels like an abandoned warehouse full of dark and mysterious things. There is so much I want to forget.

"This is really hard for me," I say finally after several minutes of silence. "I never really had any friends growing up, so I don't know how to share things with other people. I guess I'll just come right out and say it. The other day, at the cliff, I was thinking about everything I've been through and I decided it's not worth it. That it won't matter much if I'm not here. I don't think anyone besides my mother would really miss me."

I don't look at anyone's face. I look down as tears start

to drip on my twiddling thumbs. "When I came to Dartmouth, I hoped it meant I mattered somehow. That I was finally worth something. But being here, around all these people that have so much more than me, I see now how much I don't matter. Like at all in this world."

Cornrowed Connor grows enraged and slams his palms down on the table, lurching himself out of his seat.

"Goddamnit, Echo! I can't believe this is the world we live in. How can someone so amazing feel like this? Everything's so fucked up."

Connor walks across the room and grabs a small piece of paper. He returns to the table and starts writing. "Look," he says, "I haven't known you long, but you matter. It matters that you are here. You're so funny and cute and quirky and smart. You have such a deep and complex understanding of life. I don't know what you'll end up doing in this world, but I know it's going to be big and I know it's going to help a lot of people. You have greatness in your spirit. I see it."

Gabby snaps in agreement. "Ashay, brother."

"This is my number," Connor says, handing me the piece of paper. "You call me anytime of the day or night when you fall into the dark place. Do you understand? You call me anytime."

Cornrowed Connor is too nerdy to be Prince Charming, but I start to wonder if maybe I shouldn't be looking for a perfect, idealized white boy at all. Maybe a thoughtful, compassionate, dorky nature boy who wears Dockers sweatshirts is enough? In fact, this trip has also made me reconsider Earnell. He is not the Black phoenix I imagined, but beneath his ridiculous antics is a plush heart, full of love and deep concern. Isn't that what I'm looking for?

I wipe the tears from my eyes with my sleeves and reach over and squeeze Earnell's hand, which lights him up. He was already burning for me, I knew that all along, but now, he sees a glimmer of hope where there was once a closed door. *No more doors*, I think to myself.

"We should get some sleep," Connor says, finally ending the sacredness of the night. We stand. We clean the cabin. We pack. Then we hug each other like a loving family before disappearing into the darkness of our rooms.

CHAPTER EIGHT

I return to campus invigorated. One week until midterms and I feel like I can take on the world. For the first time in my life, I feel seen and appreciated just for being me. I smile at random strangers walking across the Green. I speak blessings over their lives and hope all their dreams come true. I reunite with Matthew McConaughey, telling him about the experience. He rings bells at the top of every hour to celebrate. Fall leaves ablaze with color rain down like confetti anointing the path forward. Even the autumn sun, gracious and majestic, decides to stay a little longer each day.

I didn't know it was possible to feel this alive. Nothing can stop my happiness. Not my falling grades, not the unexplainable occurrences—the cryptic letters reshuffling and the continued reorientation of objects in the world—and not the hard work I know I will have to do with Jennifer when the time comes. I emailed her asking to move our appointment to Wednesday, not wanting to dampen the good cheer currently swirling around my life.

I'm on my way to the student center now to get a math tutor. I don't want to flunk out and I hope to keep having amazing experiences like the hiking trip this past weekend. With midterms right around the corner, I know it's time to throw in my hand and seek help.

When I arrive, I glance in and see so many faces that look like mine. I am ashamed, but I bury it and force myself to walk in. The desk attendant takes my information and then assigns me to a tutor named Zach, a white boy from Rhode Island. I can tell by the way Zach coldly shakes my hand, devoid of all warmth and understanding, and the way he doesn't make real eye contact, that he isn't going to be able to help me. My RWP sensor starts beeping.

"All right, so you're here to get some help with calculus," Zach says. "Awesome. That's a biggie 'round these parts. Let me start off by asking you a few questions. Do you have a solid understanding of basic arithmetic, algebra, and functional equations? You'll need to have a good foundation in those to really grasp calculus."

I want to tell him I don't understand anything about math outside of simple addition and subtraction and that my brain doesn't relate to numbers at all. The words are my friend, the numbers my enemy. I can't even do long-form division. I started falling behind in middle school, when I also had a teacher who didn't know how to teach, and I never caught up. I made it through most of my high school math classes by cheating and doing extra credit. I can see in his empty Rhode Island eyes that he won't understand.

"All right, why don't we start with this equation. Can you tell me the order of operations? Where should we start?"

I stare down at the collection of words and numbers. *Words and numbers should never be mixed together*, I think to myself.

"Umm, maybe we should start by multiplying these two," I guess.

"Solid effort, but we're actually going to divide this side first and then we'll multiply. OK, so what's this divided by this?"

Even though it's two small numbers being divided, 32 and 4, I still punch it into the calculator and report the answer to Zach. He writes it down and then shows me how to finish the equation.

"OK, so for this next one, we have to do some algebra. If two expressions are equal for all values of their variables, the equation is called an identity. Does that make sense?"

I nod my head, but I don't understand anything he just said.

"Now, another important concept. For every x value, the slope is always zero. Therefore, the derivative of a constant function is zero. We gotta get that down before we can move on. So considering that, can you work this one out?"

My brain shuts down. I stare. I don't know what any of it means. This is what I feared in asking for a tutor at a place like Dartmouth. The tutors assume I have a baseline foundation of knowledge, which I don't have. I know they can't catch me up for the years I'm behind, but I can't meet them anywhere near what they've learned and been exposed to. Maybe Stephen was right. I start to wonder if I really deserve to be here and if I'm really as smart as I thought. Mr. Walsh, whose shadow is never far, grins from the basement of my mind like Pennywise in the sewer. I remember all the people from Cleveland who said I was intelligent. I wish they were here now.

Zach's dead eyes wait for some signal of life from me. "Do you get what I'm saying?" he repeats after several seconds of silence.

"Actually," I say while grabbing my backpack, "I was thinking I'd go home and brush up on the basics and then come back tomorrow. I just returned from my freshman hike and I'm still pretty tired. Thanks for your time, though."

"OK, yea, sweet," he says. "We're open from eight a.m. to eight p.m., so you can just stop by anytime."

I wish Zach would try harder to get me to stay. I know I should be here, but I just need someone who will be sympathetic to my situation. Zach bounces away, and with him, so do my hopes of catching up. I decide I will ask Earnell and Keli about their tutors. Maybe they can help me too.

Though I'm a little shaken after the tutoring session, I'm still hopeful from my time in nature and I'm especially looking forward to getting ice cream with Bryce tomorrow after Bible study. I've never wanted Tuesday, a not particularly remarkable day, to arrive so fast in my life.

*　　*　　*

I pace nervously around my dorm room. I know I need to study, but I'm too excited. I'm standing in front of the bathroom mirror giving myself a pep talk when I hear Manda Panda come bouncing in. I have so much energy coursing through my body, I run out to greet her and give her a hug. "I'm so happy to see you," I say.

"What's gotten into you?" She pulls away confusedly. "Wait... did you finally drink the gin and juice? Did it give you liiife?" I nod my head, even though I haven't. "Ahhhh!" she starts screaming and hugging me while we both jump up and down in glee in the middle of the room.

"I knew this moment would come," she says like a proud parent. "Look at you, glowing. All grown up and finally enjoying college. Let's take a picture to commemorate this moment." She grabs her Polaroid camera out of her closet. "Humph, only one left. I could have sworn there were more."

I quickly, and furtively, close the top drawer of my desk, which holds all the pictures she is missing, their ominous warning about the God of Opposition and his tricks sending a shiver down my spine.

"Say cheese!" Manda Panda says as we both stare into the lens and smile enthusiastically. She returns the camera and then waves the picture in the air until it's fully developed, hanging it on the wall next to her other pictures when it's done. It's our first picture together.

"I wish I could stay and drink more with you, but I

gotta run to cheerleading practice. Smoocha later," she says, before prancing out of the room.

"K, byeee," I say mockingly after she's already gone.

I return to the bathroom, preparing to resume my pep talk. When I look in the mirror, I stumble backward, almost crashing into the wall. Terror eats the excitement that was just dripping off of me. The figure in the mirror sucks me in. I can't look away. She is sitting *in the mirror*, facing away from me. A little girl, like the one I saw in the forest on the hiking trip. I can't see her face, but she seems familiar.

"Don't keep running away," she says with her back still facing me. "I was sleeping at the bottom of the well where you hid me until Jennifer woke me up." Her head starts to turn slowly in my direction like something out of a scary movie. I want to run, but my feet are pinned to the floor. Tears roll down my cheeks, the agony in the center reactivated. Soon she is looking at me, full on. I see her face and I know who she is. The same braids I wore as a child. The same shirt I used to wear before bed, all those nights curled up into a tight ball.

"You have to save me from *him*," she says with urgency in her voice. "Now he knows where I am again." She gasps in terror. "He's coming." The lights blink off and I collapse to the floor.

I wake up a few minutes later. She is gone. I sit on the bathroom floor staring at the white tile. On the outside, I am blank and cold. On the inside, the same battle I've been fighting since it happened. I thought I could keep it buried and out of sight forever but memory is like a ghost, haunting you until the pain is faced and exorcised.

I am so disturbed, I consider canceling my meeting with Bryce tomorrow. I don't want to be in the sunken place when I see him. I close my eyes and lean my head back against the wall. I try to think of what to do. There is a portal spinning in my room and I've just talked to my eight-year-old self in the bathroom mirror. *I'm going mad, just like my brother,* I think. *Should I call someone? Jennifer? Connor? Earnell? My mother?*

Thoughts of my mother whirl in my mind, conjuring her presence. I feel her everywhere suddenly. "Momma, I'm scared," I cry out. I summon another of her Bible verses. This time from the Book of Psalms. I bow my head and clasp my hands so tightly that the palms turn white.

"Though I walk through the valley of the shadow of death, I will fear no evil, for You are with me. Your rod and Your staff, they comfort me. May the Lord and all his glory and light be with me. Amen."

I inhale fully and a deep calm surges through me. *This is not the end of me,* I say to myself with renewed courage, *this is only the beginning.* The words are not my own and come from somewhere deep inside—the ancestor place, the wade-in-the-water place. Even though I don't fully believe, I trust them. I have no other choice in this moment.

I rise up off the floor and stare once more in the mirror at my face, which looks irradiated, like a Black phoenix, but without the pomp and circumstance fantasies of some man.

This is a creation of my own accord, of my own making. My eyes are flames, burning. Not with lust like Earnell's, but with a power I never knew was in me. *Chosen One*, my reflection whispers to me. *She is here*. My eyes close.

A tunnel of motion. Forward.

———— • ◆ • ————

A strange fog permeates the air around me, as if the entire campus has been submerged in steam. I am standing in line at Ladles, the only ice cream parlor on campus, uncertain how I got here. The last thing I remember is passing out on the bathroom floor after praying to my mother's God, which feels likes it was only a few minutes ago. The awning over the shop is usually bright pink with white ice-cream-cone letters, but today it's lime green with pink letters. And the parlor itself looks different, sparkling and luminous, despite the fog. I turn in confusion to a younger teen standing next to me and fire off a series of questions.

"Have you ever seen the sky look like this? Why does the shop suddenly look brand-new? Also, is it Tuesday? Is Bible study over? Is there still a week until midterms?"

"Let's see," he says sarcastically, "of course it's Tuesday. Is there another day that follows Monday? How do you expect the sky to look after it rains? It ain't all sunshine and rainbows in Hanover, honey. Are you from California or something? There's no need to study the Bible because God is dead. Look around. And college is an elaborate money scam. So my advice is to drop out and get a trade, like making ice cream, for example. I'm sure they make a killing here, which is how they can afford to remodel regularly. Does that answer your questions?"

I gasp in shock at the brashness of young people these days. I clutch my imaginary pearls and shout, "Young man, have you no decency?!" He rolls his eyes and turns around, leaving me to climb out of the cavern of his rudeness alone.

I am shaking my head in contempt when Bryce taps me on the shoulder from behind. "Hey!" he says. "I wasn't sure if you were still coming since I didn't see you at Bible study. It's so nice to see you." He gives me a big hug, and I can't figure out if it's a friend hug or an I-want-to-do-secret-things-to-you embrace.

He smiles awkwardly before falling silent. The line advances forward, but Bryce remains quiet. "Is everything OK?" I ask softly. "I mean, we don't have to talk. I was just wondering if something was up?"

"I just can't stop thinking about our conversation in the cafeteria, how real, honest, and raw it was.... And I can't stop thinking about you."

I turn toward him in total surprise. "Really?" I ask, floored.

"Yea. I just think you're so special. Thoughtful and deep. It's really rad. Without Dartmouth, I probably would have never met someone like you."

I melt. Imaginary angels descend from heaven and begin tooting their horns in delight. So this is what it feels like to be wanted. A thousand firecrackers ignite inside my soul. I look down, then toward the heavens, then into his eyes. I am as radiant as the newly shining Ladles parlor. I prepare to be loved, finally, by someone I like back.

He has more to say, but hesitates. "I think...Whew, this is harder than I thought. I think...I'm falling..."

Suddenly his face pixelates and glitches as if he's about to transform into Agent Smith from *The Matrix*. He morphs into Manda Panda, who yells, "Woo-hoo, luv you too, bitch! Roomies fa life." I pop out of my bed and realize it was a dream.

Manda Panda, who is kneeling by the side of my bed, says, "Well, I do, you know." She awkwardly runs her hand down the side of my face before getting up.

"Ew, why'd you do that?"

"To like wrap up the moment with care. I was concerned. I found you passed out on the bathroom floor last night, dragged you to bed, and then came home after a full day of activities to find you *still* sleeping, but alas, she lives! I wanted you to have some fun, but not like black out for that long."

I glance at the clock and see that it's three p.m. In two hours, I will be eating ice cream at Ladles with Bryce—for real. I'm certain he won't be professing his undying love for me. Sometimes dreams are better than reality.

The rest of the day is shot. I've missed all my classes and meetings and have managed to be less productive than I was yesterday. I plop my head back down on the pillow in a haze of drowsy confusion.

"What is the meaning of it all?" I cry out in satirical agony.

"I dunno," Manda Panda replies. "Life, liberty, and the pursuit of happiness?"

She slings her bookbag on her back.

"Study group. Toodles."

I am still thinking about my dream when I arrive at Ladles. I stop dead in my tracks when I see the same precocious teen. I pinch myself to make sure I'm not somehow still asleep. When I don't wake up, I yell, "Hey! You were in my dream last night!" He looks at me in shock and disgust, as if he is deeply offended. "Dreaming about children you don't know should be a criminal offense," he says flatly. Still rude.

"What's your favorite flavor?" Bryce asks excitedly from behind me. He immediately grabs me in an embrace. I melt into his arms wondering if my dream might have been a premonition. I stand silently for several seconds after he lets go to see if he will profess his love for me. He doesn't.

"Chocolate," I blurt out, easing the awkwardness of the previous moment.

"Of course," he giggles. "Wait, is that racist?"

I playfully tap his shoulder to indicate no offense was taken. Bryce's curly hair is pulled up into a ponytail at the top of his head, while the back remains loose. His Superman bone structure is even more visible with his hair away from his face. I am stunned by how good he looks. I forget everything that happened in the bathroom and lose myself in his attractiveness. A wide smile draws across my face while looking at him. I try to pull my cheeks forward, but they refuse.

"That hairstyle suits you," I say. "On our freshman trip, Keli braided Connor's hair and it was hilarious. He looked like a dollar store thug. Maybe we'll get her to put some in your hair one day."

He laughs and responds, "That would be awesome if I don't cut it first. I'm kind of tired of all this hair. It's a lot of work to maintain."

"No!" I yell suddenly and unexpectedly. "I mean...it just looks great on you. Don't cut it!"

He smiles bashfully. "Well, your hair is pretty cool too," he says.

I can't receive any part of this compliment because I know he must be lying. My hair looks awful all the time. I can't get a relaxer here regularly, which means it's straight on the ends and nappy at the root. I mainly keep it slicked down into a ponytail so the coarseness is less visible. I felt ugly in high school, but I feel like Igor on campus among these fairy-tale white people and their socially accepted beauty.

After we finally get our ice cream, we walk around taking in the fall evening. I feel so good walking next to Bryce. The world seems so much more beautiful with an attractive man by your side. Maybe this means I won't have to keep fighting all my battles alone.

We stop briefly in front of the wooden structure that will burn during homecoming five days after midterms.

"Out of all the things they could build, why would they build this? A giant joker in a palace. He should be in a dungeon where he belongs.... Look at him mocking us with his capricious smile. I never liked the symbology of that dreadful character. It haunts me even now."

"Me neither," Bryce replies. "Reminds me of Darth Vader, dark forces."

"Right?! I knew I couldn't be the only one who sees it."

We continue walking and find a bench just off campus.

"So how was the hiking trip?" he asks curiously.

I tell him everything. The words spill from my mouth so quickly, some of them are out of order. I'm not sure if I'm uttering complete sentences, but Bryce seems to be following along. He shakes his head affirmatively as I recount.

"I knew it," he responds. "I told you it's one of the most amazing parts of the *entire* college experience."

"Fine, you were right again," I say, attempting to flirt. He winks at me, which makes me think he is flirting back. Again I wonder, *Was that dream a premonition?* I start freaking out, pondering what to do next. I soften and try to bat my eyes like they do in romantic comedies. I cringe at myself and decide to stop. I climb back into my strength, my true nature, but try to relax more.

"I thought a lot about our conversation at Thayer," he says while pensively licking his ice cream, after a few moments of silence pass. I watch in desire. "I keep thinking about how much different I'd be if I'd came from a place like yours. Would I still be Christian? Would the trajectory of my life even be the same?"

"Probably not," I say sarcastically. Worried I have been too sharp, I try to correct myself and say, "I mean, it's possible it might have been the same, just not likely."

"That's true," he says in nonreactionary agreement. "Which is gnarly to me. How our lives can be so shaped by where we land after we leave God's grace."

I hold in my laughter from Bryce's unapologetic use of the word "gnarly." He says it exactly as I imagine someone from California would. I don't even really know what it means, but the word sounds funny. After I suppress my giggles, I begin to wonder how the trajectory of my life would be different if I were white. Would I still have been poor? I know some white people live in poverty, but would I have been one of them? Who might I be if I'd never been called a nigger, or made to feel ugly and unwelcome for the color of my skin? Would I constantly question myself and my right to exist, or would I prance through the world like Manda Panda as if it all were made for me?

After thinking about it for a while, I decide that if I were white and a man, I would walk on water too, just like Jesus. I'd make all sorts of things like computers and world-changing software since the oppression would no longer be consuming most of my energy. I would go to the moon and have a look around, because why not? There'd be no *Hills Have Eyes* gazes restricting my movement through space.

I'd walk around wearing a low-brimmed cowboy hat like Clint Eastwood with a cigarette hanging from my mouth, saying, "Go ahead, make my day." I'd have no fear since there would never be any consequences for my actions, especially the wrong ones, because I'd own the law and the jail. When it's time to die, I'd return to my white Jesus with blue eyes and blond hair—the landlord of heaven—and tell him how I pranced around the world tasting all of its glorious fruit. *Imagine*, I think.

Bryce finishes the last of his ice cream cone and then folds his hands in his lap. I have an overwhelming urge to reach over and grab one. We are sitting close, but our bodies aren't touching. I want to throw myself on him and dissolve into the heat of his masculinity. *Should I try to kiss him?* I think to myself.

I am convinced he is considering the same thing when he suddenly reaches over and touches my face, but I soon realize he is just wiping something off my cheek.

"Had a little bit of ice cream," he says. "Another thing I was thinking, from our previous conversation," he continues, "I figured out now 'how to make it right.' You have to be an ally," he says, more for himself than me. "That's what I'm committing to doing in my life. That and being the best Christian I can. If this is a world where some of us have more privilege than others, and I'm one of those people, then I want to use my energy and time putting that privilege in the service of others. That's how you 'make it right.'"

I dissolve. *He is truly just an amazing person and he doesn't even realize it*. I want him to be mine. I don't want to lie anymore. I want to drop the act right here and now and show him who I really am, a pagan with a good heart. I want to meet him in Rumi's field, out beyond expectations, lies, masks, and even religion.

"Do you like Rumi?" I ask, changing the subject. "I've been thinking about how nice it would be to experience the world as he did, to visit his prophetic field beyond labels and ideas. I mean—"

I hesitate. Trying to work up the nerve to be honest with him about me not really being a Christian and tell him how much I like him.

"It would be nice if we could all meet each other there—"

"I'll totally meet you there!" Bryce interjects enthusiastically. He's smiling now, from cheek to cheek, like I was at Ladles. "I'll be the one 'chewing a piece of sugarcane, in love with the one to whom every *that* belongs.'"

A man that can quote Rumi. I am in love.

"I have to tell you something," he says, hesitating just like in my dream. I explode inside. I want to do imaginary cartwheels all over the Green. I smile radiantly, preparing for his love confession. *I am a psychic goddess. Behold my powers.* "I'm glad I met you, Echo Brown," he says proudly. "You're a really special person." I wait for more, but he just looks off lamely into the distance. *What does that mean?! Is he playing hard to get?*

The Defiance screams in my head, *This dude is not to*

be trusted, you feel me, but desire keeps me reaching for a reality that appears to have been just a dream after all. The bubble of anticipation bursts. I sit paralyzed by confusion as the last of the sunlight betrays me, leaving without my permission. The darkness moves us past Rumi's field into a whir of quiet desperation. I long for his touch. He hungers for sugarcane and clear answers in the world.

"Ah, well, we should probably head back. I have an early class tomorrow. Wednesdays are the worst, but I had an amazing time hanging with you. I'm gonna go home and read some Rumi after I finish studying. I'm inspired."

We walk back, the flurry of the campus rushing to meet us much too soon. We stand in front of the Hanover Inn, preparing to part ways. Bryce gives me a hug. Again, I try to feel if there is more he wants to say. I hold on a little longer, to show him my desire, but he releases me like the autumn trees release their leaves. I float back down to the earth.

"I'll see you soon," he says, walking off before stopping and turning around. My hope quickly returns.

"Out beyond ideas of wrongdoing and rightdoing...I'll meet you there." He smiles.

<hr />

Manda Panda comes stumbling in at 3:00 a.m., drunk, babbling, and burping. "Hey, girl," she says. "Oh, shhh. It's nighttime. Sleepy time. Sorry."

I try to pretend like I'm still asleep as she fumbles

her way around the room, loudly slamming drawers and knocking over things.

"Shhh," she says again to herself.

When she starts throwing up, I jump out of bed, run to the bathroom, and grab some paper towels. I turn on the light and see her kneeling on the floor in front of me. Black mascara runs down her cheeks and chunks of vomit line her lips. "I'm so sorry," she says. "It's been a long night. Gin and juice is not a game, but I'm sure you know that too now. Hey, raise the roof," she says while pumping her hands up toward the ceiling several times.

I cover the throw-up with paper towels and help her up on her bed. I wipe the vomit from her mouth and ask her why she keeps getting so drunk.

"Maybe a little is OK, but not too much. I got so drunk at Professor Alexander-Grant's dinner, I threw up on her lawn. I was so embarrassed. I'm never getting wasted again. Plus, I watched my father drink himself sick my whole life. That shit will mess you up."

"Shhh," she says again even though I'm not talking that loud. "My head is killing me."

She drops her head onto my shoulder. Her long brown hair falls down my chest. I can smell the sourness of her throw-up breath. She suddenly starts crying.

"Why is life so freaking hard? I don't understand." She sobs.

"What's wrong? I thought you were having a great time here."

Her head suddenly bounces up off my shoulder. "Can I tell you something?" she says before burping in my face. "Oops, sorry."

She starts whispering in my ear even though no one else is in the room. I am shocked by what she says.

"He didn't mean to," she says. "We were having a good time. He's not a bad person. We were just caught up in the moment and I was so drunk. Even more drunk than right now."

"Did he hear you when you said stop?" I ask. She nods and then stares ahead at the curtain covering the window.

"But I know he didn't mean to. He's a good guy."

I've known many men who "didn't mean to." Men who are wolves with gnarling fangs and claws. They don't look like wolves, though. They look like regular people. They go grocery shopping and play football with their friends after work. They smile as they pass you on the sidewalk. Some even go to church every Sunday morning, as if faith can neutralize their monstrosity. It can't. It is always our bodies, and souls, that pay the price for their atrocities and all the ways they "didn't mean to." The man who raped my mother was a family member, trusted and respected. The one who raped her mother was a pastor, influential and kind. And the one who raped me was a prince, regal and popular. His name was Prince Mack and he was a known rapist in the neighborhood. No one did anything. So he was free to keep raping without consequence.

There is rarely any price to pay for taking the body

of a woman. So I understand why Manda Panda needs to reframe him as "a good guy." It's so she can come to terms with the fact that even if she tells someone, it's likely nothing will happen, especially to a white guy at an Ivy League school. And since she was drunk and wearing a very short dress, she "must have asked for it anyways." So he will get to live a normal life, grocery shopping among us despite his monstrosity, while his victim, Manda Panda, must paper over it. Crochet it into the fabric of her memory and pray the threading holds for the long term.

Before tonight, Mandy and I have been mostly respectful strangers. Not understanding each other and keeping a safe distance from our differences. In my mind, she was just an entitled prancer getting regularly drunk off Snoop's favorite drink. To her, I was probably a Black girl from some ghetto in urban America where everyone is violent and low-class. Tonight, however, we have finally seen one another for the first time after months of living together. I could not meet her on the mountaintop of her privilege, but I can certainly meet her in the dark night of her despair. Here, united by the pain of injustice, we can be more than just friends or roommates. We can be sisters.

"I think you should report it," I say again, surprised at my insistence, given my own experience. "What about the next girl? If you can't do it for yourself, can you do it for her?"

After a few moments of silence, I say, "I wish I had told. I know a couple of the girls that came after me."

Mandy leans over and gives me a hug, slathering me in her drunkenness. She lays on my shoulder for a few seconds, drifting in and out of sleep. "No more gin or juice for me," she says before crawling under the covers.

I sit on my bed and listen to her snores for several minutes. I try to put the entire night into perspective. Sure, there are so many monsters out there, but some men are not. I repeat that to myself over and over like one of Earnell's positivity mantras. *All men aren't monsters*, I say to myself. I know this because of Bryce, who is the sweetest man I've ever met, and Earnell, who is a Black Prince Charming with a heart of gold. I hope that it's more than just monsters and almost-brothers who want me, which has been the case so far. I pray a man who has basked in Rumi's field will come soon and pierce through the madness of the world.

CHAPTER NINE

I wake up early the next morning and grab breakfast for Mandy from the Courtyard Cafe, which has an assortment of delicious breakfast options. I know what I would get for myself had I gone out for a long night of drinking: grits, bacon, eggs, toast, sausage, and fresh-squeezed OJ, the true breakfast of champions. I would feast on this soul food until my strength and vitality were restored. Mandy is an athlete with abs of steel, however. I know she won't want the breakfast of champions. I try to think like a prancer. *Hmm, what does she want to eat?* I turn on my RWP sensor and scan the café for options. I settle on yogurt, granola, two boiled eggs, and a latte. I review the items one more time and feel confident in my choices.

When I get back to the room, I'm surprised that Mandy is not sleeping. I set the food on her desk and sit on the edge of my bed. A few minutes later, she comes sulking in the room, not prancing like usual.

"Hey," she says. "Why'd you get up so early? Heading to class or something?"

I motion toward her desk.

"Oh, you didn't have to," she replies. "I'm fine. It's fine. I don't even really remember what happened last night. Was I really drunk?"

"Yea, your throw-up is still on the floor. I'm super grossed out by vomit so I didn't clean it up." I pause. "You also said something happened between you and Trevor. Something awful. Do you remember that at all?"

The electricity in her body shifts. Waves of emotion penetrate the atmosphere of the room, even though her face remains stone-cold. She sits down and starts eating.

"Oh, that was nothing," she says. "I probably was just super emotional because my period is coming soon."

I know she's lying. I lied too after it happened to me. I change the subject, not wanting to push, unsure when she will be ready to face it.

"OK, then. Well, what do you have going on today? Anything fun?"

I straighten my bed and put away some loose clothes, trying to normalize the space between us despite the trauma.

"I don't have any classes today so I'm just gonna do some studying and go for a run."

I pretend to organize items in my closet, even though nothing is really out of place, just how I like it. I close the closet door after my mock organization and say, "Cool. Well, if you want to hang later, just let me know."

She nods and continues scarfing down her breakfast. I grab my bag and head toward the door.

"Hey," she says as I'm on my way out, "thanks." She smiles, but not a regular smile. The smile of someone in need of a hug, but too afraid to ask.

I am surprised at her understated reaction. I thought all that prancing privilege would make her righteously indignant if anyone ever wronged her, but I guess this kind of violation takes our voice first, then everything else.

Earnell, Keli, Gabby, and I meet in Baker Library to study for midterm exams, which are now only three days away. We book a study room for the entire morning, and then I'll have a session with Jennifer. We only have the room for a few hours, but we spend the first hour procrastinating.

"We should play a game of spades before we start studying," Earnell suggests.

"Earnell, you are really just out of your mind," Keli says. "I can't handle your shenanigans this early in the morning. Find your center and relax."

"Mmm, yes," Gabby interjects. "The center is the seat of the soul. I was just watching Venetia last night—"

"That random white woman that lives in Japan and walks through the forest picking berries and shit?" Keli asks. "I can't with you either this morning."

"Listen, Venetia provides wisdom for stressful times,"

Gabby argues. "She always says that home is not a place, but the center within us. If we learn how to tap into that, we'll always feel grounded and at peace. Isn't that profound?"

"Sure," Keli says dismissively, turning to me to change the subject. "What's up with that curly-haired white boy? Did he make any moves yet? I think he might be gay."

"Or racist," Earnell retorts snidely. "I personally think interracial relationships will never work because white people can never truly understand what we go through."

"I thought you were trying to be more open, Earnell?" I ask.

"Oh, I am," he says. "But my openness has its limits. You won't catch me kissing no blue-eyed devil."

"Help him, Lord," Keli says while laughing and playfully smacking his arm. "Help him."

"We went to get ice cream yesterday," I mention, "and sat on a bench outside of campus just talking. It was actually kind of romantic, but nothing happened. So I don't know."

"Well, why don't you give a brotha a chance?" Earnell asks forcefully. "It's some good brothas on this campus."

"Yea, and they full of themselves," Keli reminds him. "They the shit and they know it. All the girls be checking for good-looking Black men: white, Black, Asian, Latinx. Pumps up their ego too much. They walk around like they are God's gift. Look at the Alphas. They have all those women throwing themselves at them. I won't participate in that foolishness."

Gabby takes a deep breath and places her hand on her heart. She only does that when she's preparing to channel the wisdom of the elders. We know a long spiritual dialogue is about to unfold.

"I feel moved by spirit to share."

"Oh God," Earnell says. "Here we go."

Gabby looks each one of us lovingly in the eyes for way too long. "I just see such beauty in each of you. I'm being told, from the guides, that love will find you when you least expect it. And that the magnitude of your beings cannot fully be comprehended by what we see with our eyes. You are much deeper than you can imagine. The right one will see that and accept you for who you are."

"Do you smoke weed?" Earnell asks abruptly and mockingly. "Cannabis is not the answer, baby girl."

"You stupid, Earnell," Keli says while hitting him again. Keli always feels like she has to smack sense into him.

"Have you gotten yourself a tutor yet, Echo?" Earnell asks judgingly. "These midterms are going to slaughter you if you don't get your mind right, and soon."

"No comment," I retort, brushing him off.

Earnell takes a deep exaggerated sigh before launching into an epic rant.

"Friend, we had to be superhuman our entire lives just to survive. We've finally made it to the promised land, with literal white teats everywhere providing all the vitamins, antioxidants, and essential fatty acids we missed growing up and you refuse to seek nourishment? Why? So you can continue to believe you are Superwoman? You are a legend in your own mind, but it's not legendary to flunk out of college the first year. You better wake up before you're back in Cleveland flipping burgers, trying to make a dollar out of fifteen cents like the rest of your family."

"Dang, Earnell," Keli chimes in, "that's cold-blooded. You didn't have to say all that. Chill."

Earnell knows I can't fail and understands what's at stake. Beneath his frustration is a reservoir of love and care for my well-being.

Our love is always buried underneath, at least the Black people I know. We don't say, "I'm concerned about you" or "I'm terrified you won't make it" like they do in Hallmark movies. We say, "You betta get your life together before it all falls apart." We don't ask, "How are you doing? Do you need anything?" We ask, "You good?"

"You good?" can mean a range of things: "How are you? Are you hungry? How's the family?" The meaning is conveyed by the tone beneath the words, which is where we place our concern. We love through our shields, since we rarely have the luxury of taking off the warrior gear. Anything that's filtered like that, through a protective covering, will be coarse and abrasive, but it will also be rooted in deep care and love.

Earnell, Keli, and Gabby are the kinds of friends that would be on the front lines of any war in which I find myself, but don't expect them to say, "I love you. I'm here for you." Expect them to say, "You betta wake up" and "You good?"

We spend the rest of our time in the study room in silence. The weight of Earnell's comments hangs in the air. I pretend to be studying, like everyone else, but am really just waiting for time to pass. A steady stream of thoughts about Bryce, Mandy, the series of unusual occurrences, and my failing grades make it impossible to focus. When Matthew finally rings the bells, signifying it's time to go, I jump up from my seat and tell them I have another appointment.

"Must be exciting if you are in this much of a rush," Keli says.

"Trust me, it's not, but it's a necessary evil."

As I'm rushing out the door, Earnell yells behind me, "Hey. I'm sorry, but please gather yourself and fast."

I smile at the bubbling brook of tenderness beneath his words. "I will, Earnell. Don't worry."

———— • ◆ • ————

I stand at the threshold of Jennifer's door for five minutes, trying to compel myself to knock. I know something is wrong. It doesn't feel like the other two times I've been here: warm, safe, or inviting. Everything seems off, out of alignment. Maybe Earnell's intensity threw me off more than I realized. Even my RWP sensor is beeping out of control, which never happens with her. I try to talk myself out of it, but I feel her presence from behind the door as if she's standing there, waiting. Watching.

I quietly press my ear to the door to see if I can hear

her moving around, but it's eerily quiet. I don't even hear the running water of the small fountain. I convince myself she's not there, even though I know she is. I turn around, preparing to leave. As soon as I walk away, the door swings open. She is standing there. Waiting. Watching.

"I thought I heard someone," she says. "Come in. Come in. I've been eager to hear how your trip went, how everything else is going." I suddenly feel disoriented somehow. Out of place and confused. She stands aside and motions for me to enter.

I don't move. "You good?" she asks. The way she says it, like how all the other shielded but loving Black people speak, hypnotizes me and pulls me forward. I walk in a daze, as if I've lost the ability to control my own body. It moves without my blessing. I enter her office. The room rotates on its axis right in front of me. The fountain moves to the opposite corner. The desk slides across the room.

The body, still moving without my permission, sits on the couch, which is now in front of the window, instead of by the door.

The hands accept the tea in a white mug that she gives me. It's cold, which is strange, but the mind, which has stopped, cannot process. The mouth drinks. The throat swallows. Then the mouth smiles. The teeth glisten. The nose bleeds. Drip. Drip. Dripping. The hands wipe, pressing a white tissue under the nostrils. The bleeding stops.

She sits. Her eyes watch. The RWP sensor deactivates,

so there is no way to protect her from what comes next. The mind is disarmed, so it cannot build a barrier in the space between. The exposure disquiets the emotions. They blare with fright.

Then it starts. The watching. Which I knew was happening since I got here. Now to confront the watcher, finally. She is motionless on the chair across from me. She does not speak. She does not move. She just watches. The pupils of her eyes spin like all the other portals I've seen since coming to Dartmouth. The temperature drops. The water, which had been running even though I couldn't hear it through the door, stops.

The words do not come out of her mouth. They come out of her eyes through electrical pulses. They spiral directly into my brain. Living words. Luminous words that sparkle with a light of some unseen presence. The words, initially jumbled,

----

Wondering   *Picture*

            Searching   *Timeline*

You   *Answers*

        Mission   *Beginning*

Know   *Why*   *Breaker*

----

eventually organize into coherent sentences:

You are wondering why, who, what

You are searching for an answer

But there are no answers, only more questions

We are the Keepers, and when did we come?

*We arrived when you reached your lowest,
a streak of light in the sky*

*We are a collective consciousness of ancestral
forces, and what do we want?*

*We have been watching you from the beginning,
through them. They weren't watching you, we
were, and why is that so?*

*You have an important mission,
and what could it be?*

To answer the call of the beyond

Answers and questions

Know

*The inexplicable occurrences strike when you
are ready to answer the call, they test your
endurance, which this work requires*

Know

*Everything you thought you believed must be
dismantled and reassembled in a new way to
trigger the awakening*

Know

*You are a guardian of the timelines, a Chosen
One, this is the call*

Know

*We are a unified energy with no beginning
and no end, but we have known you since you
accepted the Guardianship, we have known all
of you, the Chosen Ones*

Know

*This is just the beginning, but the fall must come
before you start your work, do not be afraid*

Know

That the only way forward is through

A shrill high-pitched sound starts after those last words. The eyes close and the hands cover the ears to shield from the sound. It's so loud, like a dreadful creature of the night returning from the underworld. The nose starts bleeding again, this time dripping down all over my pants and her dark pink couch.

When I open my eyes, Jennifer has a clipboard in her hands, the water is running, and everything has been repositioned like it was on my first visit.

"I was saying," Jennifer continues, "that I'm surprised you wanted to do EMDR today. You did very well. You seemed to easily recall many things and released a lot. I'm so proud of you. When shall we plan our next meeting? It's really rewarding to watch you heal."

I blink. Cauterized by what just happened. Confused by how this Jennifer seems so different from the one that greeted me at the door and shot words into my brain through her eyes.

"Honey, are you all right?" she asks. "You look like you've seen a ghost."

The eyes stare, then another tunnel of motion, forward.

CHAPTER TEN

Her consciousness unbuttons, moving at warp speed through time and space while her body stands lifelessly in front of Matthew, staring, for hours. The body is such a faithful servant, ignoring its own needs in favor of the mission. Hundreds of timelines to travel. She is gone. Far away.

FORWARD

A dinner table. Cleveland's Last Supper. My mother has prepared a feast. We dine by candlelight. Everyone is glad I came home for winter break. They want to know about Dartmouth. What's it like living in a winter wonderland? Tonight all will be laid bare. Healing is inevitable when the truth comes out.

FURTHER FORWARD

The realm of prayers where blessings rise from the ether like mist over the sea. A transcendent dimension outside of time and the material world. I rest there for an eternity before a tunnel of luminous, bright white light swallows me whole. Then, a procession of singing ancestors. "Do you want to return as Echo Brown?" they ask through electrical impulses before the miracle.

THE END

A drowning or a rebirth. A completion of the mission or a new life cycle. A Legend or a Lost One. The end of timelines threaded by millions of choices. Events unfolding one after another until conclusions are reached.

BACKWARD

So many faces—penetrating, unfamiliar. The third week of October, a homecoming for the ages. They will worship Him first, then try to destroy Him and His games. His wicked smile taunting me again. I throw rocks at him, watch them come barreling back down. He is immune to my attacks. "Luke, I am your father now! Your mother's

God has forsaken you again. Look how the Chosen One falters," he laughs wildly. "I will defeat you!" I shout angrily.

They are all caught under His spell, running in circles, ripping off their clothes—white flesh, mad white flesh everywhere—kneeling in the dirt, praying to the God of Light, even as he, the Joker, inhales their prayers into his flaming nostrils. His chaos rules us all. He has to die.

BACKWARD

The calculus midterm exam. Pencil writes, but only doodles come out. Squiggly lines. No words. No numbers. Time's up. Professor takes the exam. Stares. His face malfunctions, switching abruptly to Mr. Walsh's and then back again. They are one and the same. They don't understand. Mr. Walsh's prophecy of failure fulfilled.

FURTHER BACKWARD

I am eight years old and the people are watching again. I told my mother, but she said it's just my imagination. They tell me they are the Keepers. They say they have been watching since the beginning. They travel through time, looking for Chosen Ones: protectors of the timelines. They never blink. Not even now, while the doctors and nurses do their poking and prodding. They stare and say whiskey man is a wicked creature, deplorable and cruel. It's all my fault for being a bad little girl. I wish my mother was here.

THE BEGINNING

In the beginning, she was intangible. An eternal concept, floating through timeless space. Then this thought disrupted her peace: "What if I can rise? And what if I can help the others rise?" Momentum spiraled, then we heard the call and transformed her from a wave to particles, to cells, accelerating her transformation. The incarnation of flesh from the infinite.

We the Keepers serve the greater purpose of activating the Chosen Ones. We balance the universe when everything bends toward darkness. And the Chosen Ones are the beacon, the light pointing home for the others who cannot see. A Chosen One does not come for herself. She comes for the others.

The cycle is constant in all realities: The concept becomes form. The form becomes story. The story becomes legend. The legend blooms into light fueling the others. The Chosen Ones protect the Legends. So it has been. So it must be.

CHAPTER ELEVEN

Zero days left till midterms. Now the verdict: I have failed my calculus midterm and gotten C's on all the others. Professor Cartwright calls me into his office and hands me back my test three days later. It is covered in doodles and incomprehensible text. I don't know what to say. "I've been having episodes," I explain. "Mental health episodes. My roommate told me I was standing in front of Baker Tower for hours, staring, until Dean Harrison came and took me to her house. I don't remember any of it. I'm sorry. I don't know what's happening to me." Tears well up in my eyes. I try and suck them back in, but they disobey me, like everything else in my life.

Professor Cartwright leans back in his chair. He doesn't know how to handle this kind of vulnerability. He tries to soften

⁘

when he sees the disappointment roll across my face. "A lot of people do just fine in the world with degrees from regular schools. It's nothing to get upset over." Mr. Walsh smiles dryly, entirely pleased with his "reassurance." Totally unaware of the way he is belittling me, cutting me down to his low expectations. He thinks he's helping me. He doesn't care what I have overcome or how much I have accomplished, like earning straight A's every year. In his mind, I'm above average at most, but definitely not intelligent enough to attend an Ivy League school. "I see it every year," he continues,

students from rough neighborhoods who think they can take on the world without having an accurate perspective on what it takes to make it in a place like this. They come here and think they can play a new game with the same rules. You can't. Find someone to help you get through this or you're going to end up on a bus back to where you came from. I always wonder why no one tells you what you're up against before you arrive." He shakes his head in bewilderment. *Someone did tell me*, I think to myself. Now Mr. Walsh will have a brother, Professor Cartwright, planting seeds of doubt inside my still fragile mind.

I knew he was a doubter all along. Nonbelievers always reveal themselves. I am numb to his cruelty now, however, even if he is right. *I am just another statistic*, despite my best efforts. My expectations for myself come crashing down. The downfall. Not even the Defiance can save me from myself now. I wonder what the House of Oppression has in store for me next?

I emerge, uneasy, from Professor Cartwright's office back out into the crisp fall air. I stand on the steps of the math building lost in thought. The unnatural chill gave way to a few summery days, which seem to be finally passing, and fall, winter's diligent messenger, hints of permanent cold's arrival. *How am I going to get through this*, especially now that the change in season is fast approaching. They say winters are both brutal and wondrous at this small, beloved college. Winters are a lot like the men who "didn't mean to."

I heard it was colder than usual last year, negative twenty-three degrees for several days. They said your nostrils freeze as soon as the cold air flows in. "Try not to breathe," they suggest. "Try to run as fast as you can between buildings." The ethereal beauty of a fresh snowfall makes up for the cold, however. That's what they say. The white snow blankets everything in sight, covering the campus in a surreal glow, just like in the brochure—a promise kept. But I've learned not to trust everything that shimmers.

I watch the sky with a low brow and my "What you talkin' 'bout, Willis?" glare, bracing myself for Darth Vader's next storm. "Can you let this one pass quietly?" I ask the God of Light as the chaos maker laughs brazenly on the horizon. *I guess not*, I think to myself. I guess some falls are destined.

"You look like a Black Xena Warrior Princess standing up there like that," Connor calls from the bottom of the stairs. "Wait, is that offensive? Sorry. Sorry if that's offensive."

I smile while bouncing down the stairs in Connor's direction.

"How've you been? Was thinking about you the other day. You haven't called so I guess everything's OK?"

I want to tell him that everything is falling apart, that winter is coming, but I know he can't really help me and he won't understand.

"I'm in Rumi's field now, out beyond all my problems. So yea, everything is fine."

Connor grabs the straps of his backpack and stares at me in confusion. "I can't tell if you're joking or serious. Do you want to go grab a bite and properly catch up?"

"Nah, but thanks. I'm running off to meet some friends. Maybe another time."

— ◆ —

We decide that the best way to release the pressure of midterms is to go dancing at a frat party on Halloween weekend. With seven weeks until finals, the semester is nowhere near over but we need to let loose and are all feeling reckless. It's the usual crew—Earnell, Keli, Gabby, and me—dressed respectively as a garden gnome, a gangster Cinderella (instead of a wand she carries a baton), and an ancestor. I'm wearing a bloody skeleton costume. It wasn't my first choice, but it was all they had left for a girl with expanding thighs.

By the time we arrive, the music is blaring and the dance floor is jam-packed with ghosts and ghouls searching for the beat. In this mostly white frat, only a few manage to find it.

"So this is what it means to be young," Earnell remarks, unimpressed.

We stand against the spiderweb-covered wall, watching in silent judgment. We are only eighteen and nineteen, but already ancient in many ways, having seen the best and worst of what life has to offer.

"I guess we should try to have fun," Keli says eventually. "I wish the Alpha party wasn't overcrowded. This looks like peak Caucasity."

We make our way to an open corner of the room and start dancing awkwardly in a circle. Nelly's "Hot in Herre" is playing. The chorus blasts, "It's getting hot in here, so take off all your clothes," at which point a girl next to us begins peeling off her sweat-drenched sexy pirate costume and chucking it into the crowd. She pulls her bra down and flashes everyone in her vicinity to the delight of her friends, who cheer and celebrate the body-positive drunkenness. Someone vomits right behind us and we shift our position in disgust. Someone else starts crawling up the stairs on his hands and knees while barking, as a friend holds a leash attached to his neck.

"Look around," Earnell says sarcastically. "This is the Ivy League. The cream of the crop. The elite. Getting wasted. Vomiting on the floor. Crawling up the stairs.

Taking off their clothes. These people will run the country one day. Take a good look and remember this."

We all comply and make a mental note of the scene unfolding before us. "White people," Earnell says, leaning into the middle of our group. "You know I brought Freddy to witness this malarkey and protect us from evil."

None of us really drinks, given the history of addiction we've all seen in our own families, but Earnell decides he wants to get drunk tonight.

"Why?" I ask. "I told you what happened at Professor Alexander-Grant's house. I'll pass."

"Well, I'm going to live it up. Keli's right. We should have fun like normal young people for once in our lives. I think I'll regret it if I never let loose. Maybe the alcohol will help."

Earnell scurries off to find liquor. Keli, Gabby, and I dance to a few more songs before making our way to the basement to watch people play beer pong. As soon as I get to the bottom of the stairs, I'm surprised, and thrilled, to see Bryce standing in the corner talking to some friends and dressed as someone from ancient Greece or one of the Lord's angels. I can't tell which it is.

"Bryce!" I shout eagerly. "What are you doing here?!" He gives me a hug and says he just felt like coming out tonight, even though this is "Satan's lair." "If we are to master the dark," he says jokingly, "we must first study and cultivate it."

Bryce introduces me to his friends, two white boys that

look like they belong to the frat and are dressed as Beavis and Butt-Head. I can tell by the way they shake my hand and avoid eye contact, just like Rhode Island Zach, that they're uncomfortable around me. We all stand in a circle for a few minutes talking. Well, *they* are talking about paddleboarding, which I've never heard of.

"Dude, the key is you gotta balance right in the middle of the board to stay up," one of them says.

"No, dude, you push your weight toward the outside of the board for optimal balance."

I feel invisible. I never get used to being erased, no matter how often it happens. White people always make you invisible when they don't know how to handle the reality of your being, even when you are standing right there.

Just like at the Dartmouth Club of Cleveland a few months ago, before I get to campus, where I am only one of two Black people in a room full of white and Asian faces. The party is at a big fancy house in the suburbs of Cleveland. I wear a sleeveless black cocktail dress that my mother found at the Goodwill and slick my hair back even though I still don't think it looks right, it never does. I stand outside the house for several moments, trying to work up the nerve to ring the doorbell. I slowly walk up the stairs, watching my Black toes protrude from the silver high-heeled sandals I'm wearing. Black shame at having Black feet with unpedicured toes, since I couldn't afford it, bubbles to the surface. The shame mutes me again. I pause and decide to turn around and leave. Just as I am walking back down the stairs, the door swings open, and a nicely manicured, severe but warm white woman calls, "Where are you going? You're part of the incoming class of 2006, right? I saw your picture in the email. Please come in!"

The woman relieves me. She is so friendly and welcoming, I regret almost leaving. She whisks me into the party and introduces me to several people. With her and her white flesh as my ally, they don't make me invisible. They welcome me with open arms. I want her to stay with me the entire night, but eventually she is pulled away and I am released to the erasers again.

I circulate throughout the room. So many faces, white and Asian, don't make eye contact. I've learned that not all minorities are playing on the same team and sometimes other people of color can be more racist than white people. I move between the groups trying to find another ally until I exhaust myself and leave. This is my introduction to Dartmouth. I should have known that it would be more of the same.

That these paddleboarders would treat me as if I am an alien from another planet. Bryce notices what's happening and becomes visibly flustered. "Guys," he says, his voice shaking a bit. "Echo is my friend and she is amazing. She is also Black, which I'm sure you have noticed. What you may not be aware of, though, are the subtle ways you are treating her differently. You're not really including her in the conversation, which is isolating. This is a party. We're here to have fun, so we don't have to go much deeper than that tonight. I just wanted to point that out and it's definitely something we can talk more about later. On that note—"

Bryce says, turning toward me, "Do you want to go upstairs and dance?"

I am so thrilled by his invitation, I don't care anymore about being erased by Halloween Beavis and Butt-Head, who stand in shock with their jaws on the floor. I eagerly nod my head yes, but not too eagerly, and follow him toward the staircase.

"See what I did with my privilege there?" he says, smiling with pride.

"Literally could you be more dreamy," I say out loud, before slapping one of my hands over my mouth in embarrassment.

Keli and Gabby do silly happy dances as we pass, which I try to prevent Bryce from seeing as we make our way up the stairs. Earnell, who's coming down, says, "Look at this, the man wins again. I'm just a Black pawn on your chessboard, but if you break her heart, I'll kill you." He raises his bottle of beer, carefree and unbothered, maybe for the first time in his life, by white supremacy and losing the girl.

Bryce and I find an open spot and dance to DMX, Ice Cube, 50 Cent, and Dr. Dre. It feels criminal to dance with someone so melanin-deficient to this kind of music, but I submit to the rhythm of the night.

"I'm surprised you dance so well," I say.

"Why?" he says jokingly. "Because I'm white?"

We both laugh. The bass-heavy songs land like bombs right in the middle of the dance floor. We have no choice but to comply with their demand that we release ourselves to the hypnotic beats. We flow, we twirl, we shimmy with glee until the music suddenly slows down. A ghoulish, digitized laugh blares from the speakers before a parade of raunchy slow jams begin. "Time for naughty fright night," the DJ announces. Bryce and I stand awkwardly in front of each other, noting that others around us start to press their bodies together seductively. I want to press myself deeply into Bryce, but I know his Bible fills the space between us.

He looks down at me and smiles kindly, like he always does. The ringlets of his curly blond hair, which is not in a ponytail now, fall down the sides of his face.

"Shall we do this?" he asks while extending his hands out in an invitation to slow dance.

"We shall," I say, taking them as he pulls me into his chest.

We slow dance like two old people at a church party. The heat of our bodies is not fully unleashed so we are not entirely comfortable pressed against each other. His body is muted by religion, and mine by fear.

As the music becomes explicitly more sexual, I feel the hardness of his longing on my hip, which I knew was there all along. *Finally*, I think to myself. I melt into him. His body feels better than I could have ever imagined. I turn around and grind my backside into him, like I've seen the girls do in the music videos and like so many others are doing now. I forget the Black shame temporarily and meet him as just another human needing to be touched and seen in Rumi's field. I don't care if I failed a course and barely passed the others. I don't even care if my mind is unraveling and I'm mentally ill. This moment has given me more value in myself than anything else in my life. Someone finally wants me.

I do what comes naturally after a moment like this, at least in the movies. I turn around and kiss him. My eyes are closed so I don't see the disgust on his face. I only feel the jerking of his body away from me, painfully away from me. The space between us again filled with the fear of crossing lines he never dreamed he would, and the consequences that often follow such actions.

"I can't," he says. "It's not like that between us. You're amazing...but...I just can't." He leaves, prancing away, just like Manda Panda before her incident with Trevor. Why didn't I notice before that Bryce prances too?

"You're amazing, but..." pounds my insides like molten lava trapped in a volcano. "But," I repeat to myself over and over. It hasn't happened yet, but I know his "but" is the cliff off which I will finally end myself. I didn't do it on the hiking trip in the woods, but this has finally pushed me over. There is no purpose to my life if no one wants to love me.

The realization rains down like hail, clobbering me mercilessly, but I don't make a sound. I don't even wince from the hurt. I run from it. Out the door, into the crisp fall air again, across the campus, and back to my dorm room to pack a few important items and the last of my savings. Six hundred eleven dollars and eleven cents. I pray it's enough. I peel off my bloody skeleton costume and snatch Jesus off the wall. "We're going home," I tell him. The portal and its spinning reminder of everything wrong with my mind taunts me. Mandy is nowhere to be found, per usual. I wonder what adventures she's getting into now. Wherever she is, I hope she's avoiding him and his fangs.

Then, away. Out to a taxi that whisks me to the airport, where I'll catch the first flight to Cleveland tomorrow, the only place I belong, where I'm a human being and not an invisible Black creature of the night that no one wants to love. Darth, resurrected from his burning palace on his favorite night of the year, trampling Jennifer's promised lands with that wicked smile, prepares to carry me back to the den of trauma and suffering that raised me. I won't leave the place that made me again. Not ever.

PART II

The Last Supper

The Last Supper. A ceremony of release. Orchestrated by us for her rising. Everything reborn in the light. A timeline of healing. Reserved only for that purpose. Home is where the Chosen One must heal. When one timeline is healed, all timelines are healed.

Old wounds, the deepest, finally mended. Pain released, then forgiveness rolling down like water.

CHAPTER TWELVE

Home.

The word takes root deep inside, but nothing grows. The soil is barren, without sustenance. I've been "home" for one day, but it already feels like an eternity. I didn't know leaving for such a short amount of time could change the core of you this dramatically. Before I left, I imagined the entire world was like my neighborhood. In just a few months, Dartmouth exposed me to wealth, privilege, and different kinds of people from all over the country. Exposure changes what grows inside a person, blossoming new ideas, beliefs, and thoughts. Then you can never go back to what you were. After Dartmouth, I feel like spring and this place, my home, feels like midwinter, dark and brooding.

I will have to make this place home again, I think to myself, but I know it's impossible. My home is the in-between now. The space between where you were and where you're going. The problem is I don't know where I'm going. Wherever it is, I'm not headed to an Ivy League degree anymore. That dream is shot, just like Mr. Walsh predicted.

Now, pregnant with spring, but deep in winter's bone, I see he was more than right. He was prophetic. It's all my fault. I should have been less stubborn and tried harder. I spend hours horizontal on my bed, ruminating. I stare at the ceiling. Full of cracks. Just like my life.

Time takes a break from ticking forward and tosses me a rope. I grab on and whir through the past. Over there where I lost my first tooth. The three of us—me, Dre, and Rone—passing the bloody tooth between us, studying it. Then Dre trying to blow air into the empty hole to see if I would inflate like a balloon. Mom hanging one-dollar bills down my pink with white lace dress for my tenth birthday. Ten candles on the cake she made from scratch. Can I blow them all out in one breath? I can. I'm a big girl. Everyone claps.

I close my eyes and wait. At first, I don't know what I'm waiting for. When a wave of regret washes over me, I realize I'm waiting for my real life, the one I should be living, to come and rescue me from this reality. I wait a few more hours. Nothing comes.

———————— • ◆ • ————————

I watch my mother, wearing her favorite apron (pink with gold stars), perfectly flip a pancake without splattering any batter. I can never seem to do that. I think it's the hesitation that gets me. She doesn't hesitate. Just a flick of the wrist and it's done. This morning is no different. The pan-cake travels halfway to the ceiling before returning to the pan on its other side. No batter lost. She may not have gone to college, but I have no doubt my mother could have been a five-star soul food chef, given the right circumstances.

I've been avoiding my family's questions about Dart-mouth. I know eventually I'll have to answer, but I try to put it off or change the subject as long as I can. Whatever I tell them, it can never be the truth. I'm too embarrassed and disappointed in myself to reveal my failure. I'll lie till I go to the grave, I decide.

"So you gon' tell or not?" Dre asks, interrupting my end-of-life planning.

"Tell you what?"

"Oh, OK. That's what we doing. We gon' play games. Mom, Echo playing games so that means something bad must have happened. Smells fishy to these eyes."

"Eyes don't smell, fool. Wrong senses. I finished my classes early because I'm a genius. So I don't have to go back until the start of second semester after New Year's in early January."

"Huh," Dre replies skeptically.

"That's real good, sis," Rone says with a hint of sadness in his voice. I pick up on it, but don't press further.

"Who would have thought?" My mother beams with pride. "Our very own Albert Einstein sittin' right here in dis' beated-up ole apartment. Didn't think ya momma knew folks like dat, did ya? I'on know what da hell he did, but I knows he was real smart. Just like you. You really somethin', girl."

My eyes fall. I quickly change the subject.

"Anybody need anything from Chesterfield? Gotta go re-up my stash of Flamin' Hot Cheetos, Starbursts, and Jimmy Dean's hot sausage. Cain't get none of that at Dartmouth."

"Oh yea, I was gon' tell you to pick up some oxtails today. S'posed ta be good luck. I wanna celebrate you finishing yo first semester by cooking a nice dinner this weekend. Oxtails, greens, black-eyed peas, cornbread, and a lemon pound cake."

"You cookin' all dat dis weekend?!" my father exclaims in glee. "Then shit, I'a be back early fo sho. Shit. Round seven den. Won't even go ta Shorty's and hustle Butch out da rest'a his paycheck. Save dat fa next week."

"Only two things can bring you home early from gambling, nigga. Food and I won't mention tha otha one in front of chirruns."

"Ain't no chirruns here," Dre interjects.

"Hush, boy, you da youngest'a of 'em all. You always gon' be my baby boy."

"But why you goin' all the way to Chesterfield? Chapman's is right up the street. Dey got all dat and oxtails." Something in my mother's voice changes. She sounds near and far away at the same time.

"Chapman's closed four years ago," I respond confusedly. "Don't you remember? John Boy moved to Florida to take care of his father. He opened Chapman's down there."

"Huh?!" Dre sits up in his chair. "What is you talkin' 'bout! Chapman's neva closed. You been doin' white people drugs up dere? You must be high."

"Chapman's not closed, sweetheart," my father interjects. "Just went up dere yesterday ta get a pack of cigarettes. Damn near seven dollars a pack now, but deys open fa sure."

"Fifteen or sixteen should be enough," my mother says, still facing the stove, and increasingly sounding not like herself. Her voice becomes hollow and wispy. Devoid of her somehow, but full of something else.

"Fifteen or sixteen," Rone says. "I'll eat dat many myself. Better get like..."

"The Last Supper," my mother interjects. "We'll have it this weekend. It will be special. Healing." My mother finally looks in my direction, locks eyes, and smiles with nostalgic serenity, as if an angel has just come down from heaven and blessed her in the light. It's strange, but my brothers and father don't seem to notice. I look down to avoid her piercing, ethereal gaze.

"Well, I'll be back in a bit," I say uneasily. "See ya'll later."

———◆———

Nothing could have prepared me for what I see on my walk to Chapman's. The Joker riding again. He rode all the way from New Hampshire in the snow and cold on his tiny bike with the big wheel to continue his campaign of terror and confusion against me. This is not possible. I don't react. I just look in disbelief at the little blue house across the street from our apartment building. The one where Chico, a childhood friend, broke his wrist after a raucous game of hide-and-seek. The too-big silver bracelet sliding right off his awkwardly turned hand. Chico was hiding in the closet. Came jutting out in a flash, tripping over his father's work boots, landing hard on his right hand, his wrist buckling, then cracking under the weight of gravity pulling him down. This is the same house we went ghost hunting in when Chico's family moved out a few years later and it stood abandoned and hollow. And the one the city tore down two years ago after drug dealers moved in and turned it into a trap house.

Standing.

I must not have seen it when I came home late the other night. Not only standing—renewed. Shining, like Ladles with the same celestial glow. Freshly painted baby blue with white trim again.

I walk up the stairs of the porch and peek through the windows. Empty, but new inside. Sparkling hardwood floors and windows. I turn the doorknob. Surprisingly the door creaks open. I slowly enter and begin swinging through memories. Playing video games in the living room for hours, washing dirt off our hands after making mud cakes in the backyard, and licking the cake spoon when

Chico's mother makes one of her famous chocolate cakes. It all comes flooding back.

I suddenly have an overwhelming urge to be a kid again. Carefree and without the pressures of almost-adulthood. It was easy then. There was a kind of freedom. We just didn't know it. We were all in a rush to be adults. We were convinced that once we didn't have to do what our parents told us, we would be liberated. We didn't know that life, for most of us, is a never-ending cycle of doing things you don't want to do, but have to, and that freedom is like the rain. Sometimes it's there. Most of the time it's not. Obligation is the defining state of being for adults. I shake my head at our naiveté, at our rush to stand in these cells of obligation.

I walk upstairs quietly, afraid someone is in the house. When I get to Chico's old bedroom, I pull open the closet where he broke his wrist, imagining him huddled in there trying not to make a sound. I see something lying on the floor in the corner of the closet. I'm shocked to see it's a silver bracelet just like the one Chico used to wear. Maybe he left it on accident? I hold it up and inspect it. *Wow*, I think to myself. *Still here after all this time.* I slide the bracelet onto my wrist and turn, looking around. The emptiness of the room unnerves me. How can something that was once full of life be so static and unused? The house has moved on, but I haven't. I'm clinging to past memories again, trying to siphon the life out of them. I wonder how long I will keep revisiting dead places trying to rebirth them.

I want to be on the other side of my past, I decide. I can't live among these skeletons anymore. How do you move on from the past? I wish Jennifer were here to tell me.

I toss the bracelet and all its memories back into the corner of the closet, close the doors, race back down the stairs, and sit on the porch trying to process this experience. My deep thought is interrupted by another familiar voice from my past, Ms. Patty, who has lived next door to us in the front of the building since before I was born.

"What you satin' ova dere fa?" Ms. Patty yells from her porch. "Don't nobody live dere. Welcome home from dat big fancy college." She chuckles to herself and takes a drink from her famous purple cup.

"I thought they tore this house down," I yell back, trying to appear concerned, yet calm.

"You ain't been gone dat long, girl. It was here fo you left. Dat lil house ain't went nowhere." She drinks again from her purple cup, whispering loud enough for me to hear, "Lord, dey go away to dem colleges and get so uppity. Don't know nothin' or nobody no mo. Mmmm, mmm, mmm." She shakes her head in disapproval. "You have a blessed day now." She smiles, syrupy and fake, then disappears again behind her drink, which is her shield from the world.

It's all off. Everything. The sun circles the sky at the wrong angles. The neighborhood is restored as if it's the early '90s again, but shining. Buildings that were gone, here again. Even the fence around the Tolver Baptist

Church, which the pastor had removed five years ago after a drunk driver crashed into it, now encircles the parking lot, untouched. I run my fingers through the springy interlacing of the metal fence. The church is closed and the parking lot is empty, but the fence stands risen, reborn.

I pinch myself to see if I'm dreaming again. When I don't wake up, I briskly slap myself in the face. Nothing changes. Still in Cleveland.

I continue my walk to Chapman's. When I finally arrive, I stand outside and see that my family was right. Chapman's is as open as a twenty-four-hour 7-Eleven.

"You're not John Boy," I say after walking inside.

Jessie, another childhood friend, comes running out from behind the counter to give me a hug. "Echoooo!! I heard you were back! How are you?!"

I am stunned. I can't speak.

"Jessie...I...you...but how?"

"Aww, come on. You don't remember me? We was in first grade together. We used to run all over this neighborhood wit dem stray dogs. Come on, Day Day! Anybody still call you Day Day?" Day Day is my nickname, which is short for my second middle name, Ladadarian.

"Of course I remember you, Jessie," I say, bewildered.

But I don't remember him like this. Cognizant. Out of his wheelchair. The Jessie I knew was hit by a car when he was eleven. He was mentally and physically disabled as a result of the accident, unable to say more than a few words. This is not that Jessie.

"Damn, girl. Why you look so surprised?"

I can't talk.

"You came up here to get the oxtails?"

Words come racing forward like lottery balls in a chute.

"How'd you know that?" I say eventually.

"Your mother told me about that Last Supper. You know. A celebration before you go back up dere wit dem white people. That's gon' be real nice. Wish I could come, but gotta work."

"She told you about that already? She just mentioned it to me this morning."

"Yea, yea. You know Ms. Aprah like ta talk. I got 'em right here for her. Threw in a few extra, but don't tell Chapman. He'a be in lata ta day. Ova dere helping the pastor out wit some things around the church. Be ova dere all da time now dat I'm working here. Basically me all day by myself now, but I don't mind it. Learnin' how to run a store. Life skills, I guess."

I barely hear anything Jessie says. I am too busy trying to make sense of this new Jessie in my mind. I give up. I decide to let the Joker have me. I jump on his bike and coast.

"Well, you need anything else?" he asks. "If y'all need anything else for the supper, jus' let me know."

"Don't you think it's weird to call it a 'Last Supper'?" I ask, remembering how strangely my mother said it earlier.

"No, not at all. Sounds like it will be a good chance to reconnect with your family before you have to leave again.

You know, in the Bible, the Last Supper was the last dinner Jesus had with his apostles before he was crucified. He laid everything out on the table. Revealed Judas. Outed Peter. It actually sounds like it was kind of a shit show. Is that the dinner where he turned over the table too?"

"Yea, he did. 'Verily I say unto you, that one of you shall betray me.' Then he got hype and destroyed the room. It's all described in the four canonical gospels."

"Word. That's what's up. Heavenly Father don't play," he says, laughing. "I'mma ask Chapman about it. He be telling me all about the history of the Bible now dat he ova dere wit da pastor all day. Anyways, I'm sure yo dinner gone be real nice. Here's your oxtails. And tell yo motha I said hi."

CHAPTER THIRTEEN

A train is coming.

"You hear the whistle?" Dre asks me.

"Yea, but it's still a ways off. Still all the way down there somewhere."

"It's rumbling. Gaining speed."

We are sitting in the big open field a few blocks from our apartment building. It's just nice enough to sit out here with a heavy jacket. This field used to be a textile factory, right next to the train tracks, but has been abandoned since before we were born. Unlike other things in the neighborhood, it has not magically rebuilt itself.

When we were kids, we would come up here to watch the trains, imagine where they were going, and dream about all the things we wanted to be when we grew up. It was our only place to escape nosy adults. It was our ghetto playroom. We were never alone. We always had five or six neighborhood stray dogs with us.

"Why you so quiet, Quamy?" I say while playfully

hitting Rone on the arm. Quamy is the nickname Dre and I give Rone. We give each other mock nicknames, which are not our actual nicknames. We only use these nicknames when teasing each other. We name Rone after the little Black boy with the square head on *Magic School Bus*. Quamy is not the boy's actual name, but it looks like it should be. We give Rone that name because his head is also big and square. My teasing nickname is Keisha, based on the little Black girl with the puffy hair also on *Magic School Bus*. Dre's nickname is Peter. We don't know why we call him Peter. We just do. You don't have to have an explanation for anything when you're a kid.

"Just thinking," Rone replies.

"What you thinking about? LaToya or Jasmine?"

Dre and I laugh hysterically.

"No, no, no. I'm not focused on girls right now."

"Then what you focused on?"

"I'on know. I just feel stuck here. Like I'm not going nowhere. You got yo' life together. You in college. You gone be somebody. What I'mma be? I'm eva gon' leave dis' neighborhood? Like befo' I die? How I'ma get da money ta do dat? I jus' don't see no way forward."

"I tole you I was gon' help you get out when I graduate. I'on got no money right now either, but as soon as I get a real job, I'a help you and Dre too."

My lies wash over me, bathe me in my own sin. Darth by my side, I allow them. I do not resist, but feel increasingly terrible. I can't help either of them now. I'm a failure

169

too. A knot grows in my stomach. Inner turmoil bubbles like stew in a cauldron. I'm overwhelmed with disappointment. *Maybe I could go back*, I think to myself. *Maybe it's not too late.* I remember what happened with Bryce and shake the thoughts from my mind. *Even if I have to get a regular job, I'll still help my brothers. I can help them with a regular job too.* Calm. Self-assurance. *There is always a way*, I tell myself, even though I don't fully believe it.

"Well, I'm happy wit my life," Dre says. "I may not have nothing. I may not ever leave dis' neighborhood, but I got people dat love me, food in my belly, and Colt." He picks up the bottle of Colt 45 sitting next to him and swallows a big gulp before releasing a deeply satisfied, "Ahhh."

"What else do you need in life?"

"Are you supposed to be drinking on that medication?" I ask sharply, referring to his schizophrenia meds.

"What it's like up dere at dat white college?" Dre asks, changing the subject. "Is er'ybody rich like on TV?"

"Yep," I say definitively. "They got more money den I ever seen in my life. It make me so mad. Here we is livin' like dis and it's people in the world dat have so much, dey'on even know what to do wit it all. Da world is so crazy and unequal."

"You got a boyfriend?" Dre asks abruptly. "Wait a minute! You got a white boyfriend?! Do he talk like dis?" Dre starts talking and motioning like he is a robot. "My name is... What's white boys' names? Like Drew Carey from dat TV show about Cleveland? Like Zack from *Saved by the*

Bell?" He continues his robotic impersonation. "My name is Zack. I cannot dance, but I am rich and white. Mew. Mew. Mew."

"What kind of sound effects are those? They definitely don't talk like that. No, I don't got a boyfriend."

"Good," Dre continues. "I don't want to have to fly all da way up dere ta knock somebody out fa breaking yo heart." He takes another swig from Colt.

I think about Bryce and imagine Dre confronting him, which would be ten times worse than all of Earnell's antics combined.

"You think I could get into community college or somethin'?" Rone asks. "I ain't dat smart like you. Seems like you cain't really do nothin' wit no degree. And I'on wanna be on da block foreva. I jus' been thinkin'."

"Of course!" I say with glee. "It's never too late, but you gotta get a GED first. You can even transfer to a four-year college once you finish at the community college. There are lots of options. It's all up to you. I'm going to visit Tarver tomorrow—maybe you come with me and then we can head to Cleveland Community College after?"

"Dats just like you, Keisha. Goin' ta school while you on break from school." Dre shakes his head.

"Oh, befo' I forget," he continues, "we got you something. Don't let this go to yo head, it's big enough as it is, but we are really proud of you, sis. You always been on dis path. You said you was gone get out and you did. Here."

Dre pulls a small package wrapped in red Christmas

171

paper with little Santas on it. "It's not much," Dre says, "but we picked it out together. Hope you like it."

I stare down at the gift and fight back tears. "Ya'll wrapped it?"

"Yea," Rone says. "We wanted it to look nice. We ain't wanna give you no bootleg present like Mom and Dad used to give us."

I want to tell them everything right then and there. How I tried, but actually haven't made it. How I had them in mind the whole time I was there as motivation to keep going. So much of me was doing it for them. How Dartmouth was harder than I could have ever imagined and not just the coursework, but everything. Trying to fit in a white world. Trying to get white boys, or any boys, to like this dark skin. Trying to understand all the new customs and cultural differences while battling mental illness. It was like going to an alien world where the aliens look like you but are nothing like you.

I start to panic. My breath quickens. Tears threaten to pour at any moment. Every emotion I have been suppressing since I came home bubbles to the surface. *I can't keep lying. I'm a terrible person. This is awful.* I close my eyes, waiting for my other life.

"Open it, Keisha," Rone says.

I slowly start to peel away the wrapping paper. They have wrapped it so nicely, I almost don't want to disturb the paper. I imagine them going to the store, picking a gift *together*, and then sitting at the kitchen table to wrap it carefully. The thoughtfulness overwhelms me.

When I finally open it, I stare down and cry. They have given me a journal that says on the front, "You are unlimited Sis, be fearless in your pursuits." They have included one of the nicest pens I've ever seen in my life.

"Nebo did the art on the front. You know he always been artistic. We couldn't find no notebook we liked at Walmart, so we got him to draw dat on it. You like it?"

"I love it."

Rone smiles chummily, like he always does when he's pleased with himself.

My conscience sits on top of me like a sumo wrestler. I can't lie anymore. I prepare to tell them the truth.

"Hey, I gotta tell ya'll somethin'," I say finally.

"Look, da train!" Dre says suddenly, stealing my moment of truth. "Where you think it's goin' this time?"

"I'on know," I respond. "Pennsylvania, probably. Somewhere in the Midwest, maybe?"

We all sit in silence. Watching the end of the train rumble off. Each lost in the heaviness of our own thoughts.

"You never thought about tryin' ta go to college, Dre?" I ask curiously. "You really good at artistic stuff too."

"I'd rather save my talents for the ladies," he says, laughing to himself.

"I thought Rone was the one spreading his talents among the ladies."

"He's not the only one." Fourth swig.

"I'm serious."

"I'on know, sis. Maybe. I'on like ta think about it. I try ta live in da moment. Like what dem Buddhist people be sayin'. I saw a show 'bout dat on PBS once. Dere's dese people dat just sit and breathe and try to be in da moment. Dey must not have no stress in dey life and no thoughts in dey head to sit and do dat 'cause I cain't sit more den three seconds befo' my mind starts racin'. Only thing dat quiet it down is my old friend Colt and my other friend Marty"— marijuana. "Maybe one day I'a go to college. We'a see what happens. For now, it's breathe in"—swig—"breathe out. Ahhh."

I shake my head in disappointment, both at him and myself for not saving him from Colt and Marty and all their consequences.

"What did you want to tell us, by the way? Befo' the train came," Dre asks.

I hesitate. The moment has passed. "Oh, it wasn't nothin' important. Thank you both for this gift. It really means a lot to me." I put the journal and pen back in the box and take off my jacket.

"Now, you know what comes next. Prepare yourselves."

"Oh no, sis. Please. No," Dre says, setting Colt on the ground and carefully replacing the cap.

"That's right! Hugs and noogies!"

I pounce on Rone first. I give him a big hug, kisses all over his face, and playfully rub my fist into the top of his head. When I finish with Rone, I stand up to chase Dre, who is running across the field.

"Your turn!" I yell, chasing after him.

"You have to catch me first! My legs longer than yours now!"

Our bodies are bigger, but our spirits are the same. Innocent and questing for adventure. I wonder if it will always be like this, returning to this field over and over, clinging to a childhood that will never again live in this world, but still beats inside of us. I wonder how we will remember it all when we're seventy, our parents long gone to glory. Just the three of us then left in our little family. The mighty three. The world different, changed in ways we can't imagine, but us, still the same when together. Forever holding the altar of remembrance between us. Hanging our little trinkets, photographs, and memories on the mantel. Honoring what was, while awaiting our own turns to journey to glory. Can we go together? It's an experience that can only happen between siblings, sharing an entire life of memories. Knowing each other in the beginning and the end.

The thought of it propels me forward, increasing my momentum. I gain on Dre, who is just a few paces ahead now.

"Don't worry, Peter! I'll catch you! I always do!"

CHAPTER FOURTEEN

Two weeks after I graduated from Henry E. Tarver High School last spring, the city condemned and closed it as a safety hazard to students. There was asbestos in the walls, black mold on ceilings, and cracks and holes of various sizes everywhere you looked. We, the students, knew we were attempting to get an education in a dump. Some of us tried anyways and some of us gave up, believing our environment was a reflection of our worth. If they couldn't bother providing clean, safe surroundings, and if many of the teachers didn't believe in us, then what real value did we have in the world? None.

The city unveiled a five-year plan to "restore and revitalize the school for the well-being and educational promise of future students." The school would be state of the art. New computers, desks, science labs, two gyms, and a football field, which they would be able to build by purchasing the empty, weed-ridden field behind the school. It would be a revitalization of not just the school system but the city itself.

So when I go visit Tarver the day after Rone and Dre give me their gift, I'm expecting to see a construction site. Bulldozers, scaffolding, orange cones, workmen busy painting, lifting, and digging. Instead, when I arrive, I am shocked to see that the school has already been restored and looks brand-new, sparkling. I walk around the perimeter, stunned. There is no football field, but the building itself looks regal. I wish Rone, who decided to sleep in, had come to explain how this all happened so quickly.

What? I say to myself in disbelief. *Huh?*

"Skipping school today? Get on in dere, girl, and get yo education!" someone yells from a car whizzing by. "I'm an Ivy League graduate!" I retort, even though it's not true.

When I get back to the front of the building, I trace with my eyes the glistening silver letters above the entrance that spell the name of the school. I imagine what it would have been like to go here now. I suddenly feel a twinge of bitterness. I feel cheated. If I had been born in the right place, like so many students at Dartmouth, this could have been my reality all along. *It's not fair,* I say to myself.

As soon as I step inside, there is total silence. Underwater silence. I am standing in the vestibule between doors. The first entrance door behind me, the second in front. When I walk inside, I see frenzied students and teachers hustle past me through freshly painted hallways. Their mouths move, but everything is quiet. I feel like I'm watching a silent movie.

I hear it on my right side first. A low hum that steadily

grows. I spin around to see where it is coming from. It gets louder and louder until it's right above me, as if it's catching up somehow and has to be synched to the present moment. A cacophony of noise. Cheerleaders practicing. A teacher yelling at a student for running through the hallways. Lockers slamming. Freshly polished sneakers screeching the floor. Just like at the hypnosis event, the sound cloud starts to descend and then—*boom*—bursts all over us. Everyone becomes animated with new life.

"Young lady, are you lost?" someone says from behind me.

"Oh no. I'm a former..."

I turn around and stare into the eyes of the prophet himself, Mr. Walsh. There is so much I want to say: *You! You're the reason I failed. Your prophecy destroyed me, planted seeds that yielded a soiled harvest. Now look at me. I'm nothing, just like you said.* Thoughts race, but no words leave my mouth. I am overcome standing in front of a man who has lived rent-free in my mind for a year.

"Why, Echo? Echo Brown! What on earth are you doing here? Do you have some time? Come to my office. I'd love to catch up!" He talks a mile a minute and then races off, expecting me to follow. I try to take it all in on the way to his office.

The same posters hang on the wall. I am reminded again of his limiting beliefs about what might be possible for me. I put a guard up, hardening my face and demeanor, preparing for battle.

"Well, tell me how it's going. How are you liking the Big Green?"

"You helped mess me up inside. Your low expectations never left me. I just want you to know the long-term impact of your words."

Mr. Walsh gets up, puts both of his hands into his pockets, and looks out the window behind his desk.

"You know, Echo," he says, still turned away from me, "when you do a job like this, you meet a lot of students. I'm ashamed to say it, but they all kind of blend together after a while. If you're not careful, you can take that blend and project it in ways you might not have intended. Miss the diamonds in the haystack. But sometimes, and I suppose this is my way of righting my wrongs, the harshest messenger can provide the elixir for your greatest transformation. They can inspire you to dig deep wells inside yourself and discover exactly what you're made of. But you know that already, don't you? You've been proving them wrong since the beginning. Excelling against impossible odds. You've been soaring your entire life. Until now. Well, I'm here with a salve to help fix what I contributed to breaking. There are so many false 'prophets' in this world leading the flock astray. I was no different." He turns around and sits back down, tracing the edges of his desk with his finger, avoiding eye contact.

"I don't know how I missed you. It's so clear to me now who you are."

The temperature drops.

Silence.

"I should have recognized you, a Chosen One. A miracle maker and healer of the timelines. Do you know your purpose?"

Cold.

Freezing.

A winding down. Time stops. I hear the second hand of the clock on the wall struggle to tick to the next moment, then give up the fight altogether.

I can't speak. He has all the words.

Hands won't unglue themselves from the arms of the chair. Eyelids won't blink. Pupils won't move. Stuck.

"Think of it this way: let's say you are a diamond," he continues.

Mind begins to awaken. He finally looks up. Locking my eyes, which are glued open and transfixed.

"If you take that diamond and you rub mud all over it, does that change the fundamental value of the diamond itself? No. If you abuse it, call it names, make it seem worthless. Why, it's still a diamond, isn't it? Despite your attacks. And if you project a career of low expectations onto that diamond, telling it to aim lower than what it is worth, what the diamond does in this world is only limited if the diamond believes you, right? You believed me. You believe it all. That's the problem. Your belief."

Mind reflects.

For the first time, I try to see beneath all the shit. I didn't know there could be a me *separate from the negative things I'd* been taught to believe about myself. I believed them, even as I acted against them. All the voices and opinions. All the reflections of my worthlessness. I picked them up like bags on the side of the road and carried them with me through the days of my life. How come no one told me I could set them down? How come no one told me a diamond might be inside all the muck?

"Yes," he says, stretching out the *s* at the end of the word. "You're starting to understand now. Yes, someone should have told you. I should have told you. You have a very special purpose."

He slowly starts to walk around his desk.

Body reacts in terror.

Eyebrows furrow.

Hands grip chair.

Mind stops.

A momentum brewing, off in the distance, like the train. A rumbling.

His sits on the desk in front of me. He looks like a mad scientist. He reminds me of Hypnotist Jerry. He speaks in a grandiose growl. He leans his head right in front of mine. He is so close I can smell his breath. His eyes lock mine, more than lock—pull some life force energy from me.

"Your purpose," he states, "is to heal what is broken."

A flash. Forward.

CHAPTER FIFTEEN

Letith us bow our heads in prayer for this, the Last Supper," my mother says with an intense, furrowed brow. "As he spoke, so we speak. As he walked, we walk. May we be forever graced by his eternal presence."

We are all sitting at the kitchen table, food steaming in front of us, despite the fact that we never all sit and eat together like this. The lights are low and candles are lit around the room. It feels more like a lair than a kitchen right now.

"Letith it be made new," my mother continues.

"Why are you talking like that?" I ask. "Like you're Jesus or something."

"As he spoke, we speak, dear."

"Letith us always be grateful," she continues, "for the bounty you have bestowed. Most importantly, letith us find the courage to live in truth and walk in faith. In your name we pray, amen."

This is not my family. They look like them, but they are imposters. Everyone, except me, begins eating.

"Father, could you please passeth the collards?" Rone says.

"Quamy," I whisper, "why you talking like dat?"

He cocks his head to the side awkwardly like a dog trying to understand human speech.

"Like what?" He smiles. Stares. Then starts eating.

"Father, brother, sister, mother," Dre says, clanging his fork against his plastic cup. "I haveth a confession to make. Colt is not a real person. When I say I'm going to visit Colt, I'm really going to drink. It's the only thing that brings me joy these days. I'm sorry for my lies. Forgiveth me."

My mother smiles. Stares. "Oh, Dre, my baby boy. You are forgiven. And howeth do you feeleth?"

"Free, Mother." He smiles. Stares.

"OK, OK," I interrupt. "What the hell is going on here? What is wrong wit y'all? This is nuts. Why are y'all acting like this? I feel like I'm in the Twilight Zone or something. Nothing here is right and I just wish someone would tell me what the hell is happening!"

I become enraged. My eyes glare. They ignore me.

"I have a confession also, Mother," Rone says. "I'm still on the block, selling. I triedeth, Mother, I really did, but I couldn't walk away. Can you ever forgiveth me?"

"Why, of course, Rone. His grace is here. His mercy too," my mother says plastically. "Of course. And how do you feeleth?"

"Unburdened."

"Now for me," my father says. "I didn't loseth the rent

183

money last month. I gambled. Gambled all of it. Is it unforgivable, this sin?"

"Edward, no sin is unforgivable or unseen," my mother says. "You are forgiven. And how do you feeleth?"

"Reborn."

"Well, I guesseth that just leaves me. I musteth warn you in advance, my sin is truly awful. As you all knoweth, something terrible happened to our dear Echo when she was only eight years old. I wasn't there with her at the hospital to console her after. Ms. Patty and Ms. Janine went instead. I told them I couldn't take it. I said I had to come home and rest, but really, I went to the crack house and nearly smoked myself to death from the pain. They told me you cried for me. Looked for me. I wasn't there for you and I'm sorry. Do you forgiveth me?"

The life leaves my eyes. Now it is me staring, glaring, at this demonic Jesus impersonator in front of me who must clearly be disowned for her sins.

I don't blink. I stare at her, coldly. Penetratingly.

I speak—my voice a whisper.

"You left me to go smoke crack? What kind of mother would do that?"

Tears fall from my eyes, but I don't make a sound.

The quaking starts first. From deep inside. My body starts to shake. Then a guttural roar. Louder than the train whistle. Deeper than the roots where home used to be planted. I scream, ferociously, at the top of my lungs.

"You left me there by myself?!"

I sweep my arm across the table, knocking the feast to the floor. I smash the plates furiously to the ground. Listen to them shatter. My "family" stare straight ahead, unmoving.

"You stupid bitch! I hate you! I hate all of you! All you do is suck, suck the life out of me. You've been nothing but a burden. All of you! Why can't you get your lives together?! Why can't you be better? Why did I have to be born here with you?!"

I continue moving around the kitchen, breaking everything in my path. It looks like a tornado has ripped through the room.

"Well, guess what? I'm not taking care of any of you anymore! I dropped out of Dartmouth. I fucking quit. That's why I'm back early. I guess we'll all be failures together." I fling my arms out to the side dramatically, as if I'm a movie villain.

"Don't ask me for nothing else. No more leaning on Echo. Depending on Echo to fix it. I'm going nowhere now, just like y'all."

Family is no more. Home is no more. Just wreckage. These pieces can never be mended. I am beyond anger. I am forsaken. Crucified by the unforgivable sins of my own mother. A Judas in a pink apron. Hate blares from my bones. I want to kill her where she sits.

"How?" I ask in a whisper, standing next to the stove

full of pots, preparing to launch them at her like missiles. "How could you do that to me? Your little girl?"

My mother looks up, finds my eyes despite the dimness of the candlelight. The rest of the family continues to stare blankly ahead.

"Because I, too, was covered in shit and didn't know it. I just wanted to put the bags down. They were very heavy. I could carry my own, but I couldn't carry that."

A moment passes. Then surrender. Big heaping sobs that fill up the entire apartment. My mouth turns up, throat stretching, barely able to contain the sound, which pours upward, cracking the ceiling. It dissolves. Only colors and light, like the aurora borealis at Professor Alexander-Grant's house. Light everywhere. Raining down, filling me. Irradiated with glowing eyes. A phoenix. Risen. Merged with the power beyond.

Bodies sit. Hands join. Heads roll up and eyes meet. Maybe for the first time. Five diamonds. Unobstructed. Words come. The Chosen One's prayer.

Let it be healed. Let it be renewed in the light. Let it be forgiven. Let it be released once and for all.

Tiny specks that look like dust. All the memories. Rising out of the bodies, past and present. So much sorrow and despair, with roots that go all the way down to the bottom of time. A line, a matrix of generational pain. A legacy of suffering. Inescapable. Birthed again and again until someone heals it. *Until someone has the power to heal it.*

Massa beats Carol Ann for dropping the honey pot. Her back takes months to heal.

My mother's mother beats her with an extension cord for leaving the bathroom light on because "money don't grow on trees."

Mom beats Dre, Rone, and me for burning roaches. Scars, just like Carol Ann's, wrap around our tiny thighs.

Massa sells Lewis's pa to a plantation down South. Lewis never sees him again. The bottle is his only comfort.

My grandfather walks off to start sharecropping in the fields when my father is only five. My father, a child, runs after him until he can't see him no more. He'll wait all night for a ghost that will never return. Only the brown liquor soothes his aching soul.

Dre inherits the family legacy of finding comfort in the bottle to escape, like Lewis and our father. Dre's little eyes watch and learn early that this is the way to salvation. Now he knows how to feel nothing.

It's not rape if she's a Black savage. It's giving her what she deserves. So Massa takes her body freely whenever he wants.

My mother's stepfather taking my mother's body freely whenever he wants, like he's been taught. The Black woman's body, meant to be taken.

Little Echo, next in line for the taking. This time by the whiskey man down the street and a wolf in sheep's clothing who calls himself prince.

We transform into diamonds, shining. New. The last of the light leaves me. I don't know if it will ever return.

I've never seen my family like this. Weightless. Unburdened. Without their pain.

"I love y'all," Dre says. "I'll see you on the other side."

A crumbling. We fade to dust. Our living flesh dissolves into particles of sand. I watch them blow away until I myself disintegrate back into nothingness.

PART III

The Rise

Even though the rise is always prophesized, it is never promised. Many factors must be coordinated to ensure a Chosen One answers the call. Willingness to escape the bud is critical. The potential is always there to transform from a caterpillar to a butterfly, but one must endure the crushing pressures of growth. Wings can only be earned. Once flight is made possible, ascension is guaranteed.

CHAPTER SIXTEEN

Landing is not easy. I travel for what feels like an eternity through a tunnel of magnificent colors, light, and sound whirring together in a dazzling show. I am disembodied. Just a wave of light and energy soaring through the universe. The tearing from the body is the hardest part. It is like carving the skin off a dead animal. We were attached. It was my faithful servant. I didn't want to let go. I watched our bodies dissolve into dust and then the tunneling started.

It seems like there is no destination, so I surrender to the journey. What's on the other side, I don't know. I hope it's my family, smiling and still shining. I promise myself I will never forget that moment of reckoning.

A compression starts at the bottom of the tunnel. It gets narrower. I feel like I'm being squeezed from all sides. There is so much pressure, like in an airplane when you drop below a certain altitude. The colors and sounds begin to dim. The speed at which I'm traveling increases. I'm flying now. Soaring. I feel the destination approaching and brace myself for impact. Faster, until I lose my sense of self. Thoughtless. Formless. Just forward. Pushing. Quicker. Until the tunnel starts collapsing. I am a wave of emotion now. Fear, anxiety, turmoil.

Then *plop*! I emerge on the other side. I keep my eyes shut tightly, afraid to see where I have landed. A soothing voice comes to me from the distance. Miles away but getting closer and closer until it's right in my ear.

"Echo, dear, welcome back. It's OK, you can open your eyes. The first time is always a bit jarring."

I open my left eye just enough to get a peek at who is talking to me. When Dean Harrison's Mr. Spock face is revealed, both my eyes pop open and I reach my arms around her neck. I am thrilled to see her after everything that just happened. She grants me her neck but does not wrap her arms around me like a normal person. *Still a weirdo*, I say to myself.

My memory stalls for just a minute or two. Soon it all comes rushing back. The Halloween party. Humiliation and defeat. The taxi to the airport intercepted by Dean Harrison outside my dorm—her pleading, begging me to come home with her. "Please, I have so much to tell you. If you still want to leave after we talk, I'll drive you to the airport myself." Something in her voice—uncharacteristically full of emotion—convincing me to follow. Her house dark and brooding on the edge of the woods. Then the tea that smells like dandelion. It's too hot to drink so I inhale the steam. The tea spinning counterclockwise again. Just like in her office, her spoon clicking the side of the mug before stirring. Moving in slow circles until my eyes droop. My entire body feels so heavy. And then I'm back in Cleveland. A city I just watched dissolve into dust.

"I'd ask you if you wanted some tea, but I think you've had enough for one night. It's my way of helping you relax before the journey. Too many thoughts or too much anxiety and it doesn't work. One has to be on the right frequency to travel between the planes. What do you remember?"

"I was in Cleveland. Nothing was right, but I saw my family. We made amends. They were all talking like Jesus. Then we crumbled to dust. How did I get back here with you?"

"You must be tired. Why don't you get some sleep and I can explain everything tomorrow? I promise it will all become clear soon."

"No," I insist. "I want to understand what happened. Where is my family? Are they alive? Are they safe? Was I dreaming? Did I imagine it all?"

Dean Harrison inhales slowly before glancing up at the clock on the wall.

"Words fail this experience, but I'll try. Reality is multilayered. There is no *one* reality. There are many, and they are intertwined. Connected. Multiple timelines running concurrently, all happening at once because time is an illusion. Existence is a vast, vibrating field of pure energy. What happens in one part of that field ripples, like when you skip rocks on the sea. Eventually the whole sea will feel the impact of that one rock you threw.

"You are a healer in the field, a Chosen One. There are many Chosen Ones sharing this work, mending cracks in the timelines. Holes, dark places caused by trauma and too much suffering. You can help repair these things. That's what you were doing with your family: healing the ancestral lineage from wounds that have been passed down for generations. This work is done outside the laws of physics, where anything is possible. Buildings that have been torn down reappearing, for example.

"Healing ancestral wounds involves not only the living, but many passed on. There are experiences and interworkings that we in this flesh form can't fully understand. So yes, you went to Cleveland, but in the astral sense, which means your body didn't go, but your consciousness did. The body is material so it is always fixed in one location, but your consciousness is not. In fact, your consciousness is everywhere all the time and is not limited to the confines of your body. Astral travel also unfolds in your sleep since it is not dependent on the body. Maybe you're already starting to have those kinds of dreams?"

I remember my dream about Bryce at Ladles and wonder if that's what it was, "astral travel." It seemed very real until I woke up to Manda Panda stroking my face. I don't want to confirm her science fiction malarky so I don't mention it. Instead, I continue to stare at her in total disbelief.

"I see your skepticism. You don't believe me. Just let me

finish explaining. All will be made clear. You didn't travel to the Cleveland you knew. You traveled to the Cleveland where all that unresolved ancestral pain and suffering went to fester until the Chosen One came to heal it. A Cleveland between physical worlds, but no less real. The healing work you did there will ripple forward in ways you can't control. In fact, that work will even ripple here eventually. You'll know the signs when you see them, the miracles that happen in this time-space reality as a result of your work.

"What makes someone a Chosen One is the ability to create those ripples, which can impact how people behave in timelines throughout the universe, including this one. Ultimately that change in behavior is what begins to heal ancestral lines."

She has clearly lost her mind. Did she give me drugs? Does she work for Hypnotist Jerry? I attempt to sit up on the couch, but my body feels weak and a million miles away.

"It takes a few hours to regain strength and proper orientation."

I lean on my forearm since I can't hold myself up.

"You want me to believe my consciousness left my body, traveled to a plane between physical worlds, and healed my ancestral lineage. Sure."

I laugh mockingly, like the Joker.

"Am I Jesus, then? Oh my God, now that's *ironic*. A quirky, Black, poor pagan girl from Cleveland with expert knowledge of the Bible, thanks to her mother, is the modern-day Jesus. Behold, humanity, the second coming has arrived! What folly! What poppycock!"

Mad laughter fills the room.

"You are not Jesus. In fact, there was no Jesus. I mean, there was a man known as Jesus and he too was a Chosen One, healer of timelines, one of the most powerful ever. He channeled the Holy Spirit—an energetic consciousness even more powerful than the Keepers—into this world, but he was not the 'Savior.' Look around, nothing is fixed. That narrative is just a myth created to survive the chaos and harshness of life, to help people decipher the forces of opposition, or the 'cosmic Darth Vader' as you call it. The only way to defeat those forces is to surrender to what exists and heal what is broken. Then you will know how to ride out the eye of any storm with steadiness and control.

"So no, you are not Jesus. And don't be fooled: You are not responsible for saving anyone. You just have to save yourself and then the healing work may be done through you." Rage claws its way out of my weak and slumped-over body.

"What do you think I've been doing this entire time?! I've been saving myself since I was born. My load is already heavy enough and now you want me to be some 'healer of the timelines.' No. I refuse. And how dare you play games with my mind like the Joker. What, do you have some cult of Chosen Ones you want me to join? Some Saviors of the Light group that has all the answers? No god has ever saved me. I highly doubt your god of magic will either. I've heard what you have to say. I'm going home for real. I'm done with this place. Your tricks won't stop me."

She tries to hide it, but I see the disappointment roll across Dean Harrison's face. She wanted something else from me. A different reaction. I feel bad. I hate when people lose faith in me. My eyes dart down toward the floor.

"You should release the Defiance from the dungeon. They are one of the most important navigation tools in your life. Whenever you get off track, they will always have your back. They are your intuition."

"How do you know about the Defiance?"

"Nothing is hidden. You just have to know how to access it. How far has your stubbornness ever gotten you? Are you really where you want to be? You are afraid you will fail so you'd rather run than witness your own fall. I want to tell you, as someone who has taken this journey..."

She pauses. Adjusts the ring on her finger. Her body grows heavy. Weighted with a wisdom I can't yet understand. She suddenly looks ancient, a thousand years old.

"This is not something you can walk away from. Your destiny. The calling. Nothing can stop the call. The call is why you exist. Either you keep fighting and it will destroy you. Or you accept the call and become what you must. Either way, there is no escape."

The gravity of her words demands my compliance. I know she is right even without the Defiance ringing in my ear: *She tellin' the truth, you feel me? Hah, finally, someone with some sense. Yasss, bitch, yasss.* She has laid me bare, marrow to flesh. There is no use continuing this parade of sorrow and self-pity.

"Find a better tutor. More than one. Learn how to access the knowledge of the field. This coursework won't be hard for you once you unlock your mind. Now, it's way past my bedtime. I'll see you in the morning."

"Wait!" I yell as she walks away. "Who are you?"

"Yoda," she jokes. "Rest well."

Morning, like the end of the color tunnel, comes slowly. My body finds no rest, instead tossing and turning on Dean Harrison's freshly laundered sheets in the guest room by the kitchen. My thoughts spin themselves into perfect webs of confusion trying to make sense of everything Dean Harrison told me.

When the sun finally begins her ascent, chasing the dark and all its unanswered questions back into the hills, her rays wash a new peace over me. I rise from the bed, tell the Defiance we've got work to do, and then start sprinting back to the life waiting for me on the other side of fear and self-doubt.

CHAPTER SEVENTEEN

The student center is not open yet, but I am already sitting in the hallway in anticipation. I will ask who is the best tutor. The one everybody raves about. I want that person. I'll take a new approach. Instead of pretending, I'll tell them I don't understand anything about math. It's a foreign language to me. So teach me from the ground up.

I am sorting out my thoughts when I hear the elevator activate. It's still early, but I hope it's the staff on their way up. I want to grab a table in the back and get situated. Maybe they will wonder why I am here before they are. I try to look natural. I stand, but then decide to sit back down with my hands lightly folded on my lap. All of my tension evaporates when I see Earnell come bouncing off the elevator, whistling "Get Low" by Lil Jon to himself. I hear his whistling before he steps off the elevator and wonder which staff member would be singing such a ratchet tune. I should have known it was Earnell.

"Oh my God! Earnell! What are you doing here?"

"Well, I guess I could ask you the same thing, Negro Brown. And why are you looking like the Secret Service wearing that baseball hat and sunglasses? Are you hiding from someone? The mob? The KKK? That Christian white boy you ran away from last night? I've never seen you move that fast."

I don't admit it, but I am hiding from Bryce. I hope carefully placed hats, scarves, and sunglasses will prevent him from recognizing me for the rest of the school year. I never want to see him again.

"I'm not hiding from anyone. It's way too early for your shenanigans. So don't start. Let me just sit here in peace until they open. . . . I almost caught a plane back to Cleveland last night, but forces bigger than me intervened."

Earnell's tone shifts immediately. He places a hand on my thigh, the pressure of his palm alternating between caring friend and desirous lover. I don't move it.

"I shouldn't have said that to you the other day—"

"No, it had nothing to do with that," I say, interrupting him. "I know you were just trying to help."

"What happened? Why were you about to go home?"

I know I can't tell Earnell about the astral travel. I focus on my sliding grades instead.

"It just seems like everything I've worked for is crashing down. I didn't pass my calculus midterm. Got C's on all the rest. I've never failed a test in my life. You were totally right this whole time about getting help. I feel like a complete failure."

Earnell takes an exasperated inhale.

"I've been thinking about the conversation we had in that study room and have arrived at a new place of understanding. What if I was wrong? What if I told you that you can't lose?"

"What do you mean?"

"Hang with me here. Even if you leave this godforsaken place, return to Cleveland, get a job trying to make a dollar out of fifteen cents—and to be clear, I don't want that for you at all—you will find another way to do what you came to do. This path we are on was started long ago by the ones that came before. It's ancestral. After everything they went through, if they did it, then damnit so can we. We are our ancestors' wildest dreams. Their spirit lives in you. It lives in me too and it will never stop. So as Dr. King once said, 'I have been to the mountaintop.' Seriously, look around, we are literally on a mountain. 'I'm not worried about anything. I'm not fearing any man. Mine eyes have seen the glory....' We can't lose. Your spirit won't allow it. Purpose is bigger than our fears and limitations."

"Wow, Earnell. That was really deep and sounds a lot like what Yoda said."

"Wait, from Star Wars? Yoda quoted Dr. King? In which movie? I need to watch this."

"I'll see if I can find it," I say jokingly. "That was very inspiring."

I bounce up and start shouting lines from Dr. King's speeches: "Mine eyes have seen the promised land! I've been to the mountaintop!" The Black shame simmering in my center crumbles beneath the prodigiousness of Dr. King's words.

Earnell, finally accepting his duty as a Call preacher, joins me. We continue our dramatic recital until a white, blond staff member exits the elevator and says, "Umm... what's going on here?"

"Nothing much," Earnell says, enlivened. "Just a couple of new age negroes remembering who we are and finding our way home. You are welcome to join us."

———— •◆• ————

The math tutor is only the first step in fixing the mess I've made. I convince Professor Cartwright to let me retake the midterm in a week. I explain my new approach of asking for help. "I was just afraid to fail," I say, "but now that I've actually failed, I'm not afraid anymore and want to fix this." He is moved by my plea. "I'm glad you came back," he says. "I'll always have a second chance for someone who doesn't give up. Happy to help in any way I can, Ms. Brown."

I hunker down, taking hours of tutoring each day. I pore over the textbook, trying to understand. I work and rework the problems on the old exam and the practice ones the tutor gives me. This tutor, unlike Zach, understands my limitations and my strengths. Tracey, but I call her Tray Tray—the "hood name" I give her on our second meeting—also comes from privilege. She was raised in Cape Cod but, thanks to her wealthy parents' foundation, spent her summers volunteering in countries with big education deficits.

"It changed me," she shares after one of our study sessions. "Seeing people with so little who were as gifted and smart as me, but just hadn't had the luck of being born in the 'right' place. I learned from that experience that so much about whether you make it in life or not is about positioning. Where you happen to land first, and nothing else. I vowed to use my time and energy to help others who may not have had the same access and opportunity. I mean it's the least I could do based on all that has been given to me. It's the only way I could live with it, the imbalance in the world."

Tray Tray, unlike Zach, can see me thanks to her (white savior) volunteer work and that's how I know she can help me. I don't feel embarrassed to speak up when I'm confused about something. She has a knack for teaching and frames the lessons in a way I can grasp. I feel like I finally have access to math for the first time. I wonder if this is what Dean Harrison meant about unlocking my mind?

"Think about math like building a house. Once you have the foundation, you can build a really sturdy structure, but if the foundation is screwed, the whole thing is compromised. Most of the people I work with never had a solid foundation in math. So let's start there. We'll worry about the more complex problems later. We don't have much time, but let's make sure you understand the basics."

*   *   *

For the next week, my life is only math. A new understanding of the subject takes root in my mind. Hope rises like a balloon escaped too soon, but skepticism drags me back into the trenches of my own insecurity. *What if I still fail?* This blow, if I don't succeed, will be more devastating than the first. This time, I tried. I gave it my all and I still failed. Then I'll know for sure, I am not good enough. *I always knew I was worthless.* I sink, then a flash of memory. The diamond. The irradiation. And the Defiance, newly released from the dungeon, galloping across the horizon toward me. Their message on fire with determination and possibility: *The battle, hah, cannot be lost by those who persevere, hah. Bitch, pick up that pencil and soar! Looks like another TKO for these obstacles. You got this, you feel me.* I don't believe, but I obey.

I speak Dr. King's words aloud again to myself interspliced with Lil Jon. The Defiance on horses, nearby, watching. Waiting. "I'm not worried about anything. To the window, to the wall. Get low, get low, get low. Mine eyes have seen the glory," I whistle and recite until courage burns where worthlessness once did.

CHAPTER EIGHTEEN

It's amazing how quickly Prince Charming can lose his throne and fall from grace. How something you believed so strongly can change in your mind in an instant. *How could I have been chasing an idealized version of white men? When has a white man ever saved me?* I shake my head in disappointment.

I haven't seen Bryce since the frat party, which I attribute to my cleverly crafted getups, but Earnell says, "Anyone with functioning eyes can see it's you. Oh, look, it's Negro Brown in a baseball hat and sunglasses. Oh, hey, there's Negro Brown in a big winter coat and a scarf. Oh my goodness, is that Negro Brown again in a shawl, headwrap, and more sunglasses? Yes, yes, it is. The more you hide, the more you are revealed."

"Shut up, Earnell. Only negroes know it's me. *They* can't tell."

"Everyone knows it's you."

Earnell is a fool, I think to myself while grabbing lunch

in the café one day before my makeup exam. *I'm clearly a master of disguise. A real Houdini.* I am about to rain down more self-congratulations when I feel someone tap me on the shoulder. Spooked, I spin and see Bryce standing behind me. A deer caught in headlights, my eyes bug out of their sockets, but thanks to the dark shades, Bryce can't see.

"Hey," Bryce says. "Do you have a minute to talk?"

"Talk about what?" I laugh uneasily.

"You know, the party," he says embarrassingly. "I just want to...I feel like we should process it."

As if I owe him that. Why do white men always act as if it is someone else's job to help them work through their feelings? The world has given them everything and they can't even carry their own emotions alone.

"There's nothing to talk about," I say dryly. "You don't need to explain anything to me. I get it."

I tell my body to grab my tray, pay, and find a table, but it doesn't obey. I remain frozen in front of Bryce with too many scarves wrapped around my neck and the Defiance screaming *Run* in my ear.

"Look, I'm attracted to you too. I think you're beautiful, smart, and cool. I love our time together, but it's just... there's already so much pressure in my life. The diversity work is super important to me and I'm committed to it, but an interracial couple would be a lot, especially in a place like this. The judgments, the questions would be crushing. I'm already trying to make everything in my life work.

Trying to do well in classes. Trying to be a good Christian and not disappoint anyone. This would just be too much, as much as I want it. I can't handle it."

What does he know about pressure? As if I'm not dealing with the same and more, but I am still willing to risk it.

I remove my sunglasses and look into Bryce's eyes. I see for the first time: There is no prince here. No shining white knight who is going to rescue me from my problems. Only a scared little boy afraid of being judged by others. No one ever comes to rescue me anyways. I should have expected this.

"You're a coward," I say finally. "What good is any of that diversity work if you run for the hills when the stakes are high? I guess it only applies in theory and not practice?"

He stands, unmoving. He lingers right next to me, waiting for me to soften and take care of his conflicting feelings. If only I could tell him he's still a good person and it's all going to be OK. If only I could make him feel better about his privilege, again. Not wanting to date me does not make him a bad person. Not wanting to date me because he is afraid of what others think makes him a coward. No, there is no prince here.

I grab my tray and walk toward the cashier. I feel his silent eyes piercing my back, but I don't turn around. When I find an empty table at the back of the café my body slumps. My appetite is gone. I begin to wonder if Blackness makes me untouchable. If the only Black man interested in me is my like-a-brother best friend and white men react like this even when they are attracted to me, will I ever find a romantic partner? Will other men also be scared to date me because of the consequences of being attached to a Black body? *What's wrong with me?* I think to myself. *Something must be wrong.* I inhale the tears, not wanting him to see me cry. I put on another disguise: the mask of strength. Emotion wells in my chest, but my eyes go dead, cold. It's what's needed for the protection of the soft parts underneath. There are so many soft parts, but no one seems to care that I need to be nurtured also. That I need a little tenderness too. They have built me for the battle, to withstand the hits. I just didn't know there would be so many blows and that strength could be so suffocating.

The wind carries me back to my dorm room. I can't walk on my own in this state. I float, lifelessly, until I somehow land in my bed. I need to study for my exam tomorrow, but not even that can generate the energy to rise. I remain horizontal and motionless. Counting cracks again until a haze of sleep and exhaustion washes over me.

———— • ◆ • ————

I sharpen all three of my pencils and lay them on my desk. The tips are so pointy they could prick blood from your fingertips. I arrange them from shortest to longest. Then I change my mind and decide they look better longest to shortest. Controlling the pencils, which is the only thing I can control in this moment, helps ease my nerves. By the time Professor Cartwright comes shuffling into the room ten minutes late, I have already gone back and forth three times.

"Now, now," Professor Cartwright says. "Don't be scared. You look like you've seen a ghost. You'll have forty-five minutes to complete this and then I'll grade it right after. Just breathe and do your best."

He hands me the exam. I pick up one of my extra-pointy pencils and glance through the questions. Even though I have studied nonstop for a week, the questions look complex and intimidating. I start panicking internally and prepare myself for failure. *I knew I was gonna fail.* Despite my lack of self-confidence, I work through each problem methodically, as best I can. By the end, I'm convinced none of my answers are correct. I still have ten minutes left, but instead of looking over my test, I read all the announcements on the side wall.

"All right, time's up. Do you need an extra five?" Professor Cartwright asks.

I walk the exam up to his desk. Tears begin to well up in my eyes.

"I just want you to know that this time I tried really hard. I'm sorry if I failed again."

He smiles compassionately, which is the first time I've felt him recognize my humanity. "Let's just take a look. Have a seat. This will only take a few minutes."

I rearrange my pencils again and resharpen them. When that doesn't bring satisfaction, I push back the skin of all my cuticles. Manda Panda gets manicures at the nail salon next to Walmart off campus. Her nails always look great: light pink, baby blue, and purple. I wonder how my nails would look with a manicure. I still appear young in the face, but my hands give away the struggle that has been my life. They look like working hands, rough with brittle, dirty nails. Shame, both for my hands and my impending failing grade, rocks me.

A few minutes is really almost twenty-five. That's how long it takes him to finish. I don't know if the extra time is a good thing or a bad thing. He walks the exam over to me. I try to read the expression on his face, but he doesn't give anything away.

"Are you going back to Cleveland for the break, Ms. Brown?" he says, sitting on the table next to me.

I want to throw up. There is no reason to make small talk unless I have failed. Is he going to tell me to stay there? Why does he want to know this?

"Yes, I was planning on it. See family and friends, you know."

"Well, you can tell them you aced your calculus exam." He hands the paper to me.

"I'm not often impressed, but I'm blown away by what you were able to do in a week. Well done. I hope you are proud of yourself. Get out of here and enjoy your break. You've earned it. Now I've got a dinner to get to. I swear, ninety percent of my job is going to fancy college dinners."

He packs his briefcase and rushes out. I try to get up,

but I can't move. I watch as tears rain down on the paper, smearing the black ink and my pencil markings. *Me, I got an A on a calculus exam?* I thought this was not possible. I imagined failure even as the Defiance spoke of victory. I wonder what else I can do that I thought was not possible? I reach down into my well of memories and remember all the times I thought I couldn't but did anyways. Just like now. I never fail when I try.

I begin to allow the possibility that it could be me. That I might be a Chosen One. If I'm capable of this, what else could I be capable of? *Me? A poor Black girl from Cleveland?* They never make heroes that look like me, but maybe it's time for a new legend.

I rise triumphantly, stuff the exam and pencils into my backpack. *A Chosen One*, I say to myself. I like the sound of that.

CHAPTER NINETEEN

The final six weeks of the semester bow to my newfound mastery of collegiate subjects. Tray Tray specializes in math, but she has enough knowledge to guide me through all my classes. If she doesn't know something, she figures it out and comes back with the answer. I thought about getting another tutor, like Yoda suggested, but she's the only one I trust. By the time finals arrive, I have been training in Tray Tray's secret library lair for weeks.

She quizzes me like we are on a game show with everything at stake. "Under our Constitution, some powers belong to the federal government. What are those powers?" I answer: "The go'ment, like my parents call it, can coin money, regulate commerce, declare war, raise and maintain armed forces, and establish a post office."

"You just won a hundred thousand dollars!" she exclaims excitedly. "Which author won the Nobel Prize in Literature for his realistic and imaginative writings, combining sympathetic humor and keen social perception?"

"Uh, I'll take the hottie known as John Ernest Steinbeck for two thousand, Alex."

"You are correct. Final question. If you get this right, you will walk away with one million dollars. What is the worst movie of all time?" Tracey asks, jokingly.

"Tell my momma, we movin' on up to the East Side. Alex, what is *Birth of a Nation?*" The imaginary crowd goes wild as we jump around in a circle to celebrate our winnings.

I prance into the testing rooms during finals week, wielding my freshly sharpened pencils like lightsabers. "May the Force be with me," I whisper before I start.

After finals, I rush home to my dorm room, burst through the door, and proclaim: "Hear ye, hear ye: I have completed my first semester of college and I feel great!" Manda Panda bounces up off her bed and screams at the top of her lungs, "Ah!" I run to my closet and pull out the triangular birthday hats and party blowers we have been saving for just this moment. We put on our hats and jump around the room in glee. Manda Panda blasts "The Final Countdown" by Europe. I put my sunglasses on in preparation for a dramatic karaoke joint performance. As soon as the music starts, Manda Panda and I move intensely. When the lead singer reaches the chorus, Manda Panda starts twerking, but she is so remarkably off beat, the African pulse still beating in me after all these centuries forces me to stop the music.

"Mandy, no. That's not it. Who twerks to eighties music anyways?"

"What? Then how do you do it? Show me."

"Well, I definitely don't know, but I know that's not it."

"Who are you, the beat police? This is a celebration, bitch!"

Manda Panda presses play and the music blares. She continues her bad twerking until I join. I'm not the best dancer, but I manage to find a beat or two. I grab the gin and two shot glasses from her closet. I pour us each a shot and mix in a little orange juice. We toast, lower the music, and then collapse on her bed.

"Can't believe we made it through our first semester," Manda Panda says while lying on my chest. "Let's save this moment forever." She pulls out her camera and snaps a picture.

"You think you'll remember me in twenty years?" she asks while looking at the developing Polaroid film. "Your wild first-year roommate?"

"How could I forget?"

"We'll be so old by then. Like have gray hair and stuff."

Silence.

I stare at the ceiling trying to summon the courage to ask her about the aftermath of that terrible night.

"Hey . . . I wanted to ask if you ever ended up reporting him? Have you seen him around?"

Mandy's body grows cold and heavy.

"I see him everywhere. At the gym. In the café. At first, I would run in the opposite direction, find the nearest bathroom, and melt down. Like have a total panic attack. But one day I just decided to stop running. I pushed my chin up. I walked right past him. I don't know if he saw me. Now I just walk around without asking permission. I'm working on not letting it define me or draw limits on how I move through space, but it's hard. At least I'm trying, I guess."

Tears well up in my eyes. I am so proud of her. I have watched her struggle for the past month. The days she didn't get out of bed. The secret crying in the bathroom. The dead, despaired look in her eyes. She still made it to this moment of glee and celebration, and she gets to keep all the rest of the moments of her life despite what he took from her. Make them her own.

"The battle cannot be lost by those who persevere," I say.

"Yea, it is a daily battle. I filed a complaint. They said they'd look into it and get back to me, but I know they never will. I was so afraid walking in there, like I was shaking while I filled out the form. Thanks for pushing me to do it."

Manda Panda suddenly jumps up from the bed and changes the song on her iPod, turning the music back up.

"You know what, fuck these men and their shitty love.

Always takin' shit that don't belong to them. Fuck these men and all their bullshit!" she yells at the top of her lungs.

Tina Turner's "What's Love Got to Do with It" starts blaring from the speakers.

"Why do you have so much eighties music?" I ask.

"The only thing I love more than a little drinking is eighties music. It was a vibe, a wave that'll probably never come again. Savor it."

I try to let go of the hope I had in finding a relationship here. Throw it away like Manda Panda is doing with Trevor, but the shadow clings to me. I think back to my anticipation and excitement over Bryce. If just the possibility of love is that invigorating, what is actual love like? I don't know if I'll ever find out. I feel worthless without the hope of love.

I start stomping the ground screaming, "Damnit!"

"What are you doing?"

"I'm trying to release something by stomping it out."

"Ooh, that's a good idea. I'm gonna stomp on Trevor's head."

Manda Panda starts stomping and yelling, "Die, Trevor! Stupid man-boy-looking bitch! You took my body, but you will never take my freedom!" she screams while imitating Mel Gibson in *Braveheart*.

We stomp harder until the whole room shakes. Luckily, we are on the first floor so no one is beneath us, but I'm sure our neighbors must be wondering what's going on.

"Do you think he's dead now?" she asks, out of breath.

"I hope so."

"We should stomp more to make sure."

Manda Panda continues pounding the ground with her feet while screaming, "Die! Die! Die!"

Her screams come from deep within her belly. They are guttural, visceral, like a mother giving birth. I know she is trying to erase him from her psyche, but I've learned the only way to extract the pain is to heal it out. I don't stop her, though. She is taking her revenge for being punished by a crime she did not commit.

"What about now?" she asks in exhaustion with no more breath to spare.

"Yea. I think we did it that time."

When we finally finish our catharsis, all I can hear is our beating hearts. Hearts that know how to survive. Hearts that know how to persevere. *We do need our hearts*, I say silently to Tina. *We always needed them*, even though I've spent a lifetime trying to shut mine down. I decide as long as mine is beating, I can try. I can keep going. Every beat is an invitation to stand again, wipe the sweat from brows, the tears from eyes, and ask, "What next?" I don't want to be a warrior, but being a woman in a world full of men is to learn to take up arms constantly. Women's hearts are vast, unlimited, ever expanding to absorb the runoff. All the pain that the men refuse to feel is passed on to us. We make magic out of it.

I kiss Manda Panda on the forehead as she is falling

asleep. "Night, sweet girl," I whisper. When she is snoring, I take one more shot and pass out until dawn arrives.

We meet at Denny's on our last day before heading home for winter break. We are celebrating our academic victories. Four Black kids from Nowhere, urban America, made out like bandits with GPAs ranging from 3.45 to 3.73 despite rocky midterms. Gabby's was the highest. She thanks the ancestors for "ordering her steps and guiding her path to success."

"Nigga, it wasn't the ancestors," Keli scolds. "It was hours of studying, tutoring, and praying."

"No, actually, I have to agree with Gabby on this one. They were definitely watching out for us." Earnell winks at me.

"Finally, some validation. Thank you, Brother Jackson. At least one of us can see the light." Gabby sticks out her tongue at Keli in playful scorn.

Lessons about the power of accessing seem to come from everywhere now. I remember Dean Harrison's advice. If she was right about that, was she right about everything else, including the magic? She was certainly right about the miracles, which was confirmed when I spoke to my mother yesterday after the test. In one phone call, she revealed four miracles. Then I shared mine. Five in total.

"I got somethin' I gotta tell you," she says as soon as I answer the phone. "It's been heavy on my spirit and now that I'm in AA, I'm working on makin' 'mends to the people I ain't done right by. That's the eighth step. And I...oh boy, this is hard. I don't know how to say dis', but..."

I wait for her to say what she already did in the other realm. I never thought she would tell me the truth in real life. She has been so burdened by it, I was sure she would carry it to the grave.

"Baby, look...you know when dat thang happ'n to you when you was younger? And I wasn't dere for you? I shoulda been dere for ya. It's just, I couldn't handle it. Lord knows I been through er'y battle dere is, but dat... dat was mo' den I could bear. I want you to know I stood outside dat hospital fo' an hour. Tryin' to find da courage ta go in.

"I couldn't watch my baby girl be destroyed like I was. I ain't neva recovered and I couldn't believe, as much as I tried ta protect you, dat it found you too. Right den and dere I decided dat it wutin' no peace, no justice, no rightness. Not in dis' world. And I went ta da only place I could thank of ta find freedom from all dat. Righteousness don't matter in da crack house. Neither do peace or justice. Tried to kill myself dat night, but somethin' stop me. Some force put a hand on my shoulder. Was da same night Cleveland had all dem colorful lights in da sky. First and only time. Dat's where I was while you was goin' through all dat. In da crack house. I ain't gon' ask for yo' forgiveness—"

"I forgive you," I interrupt. "You were a diamond covered in shit. I forgive you."

We are silent, only for several seconds, but it feels like an eternity. That's how long we have both carried this sin, not even our own, finally released.

"It won't happen again in our family," I tell her. "I don't want any kids. It can end with me. Unless Dre and Rone have kids, which we should pray to all the gods never happens."

Laughter. Joy. Tears. Healing. A miracle. I know her realization is somehow linked to the work I did in the healing timeline.

Not only that, but Rone enrolled in GED classes so he can register for community college eventually. Miracle number two. Dre traded his old friend Colt for slightly less alcoholic coolers. Baby steps, and still miracle number three. Dad worked long hours at the welding shop to retrieve the rent money he gambled, which saved the family from eviction. Thinking about someone other than himself, miracle number four. My forgiveness—the fifth and final miracle. Every forgiveness, the choice to let go, is a miracle of grace we bestow upon one another for being human and eternally flawed.

"Negro Brown, you're awfully quiet. Are you OK?" Keli asks.

"Yea, just reflecting on the semester and the fact that we actually all did it. I'm so proud of you guys. I couldn't have done it without you. Every winner needs a strong crew. I love y'all like family."

Earnell dabs his eyes with a napkin.

"Earnell?! Are you crying?" I ask, shocked.

"What?! No! I think it's just windy in here. Something blew into my eye."

"But there is no wind and all the windows are closed because it's the middle of winter."

"Leave him alone, Keli!" Gabby shouts while putting a caring hand on Earnell's shoulders. "It's OK, my friend. We, and by we, I mean us and the ancestors of past and present, accept and support your feelings. They, too, remember the joy of a Grand Slam with extra bacon," which is what we've all ordered.

"See, there you go again," Earnell replies. "Ruining the moment. I'm proud of you guys too. Y'all my road dogs."

Earnell smiles, then places his hand over mine, which is resting on the table. He leaves it there for longer than a friend should, just like his hand on my thigh outside the student center. Gabby, Keli, and I all stare in silent, but knowing, surprise.

Snow falls on the white pine trees outside the tightly shut windows. Still no wind to speak of, but Earnell has cried three times tonight and again grabbed the hand of the girl he has liked since the beginning. Finally making his feelings known.

I ride off into the new year, basking in the glory of friendship, miracles, and A-pluses.

CHAPTER TWENTY

Dean Harrison was right, she is Yoda. She is ancient like a redwood trunk in a California forest. Her wisdom predates time. Now I know my life will be divided into two parts: Pre-DH and Post-DH. I will never be the same after what she told me. After the five family miracles, I yield to her knowledge. I return from the real Cleveland after a long winter break determined to learn everything she has to teach. I accept the inexplicable series of occurrences happening around me as part of my transformation. I cherish my role as a traveler of the realms. I release myself from the stigma of any imbalance or impossibility. Now, there is only Yoda and Luke answering the call to heal the universe.

My questions lead to more questions and astounding answers. The Keepers, who have been watching me through other people since I was born, are an ancestral force that respond to disturbances in the living field. Once I answer my calls, I can become a Keeper or like Yoda if I want to continue working in the realm of form, guiding new Chosen Ones. The choice is mine. When darkness is legion, the Keepers answer the calls of the Chosen Ones throughout the universe to balance and heal the field. The Chosen Ones exist as waves of hope and possibility in the quantum realm until they are activated by the Keepers. The quantum realm is the space before time, from which all other realities emerge. It is infinite, containing all possibilities and potentialities. My primary job is to help balance the timelines, which are the various realities in which life can occur, from heavy pain and suffering.

"You said there are many Chosen Ones; how many?" I ask. "I kind of wish I was the only one since then I'd be more special. Then I'd be really important."

"That's too much power and responsibility for one person. You are never the only one. No single person can heal all the timelines. It's a coordinated effort between many different beings throughout time and space. Anyways, it doesn't matter how many there are. The quantum realm delivers what's needed in the right time.

"A few more things you should know: After your initiation, the Keepers stop watching. You will have to contact them when you need assistance. They are your access point to performing miracles and traveling between realms. They control the portals, mainly to prevent Darth and his shadow workers from wreaking havoc on the healing timelines. On the night you went to Cleveland, I summoned them to open a portal."

"How do I summon them?"

"The portal on your wall is like an access key that will follow you wherever you go. It can also deliver premonitions and warnings. For contacting the Keepers on demand, you'll have to figure it out on your own. It's different for everyone. For me, it's the teacup. Stirring a certain way and clinking the sides of the cup sends them a signal. Your summons seems to be EMDR. It's unique for each of us, like fingerprints. You can try in therapy."

"On my own?"

"Your purpose and your journey depend solely on you."

———————— ◆ ————————

I eagerly jolt across the Green to Jennifer's office my second week back on campus. I'm sweating and out of breath by the time I knock on the door.

"Oh my goodness," Jennifer says in surprise. "Have you been running? Is someone chasing you?"

She tilts her head out and looks down the hallway behind me.

"I just felt like running today."

"OK, well, I guess any exercise is good. Come in. Grab some water. Sit."

Her office smells sweet like freshly cut grass, not lavender or rose anymore. I notice new air fresheners hanging on the wall behind her. Garden Fresh and Fields of Spring. I inhale deeply to soak in the scent.

"Smells good in here now, like spring," I say, uneasily

trying to deflect from the pressure of figuring out how to call the Keepers.

She smiles softly. "So, tell me. How was your trip home? I want to hear all about it."

I don't want to talk about my life right now. I want to figure out how to use my supernatural powers. I wish she could just sit there silently while I try various methods, but that would be ridiculous. The thought of it makes me giggle.

"Is something funny?"

"No, I'm sorry. I was just thinking about something that happened in class the other day. My trip home was fine. My family is doing a lot better than when I started here in the fall. Everyone's hanging in there."

"That's wonderful. I'm glad to hear that."

Since the Keepers stare, I assume I should call them through my eyes somehow. I try an assortment of things: opening and closing my eyes, pulling the lids back and bulging them out, rolling them in circles, even crossing them. I have to be subtle. I quickly do these things when Jennifer looks away or writes something on her notepad. None of it works.

"Have you had any more episodes of seeing things that weren't there?"

"No, actually. I think it's finally stopped."

"Wow, that's incredible. I wonder if the work we're doing here had an impact. I'm sure it must have. You're really making strides."

Next, I try breathing differently. I learned in yoga class that the breath is the gateway to the soul. I wonder if my breath sends a signal. First, I inhale deeply, trying to fill myself up with oxygen. When that doesn't work, I try the kundalini breath of fire, which also comes from yoga class. It involves snapping the belly in quickly and forcing air out through the nostrils. It looks like you are panting like a dog except your mouth is closed.

"Are you OK?" Jennifer asks concernedly. "You seem distracted. Everything all right?"

Nothing works. I grow frustrated. Tension builds in my brow.

"I'm just trying to work through something but can't seem to get it."

"What are you trying to figure out?"

"The ways of the universe."

Jennifer laughs at my melodrama.

"Aren't we all? I've learned in my life that the more you chase something, the harder it is to catch. Sometimes you just have to relax. Let the answer come to you."

I accept her advice mainly out of exhaustion. I've done everything I can think of to call the Keepers. I scan the eclectic objects in Jennifer's office to take my mind off this impossible task. She's added some things since last semester. A signed tennis ball on her desk. The only tennis players I know are Venus and Serena Williams, who I feel like are my sisters even though I never met them. Every time a Black person achieves anything, all of us feel a kinship and claim to their accomplishment. Public figures become more than just people with extraordinary talent. They become family. Close enough to feel like you know them, but distant enough to realize you will probably never meet. The strange looking glass of celebrity.

My eyes keep moving around her office. A framed picture of a brown-haired, dorky-looking white man with big teeth. *He's not cute at all*, I think to myself. *So why would she hang him on the wall? White people.* I shake my head in amusement.

"That's Jerry Seinfeld," Jennifer says, noticing my gaze. "One of the greatest comedians ever."

"Huh, never heard of him."

"You know, Echo, we've met a few times now and I'm wondering if we shouldn't try to deepen our work? Are you open to that?"

"What does that mean?"

"Unpacking some of the more difficult things that happened to you. Only if you feel ready, of course."

My enthusiasm for contacting the Keepers wanes. A wall erects between us. Haven't I done enough work? Aren't I healed after everything I experienced in astral Cleveland? Now she wants me to excavate more bones from a padlocked graveyard. I become enraged.

"I'm not trying to push you," Jennifer says, noticing my anger. "I just don't want you to stay burdened by things you can let go of. You'll be amazed at how freeing this work can be if you do the work. I know you are not Christian, but there is a Bible verse that always brings me peace when I have to face something big. 'Come to me,' it says, 'all who labor and are heavy laden, and I will give you rest.'"

"Matthew Eleven."

"Yes, that's right."

"My mother used to quote the Bible to us all the time. She came back to that one a lot. She had a big load also."

"For me, it means we don't have to carry our troubles alone. Others can help us. And the only way we truly find rest is by assisting each other with these heavy loads. I know I've said this before, but you can lay your burdens down in this room. I am a friend of your soul."

Something about her sincerity breaks me. A flood of tears. How could she know this is exactly what I needed, to be gently nudged into my own salvation?

Jennifer moves her finger back and forth while I tap the tops of my thighs. I take a deep breath and close my eyes. An open door inside. I walk through it with my eyes still shut.

"I just wonder why it happened to me," I say with a quivering voice after a few moments of silence.

"I mean that kind of thing happened to all my friends who were girls and even some of the boys. Some people are truly monsters. Demons disguised as flesh...He told me he had books in his apartment. He knew I loved school and reading, those sorts of activities. I was hesitant initially to follow him, but I really wanted to see what books he had."

I pause, crying quietly to myself.

"I was so young and confused, you know? I didn't understand what was happening, but I still feel like it was my fault somehow. It felt so terrible. So, so, so bad. Like being slowly ripped apart. Eventually I stopped resisting. I stared at the ceiling and started saying some of my mother's Bible verses aloud. 'Though I walk through the valley of the shadow of death, I will fear no evil: for thou art with me. Thy rod and thy staff they comfort me.'"

A winding down of time. A chill in the air. Then their voices, the Keepers, pouring forth from my own eyes, which suddenly fling open. I look over and see that Jennifer is frozen with her fingers in the air, preparing to administer the EMDR. They continue their channeling, sending electrical pulses through my entire body.

So you have reached us on your own through the words of your mother's God.

Welcome.

How can we strengthen you in this moment?

"You came."

We did, and now you know how to reach us.

"Yes, but why didn't you come every other time I've quoted the Bible?"

We can only hear your call through any collection of words by which you are moved when your emotional frequency is elevated. It is why we came the night you prayed on the bathroom floor. You, overwhelmed by our presence, passed out, but we still prepared a portal while you slept so you could travel in your dreams.

"Wow, do you know everything there is to know?"

Yes.

"What is 347,589 divided by 3 and then multiplied by 12?"

1,390,356.

"Impressive. Why didn't you give me the answers to my calculus exam?"

Your journey is by design. We cannot interfere with the events of your life. We can only watch and set the momentum in motion.

"Why didn't you stop it from happening? Why didn't you stop him?"

We can only bend the arcs of time when something might be life-threatening to a Chosen One. This tragedy was not, thus we could not interfere.

It is critical to understand that you are not responsible for what he did. He was a monster on your path. There will be many. Once you accept that you are not to blame for disturbing behavior, the ghost of his sins can be released from your psyche.

We can help you see it differently if you would like?

No other event has paralyzed me more: impacting my self-image, self-esteem, and ability to form relationships. It made me deeply distrustful of others and convinced me that I am a terrible, dirty person. I wonder who I would be without the weight of this constantly throbbing at the bottom of my mind.

"How would I see it differently?"

We will prepare a portal.

BACKWARD

Here we are in the same dingy room I've been running from my entire life. I freeze. Then I see her in all her innocence. Hair plaited. She is so young. *I am so young.* Prior to this, I've been remembering myself as an adult. Not as a real grown-up, but the qualities of one projected onto my child self, which allows me to keep holding myself responsible for what happened. *I should have known better* is what I repeat in my mind over and over. But how could this child, this sweet, innocent child, have known better? The realization electrifies me.

Then the crime. I am pinned beneath him. Helpless. I can barely watch. A violent rage takes over me. I lunge toward him, knocking him down. My fists land decisively against his face until he transforms into a disfigured, frightened creature. I see him for the first time as he truly was: a sick coward. He shrinks away from me, scurrying around the room before jumping out the window to his death.

I grab the little girl's hand and tell her she is free now.

"You saved me," she says. "I knew you would."

A release. A thousand sparks inside as if each of my cells is rejoicing all at once. A radiation. A lifting. So many thoughts: *I did not cause this. It was not my fault. I was help-less. He was a pedophile who preyed on children. Something was wrong with him, not me. Nothing is wrong with me.*

Do you see now?

I am silently overwhelmed.

We have not registered your response.
Do you understand?

"Thank you" are the only words that manage to leave my lips. "Thank you."

I sit in stunned silence and return to the present moment.

"How do you feel?" Jennifer asks after she unfreezes. "Did you discover anything new?"

"I feel like my whole life paradigm shifted."

"Wow," she says. "That's the power of EMDR. It is a deeply transformative practice. I've seen it change lives more than once. I think that's enough for today. Go home and rest."

I walk slowly toward the door, trying to process everything that just happened—the enormity of the shift that has occurred inside of me.

"Beloved," Jennifer says, prompting me to turn around, "I pray that in all respects you may prosper..."

"And be in good health, just as your soul prospers. John 3," I respond.

Loving gazes pour from each of us and fields of healing erupt where walls once were.

And so, Luke Skywalker discovers her abilities and joins the Jedi of Chosen Ones, answering the call to heal what was broken, and defeating Darth and his army of wicked creatures. The darkness is legion, but so is the light, especially once you learn how to wield it.

CHAPTER TWENTY-ONE

Second semester, unlike the first one, is a breeze. Three weeks in, I feel renewed, like I'm on top of the world. I've finally figured out this college game. The course load is a mix of interesting and daunting. I'm taking Government Two: The International Political System, Religion One: Patterns of Religious Experience, Theater One: Introduction to Theater, Introductory French, and my least favorite, most daunting class this semester, Economics One: Economic Principles and Policies. Even though I hate economics and anything to do with numbers, I've learned how to study and work with a tutor.

I've been most excited about theater class this term. There are no exams and I like the idea of dressing up and pretending to be someone else. I'm terrified to do this in front of other people, but I'm pushing myself to step outside of my comfort zone. The theater professor, Mrs. Nielson, is quirky and far removed from the box. She wears colorful clothes, her hair is always frazzled, and the syllables of her words stretch out for dramatic emphasis. *Does she talk like this at dinner with her husband and kids?* I wonder how someone finds the courage to so freely express themselves. I'm scared of her freedom and what she will make me do, so I hide in the back of the class. I know she's going to find me eventually, but for now this is safe.

Another semester means more racial conflict. This time mostly generated by the *Dartmouth Beacon* and their controversial slate of guests, including Rush Limbaugh, Congressman Ron Paul, and Dinesh D'Souza. Now, three weeks into the semester, the *Dartmouth Beacon* has written a scathing proclamation to President Roberts demanding the end of affirmative action for incoming students. The air on campus is thick with tension and disagreement, which is the perfect time to secretly infiltrate a *Dartmouth Beacon* meeting, according to Keli.

"If we are going to make it in this world," Keli says, "we have to know how they think."

"Yea, but don't you think four negroes walking in together will be suspicious?"

"That's why we don't walk in *together,*" Keli says. "We go separately and pretend to be like Daniel. Just Black individuals down for the cause."

"Um, I'm afraid," I say. "They are going to know we don't belong there. We're gonna need all the deities to get us through this...and Freddy."

Earnell reaches into his bag and pulls out the *Nightmare on Elm Street* doll. "Gotcha covered."

Right before we leave for the meeting, Earnell gets on his knees and leans over the side of his bed.

"Oh my God, what are you doing, Earnell?" I ask. "And why are you dressed like a rich white man from Connecticut?" He is wearing Dockers pants and shoes and a powder-blue, collared, button-down shirt with a sweater tied around his neck.

"I'm praying and I suggest you all join me. And to blend in. Duh. Is that what you're wearing? That ridiculous 'disguise' is going to be a dead giveaway you don't belong."

My jeans, black turtleneck, and trademark black sunglasses are insufficient for conservative infiltration, apparently.

"I don't care what they think," I reply. "I'm not saying anything when we get there. I'm just going to sit in the back quietly and cause no problems, like in theater class." I turn and look at Keli. "And please don't get into a fight. You know I'm not a fighter. I will run."

"Look," she responds. "If anyone steps to my face, I will start throwin' bows. It's not up to me. It's up to anyone who wants to try me."

"Come here, girl," Gabby says. "You need this most of all." Gabby lights a plume of sage and douses Keli in the airy white smoke. "If this doesn't help, nothing will."

"Amen," Earnell says, hoisting himself up off the floor. "I feel protected by the blood of the lamb. Let's go."

The meeting begins with the Pledge of Allegiance "to honor this great nation and the rule of law." Already I want to leave. I don't look at Earnell, Gabby, or Keli, since I know I would burst out laughing. Instead, I focus on the flag they have hung across the blackboard in front of the room. The room is mainly full of white men, a few white women, and two other students of color, one South Asian and one East Asian. I expect to see Daniel, but he doesn't make an appearance. He probably would have outed us anyways. We didn't think about that at all.

The first part of the gathering is business: which speakers to invite next, minutes from the last meeting, and whether they should stage another affirmative action protest in the middle of campus. The second part is a debate about freedom of speech and whether there should be limitations for certain people based on beliefs and ideas.

"I can start," Stephen Clark, who is chairing the meeting, begins. "In my opinion, free speech is only complicated due to certain groups, mainly far left-wing liberals, attempting to put restrictions around what conservatives think, feel, and believe. The answer is simple. Let us believe and speak about whatever we want to our willful audience. Then there is zero problem. Not sure why that's so hard to grasp."

I am burning. I hate Stephen Clark and his squinty little eyes and his squeaky little voice. I cover my ears and count the stars on the flag even though I already know how many there are. I can still hear what they are saying, though muffled.

"People have a right to 'hate' speech publicly if that's what they believe."

"There shouldn't be any 'safe' spaces that allow the voices of some but deny others. It's unconstitutional."

"This is really a discussion about who gets to draw the line between morally acceptable and unacceptable speech. I definitely don't want them deciding that for me."

The young conservatives feel very persecuted, like the whole world is out to get them. I never knew white people—white men—could feel like victims. How? When so much has been given. How, when the privileges afforded them for generations are as thick as the molasses from an old sap tree? They want the entire world. They want the world of their ancestors, to be free to take whatever suits them—land, people, riches. Not just privilege but vast, unchecked power. There are too many voices now and experiences demanding inclusion. This is not the world they know in their bones. Considering the impact of their words on someone else encroaches on their right to hate freely and, when in power, oppress freely.

I don't say any of that out loud, of course. I sit quietly still staring at the flag and the clock, which are my safe anchors in this room. Gabby, Keli, and Earnell have also been quiet for the duration of the meeting. Until Stephen says there should be limitations on protests against public servants, particularly police officers and people elected to serve "this great nation." I can feel the tsunami of Earnell's rage coming. I look at Gabby and Keli—we know it's time to prepare for battle.

"Hey, just gonna chime in here. Faithful conservative since birth. Earnell. Yea, I don't think we're thinking about this in the right way. Public servants and police officers are people also. They are not without flaws just because they are in a certain role. If anything, we should be even more vigilant and speak up when wrongdoing has occurred."

A hellscape of discussion. World War III of beliefs. Jennifer's ideological tennis ball jockeying back and forth, building to a crescendo of Earnell's raw emotion for this brother. Earnell stands and begins shouting:

"These dumb opinions are easy when you never been through nothin'! When the toughest choice in your life is what college to go to."

"You don't know what I've been through," Stephen retorts.

"I don't. But I know that if you have been through what I've been through it's almost impossible to believe what you believe."

A force field of energy starts building behind my eyes. Then words by Dr. King: "Until justice rolls down like water and righteousness like a mighty stream." So much pressure builds, I furtively shake my head to try and release it. It doesn't work. More energetic intensity. Then beams of light spinning around the retinas before shooting out of my pupils, bathing Stephen in a bright white light. He freezes, hypnotized by the glare.

"Show him," I say, beckoning the Keepers. "Show him

his ignorance." Messages from the light pour out. Black men who have been shot and killed by the police, incidents that never made the news, flow into Stephen.

> *He thought I fit the profile of a burglary suspect.*
> *I was twenty-one. He was acquitted. My mother*
> *hasn't gotten out of bed in a year.*

> *He thought I was reaching for a gun. No weapons*
> *were found. I was twenty-nine. No charges filed.*
> *My family marched for justice that never came.*
> *He retired and moved to Florida.*

> *He yelled, "Show me your hands!" and then*
> *shot before I could get them up. My head landed*
> *on the steering wheel while my six-year-old*
> *daughter cried in the seat behind me. They give*
> *her risperidone for the anxiety and nightmares.*
> *She keeps asking if I'm ever coming back.*

So many. Too many to count. Their faces and stories burn into Stephen's mind now, wrestling with his blind conservativism.

The light begins to retract. I take several deep breaths to try and steady myself. I don't know what just happened or why, but I'm deeply affected by it. I can see that Stephen is also. Something shifts in his eyes. One of his guards stands down. There is a receptivity present that wasn't here at the beginning of the meeting.

Earnell is still enraged and doesn't see it. He leans forward on the table, burning.

"There is not a day that goes by when I don't think about my brother. Not one." He points his finger at Stephen. "Imagine someone you love, a sister, a brother, or parent, is senselessly ripped from you and there are no consequences for the person that took them. Imagine! You are debating rights and freedoms, but what about justice for those who suffer when the law sides with the hateful? What should we, the ones forced to reckon with the flaws in your police and public servants, do? Sit quietly in cruel acceptance? I think the fuck not. You're delusional. Keli, Gabby, Echo, let's go."

We stand and begin clapping for Earnell while marching toward the exit. Everyone watches silently as we leave.

"Hey," Stephen calls out before we reach the door. "I'd want consequences if it was my family and I'd want a right to speak up." He tries to build a bridge toward us, but it's too late. We are already in the water, swimming against a tide that comes from all sides. We've been in the water our entire lives and don't know what it's like to bunk in a cabin on land. If we had, we wouldn't think the tide was so bad either and it would take a miracle of the light to convince us also.

Earnell is quiet for the rest of the evening. A silent

Earnell is unusual. I know he must be ruminating over his brother. We order milkshakes in the late-night café. A band onstage plays soul music. Hits by Otis, Sam Cooke, and Aretha. Gabby snaps and sways along.

"It was worse than I thought," I say.

"A real slap in the face," Gabby says. "How can they believe all that crap?"

Keli places her hand on Earnell's shoulder and asks, "How ya doin', buddy?"

"When will we be equal?" Earnell asks wearily. "When will they understand? One hundred more years? Two hundred?"

"More like a thousand," Keli responds. "Probably never."

The smoke of sorrow, which always follows the flames of rage, settles on the table and doesn't lift even after we leave. No one sits there for the rest of the night. The band's last song is "Don't Let Me Be Misunderstood," by Nina Simone.

———•◆•———

Dean Yoda takes me out to dinner every week now, instead of meeting at her office, to check in and see how I'm doing. I eat as much as I can each time. Campus food is great, but not as delicious as restaurant food. Last week we went to Molly's, which has the best bread around. They bring out a basket of warm bread and honey butter. I finished most of it myself, then asked for another. I ordered calamari to start, fish and chips as my main course, and apple pie for dessert. It was so delicious, I could barely keep up conversation. After I finish, I suck down the large glass of water on the table, pour another, then repeat. I am nearly in a food coma, like after the lobster dinner, when it's all done.

Tonight, we are at the Indian restaurant down the street from Molly's. Indian food is my favorite. It's so different from the food we eat in Cleveland, but I fell in love with it instantly. The spices, the naan, the curries. If I go to heaven, I want them to only serve me Indian food. I don't eat anything for breakfast on the days Yoda takes me out so I can leave room in my stomach for everything I will eat later. I walk into the restaurant beaming, full of glee.

"Hi, Dean Harrison!" I call out. "I came starving."

"I know you did," she says, smiling knowingly.

I tell her about the Keepers and the light at the *Dartmouth Beacon* meeting a week ago, about how it shifted something in one of the biggest conservatives on campus.

"I'm proud of you for figuring out so quickly what works for you, and for that incredible, life-changing realization. Some people carry pain their entire lives. It also makes perfect sense that scripture would be your conjuring tool. You have always been called by the words, even Bible verses though you are not Christian. I find that strange."

"*You* find something strange," I say amusedly. "This coming from the weirdest person I know. How did you become like this?"

"I, like you, was called forth...."

"Oh my God, it was a joke," I say, laughing. I take another long sip of water before launching my next question. "Why can't I just get people to do what I want? Like why can't I turn Stephen Clark into an ally?"

"That's not how it works. What we really do is influence deeper insight, which can alter how someone sees the world. Once that happens, change is inevitable. We work to inspire new realizations. After that, it's up to the person."

I want to ask Dean Harrison another question, but I don't want to offend her since she rarely shares anything about herself. I try to think of how to frame it, but before I can finish the thought, she interrupts me.

"I'm afraid of many things. I just don't allow that fear to define me and my choices."

"What! You can read my mind?"

"I accessed the frequency you are emitting."

"Well, I guess there is no privacy here, then."

"If you don't want me to do that, just say so."

"Have you been reading me every time we meet?"

"Here and there, mostly when there is some change in your energy field. There was sudden distress and I wondered what it was. Know that you can ask me anything. In the beginning I was a bit of a firecracker. Very hot around the collar. Through many lives comes the calm of knowing and release from the fear paradigm. It is simply futile to resist or give in to fear. Life will never be without turbulence, but it's easier to accept what is happening rather than fight it. That wisdom applies in every field, all realms."

I consider what Dean Harrison says. I've never met anyone as calm as her. I wonder if she is Buddhist. In religion class, they say that a Buddha is the highest flowering of human consciousness. One is without inner turmoil and can access universal wisdom for the benefit of others. Does that not apply to Dean Harrison? I don't know how not to fight. I've been resisting my entire life. I wonder if I'll be a Yoda or a Buddha one day: graceful, calm, and wise. For now, I'm still a wellspring of curiosity, confusion, and determination.

"No, I am not a Buddha, just well-practiced."

"Hey!"

"Last time, promise," she says, smiling.

While Dean Harrison signs the check after dinner, I suddenly feel an overwhelming sense of gratitude to her. Though she has pressed how inescapable the call is, there is still a choosing. An acceptance. She chooses to give freely so much of her time and wisdom. No question is stupid or off-limits. There is never judgment or frustration. She is so clear and unobstructed without internal friction. I wonder if adults—real adults, not nineteen-year-old beginners like me—should spend more time ironing out their insides before they try to teach us anything. Maybe if they faced what they have buried, they could be more available and hold better space for us.

"We all do the best we can," she says.

"Hey!"

She smirks and hands the waiter the check.

"You said you were Yoda. Can I call you that?" I ask, taking one final swig of water.

"No, please, I wouldn't like that at all. It was just a metaphor."

CHAPTER TWENTY-TWO

I'm always afraid of what Professor Nielson will make us do in her workshops. We haven't read any scripts or done anything related to theater five weeks into the semester. Winter Carnival is only a few days away and midterms a month out. At this point, I have no idea when we will start actually performing. "Before you can do theater, you must examine yourselves, which is a lifelong practice," Professor Nielson says with her stretched-out syllables. "College will end. Self-study won't."

I'm tired of examining myself. There is so much to learn. I thought there would come a point when the learning was done and you can stand on the mountaintop of self and claim victory. I wonder how much more I will have to figure out.

All of the initial theater classes are dedicated to self-study. In the first session, we sketch our childhood inspirations and present them to each other. I choose Maya Angelou (who reminds me of Dean Yoda) since she overcame similar obstacles as me and seemed very internally balanced in her later life.

"Maya Angelou," Professor Nielson says, stretching out her syllables even more. "Interesting. That tells me a lot about you."

"What does it tell you?"

"That you have the soul of an artist or healer."

Professor Nielson asks us to split into small groups and discuss our fears and angers in the second class. Each person has to sit in the middle of the circle when it's their turn to be "witnessed in raw form."

"How can you transmit the range of human emotion," Professor Nielson says intensely, "if you don't know what's buried inside? Usually fear and anger are pushed down the furthest."

Today, in class, she tells us, "We are going to do mirror work."

I don't understand what she means until she starts setting up full-length mirrors against the wall in front of us. *Oh dear God*, I think to myself. *What on earth is she going to make us do?* Fear rides through my bones.

"The mirror can tell you a lot about yourself," she says. "Most of us look at our reflection almost every day, but do we really see the soul looking back?" She sounds like Hypnotist Jerry. "If you cannot behold yourself, how can you expect as much from an audience? You must know who exists within you before delivering them to others in a meaningful way." I begin praying: *Our Father, who art in heaven, please protect me from this woman and her witch-craft.* "Today you just might confront the higher being that lives inside."

I look around the circle to see if anyone else is freaking out. I make eye contact with a blond girl standing across the room from me. Her eyes are wide with fright, con-firming I'm not the only one terrified by what is about to happen. My feet are running out of the room and into the safety of the hallway. Just my imaginary feet. My actual body is frozen.

I don't know why I'm so afraid to look at myself in front of others. Probably because the mirror has never been my friend and has only been a place of critique and pain. I real-ize Professor Nielson is right. I don't think I've ever actu-ally seen myself outside of superficial projections of how I imagine others view me.

"So here we go," Professor Nielson says before dramati-cally turning off the lights. "I want you all to take a deep breath. Come into the room. Feel yourself in your body. Flesh and bone. A living miracle. Buddhism approaches the possibility of life occurring like finding a needle in the ocean. Extremely rare. So there is no question about your majestic preciousness. Only a matter of you seeing it.

"Before I turn on the lights, I want you to imagine that you are a newborn baby seeing yourself for the first time. Fresh eyes. A new way of witnessing. So take a deep breath and close your eyes. When I tell you to open them, do your best to let go of any judgments, critiques, assumptions, or beliefs and just see."

I try and inhale as much oxygen as possible, but my chest is so constricted with fear I only manage to pull in small gulps. When the lights come on, I watch myself struggle to breathe, which is exactly what a newborn would be doing anyways. I can only look at my reflection for a few seconds before I have to look away in disgust. *Why am I like this?*

"You can sit or stand, but keep breathing. Keep looking. Let the layers of who you thought you were fall away like autumn leaves."

I have done the work. I have killed the monster in my psyche, yet all I see when I look forward is a beast. An unlovable creature of the night. What's the point of having a "precious human life" if my experience will be filled with so much suffering?

"Let pass whatever emotions may arise. Shame, fear, anger, sadness. Treat them as you would a guest who is here for a short time to teach you something, but ultimately moving on. Say to your reflection: 'I accept you. I love you. I believe in you.'"

Has she lost her mind? No way. The words refuse to even come near my lips. *This is so dumb.*

I glance around and see that I am not the only one struggling with this activity. Several people can barely look at themselves. I am so deeply uncomfortable, I contemplate leaving the room altogether.

"You may be wanting to escape. I invite you to stay

with us. Dig deeper. This work is hard. If you can't make those statements, simply say, 'I see you.'"

My dark brown eyes plead for a validation I cannot provide. I say it, but without looking at myself.

"Maybe you are waiting for someone to come and tell you that you matter, or are beautiful, smart, a good person. Or maybe you're waiting for someone to come rescue you. I want to tell you that after fifty-seven years on Earth, I've learned that nobody saves you. We only save ourselves. Can you find the courage to go get yourself, again? I know you've done it in the past after each disappointment. I can only imagine the things that have happened to you. The deep well of pain that must be throbbing in the center. You are not your pain. Take a moment to let that marinate. You are not your pain. What are you, then, beyond suffering?"

I have never considered that I might be something other than an aggregate of all the bad things that have happened to me. That's what I see when I look in the mirror, an inventory of dreadful experiences. The realization destroys me. *How sad*, I think to myself. *I don't want to go to my grave having only seen myself this way.*

I try to find strength. I recite a few Bible verses in my head, attempting to conjure my mother's presence or the Keepers, but it doesn't work. I feel dead inside and totally alone until I hear Shaquanda say, *I have always loved you. Since you were a little girl. I remember how you shined, the luminosity of your being. You still shine, even now, after everything that happened to you. Nobody can take your light from you*. The Defiance, sitting behind me like proud parents. Shaquanda, softer than I've ever seen her. I didn't know she could be this gentle. *Yea, and I said this girl is something special, you feel me? This girl right here got a special purpose*, Damon says. *How the heavens rippled, hah, with your arrival, hah*, Terrell chimes in. *How existence itself bowed to your majesty.*

I blush. A wave of airy elation washes over me. I feel full, enlivened. *You ready to meet your true essence?* Shaquanda asks. She puts her hands on my shoulders. Terrell and Damon both place supportive palms on my back. I take a deep breath and look into the mirror.

A me unlike any me I've ever seen. My higher self, who is wise even when I'm not. The best possible version of me buried beneath all the shit. Stunning. Glowing. Ethereal, with otherworldly beauty. My energy looks perfectly balanced: femininity, power, and softness all integrated. The inner turmoil that has driven my life, quieted.

She uncurls, my reflection, and smiles so lovingly I can barely behold her compassion. She raises her right hand and folds her fingers into Gyan Mudra. Finally, she speaks. "Holy are you and all who live. Part of the path is forgetting. I am your home. Only self-love can save you. Come as often as you need to be reminded. The heart knows the way." She returns to her celestial position. The Defiance clap gleefully behind me. They play "At Last," by Etta James, to commemorate the moment. I mumble along with them: "At last, my love has come along…and life is like a song."

I am not the only one singing. Several other students hum, some dance, and two shed tears. A few participants seem to be unmoved and unchanged, glaring around the room at an awakening they don't share. *Maybe next time*, I wish for them. Still, the shift in energy across the room as a whole is dramatic and overwhelming.

"Yes!" Professor Nielson cries out joyfully. "Embrace yourself! Sing, dance, twirl. You have found the fountain of life...at last."

True homecomings are like this. A joyful reunion with what was in you all along. The path back may be muddied and overgrown with weeds, but have faith that your heart, like the camel in the desert, will never lead you astray. A Jedi's greatest asset then is not magic but self-love.

———————— ◆ ————————

Fairies ice-skate across the arena. Even I have feathery white wings tonight for the forty-fifth annual Winter Carnival. Who knew late February could be so enjoyable. The campus has been converted into a snowy paradise complete with snow sculptures on the Green, white angels hanging from light poles, and white lights that dance with glee as soon as the sun goes down. Unlike everything else, this looks exactly like it did in the brochure: magical. Christmas was seven weeks ago, but the speakers blast all my favorite holiday songs: "Santa Baby," by Eartha Kitt; "It's the Most

Wonderful Time of the Year," by Andy Williams; and "This Christmas," by Destiny's Child, to add a little spice to the mix. I blow a kiss at the DJ to show my appreciation.

"Well, aren't you suddenly flirty?" Keli says, holding on to my arm to steady herself on the skates.

"I don't know why you grabbing me, I can't skate neither," I respond.

"Yea, but we can use each other for balance."

Earnell, who took ice-skating classes when he was younger at the local YMCA, whirls around the rink, spinning and elegantly extending his limbs like a snow king. He keeps yelling over to us, "Watch this, ladies," before each of his tricks. We can't clap since we are holding on to each other for dear life.

Gabby sips hot chocolate and waves eagerly every time we pass by. "Outdoor activities in the freezing cold are not my forte," she reminds us when we all agree to attend the festivities together.

"But I mean," Keli continues, "you've got a different energy. Walking across campus winking at cute boys. I saw you. Now blowing kisses. Give me some of whatever you're taking. I wanna be an easy, breezy Cover Girl too."

Keli is right, I have been aglow since meeting my higher self in theater class. I feel like I'm floating through the world and everyone is a friend. I can't believe how different I am inside compared to when I first got here. It's like my self-image was a deformed monster, but now it's a sparkling siren who can't stop singing love songs. Charm suddenly oozes from my pores. I've never had this experience in my entire life. I keep waiting for it to pass, for my familiar brooding nature to return, but so far it hasn't. I'm elevated. *Am I enlightened?* I wonder after Professor Demeton discusses this state of mind in religion class. "Imagine a state of being so profound, you become one with all life. Your thoughts dissolve, and you live in bliss." I still have thoughts so I guess I haven't arrived, but I do feel blissful. *Maybe I'm one step away from Buddhahood.*

Ice-skating is followed by a lovely walk across campus to the snow sculptures. Unlike the wooden joker for homecoming, the snow creations are glitzy and dazzling. There's Tinkerbell, an ice castle, a frozen forest of ancient trees, dancing elves, and a nativity scene.

"How come nobody ever built stuff like this in Chicago?" Keli remarks. "Winter there would have been so much better."

"'Cause poor people too busy trying to survive," Earnell replies bitterly. "Don't have the time or energy to play in the snow when dem bills gotta be paid and dem babies gotta be fed."

"I know that's right," Gabby agrees. "They stay making sure joy is limited for poor Black folks, but we always manage to find a way to cultivate it in our souls. Like this one over here"—she says, pointing to me—"have you ever seen her so vibrant and free? You really need to tell us if your wild oats have been sowed."

"Oh my God, shut up!" I say playfully. "Why is everyone

so concerned about my lady parts all of a sudden? I am unsowed!" Earnell gleams at my confession, touching my arm, softly suggesting he might be the one to get the gold. He won't, but I'm overflowing with love and want to be deeply connected to others around me, so I turn around and hug him. I press my entire body into his chest. He is slightly disappointed when I do the same thing to Gabby and Keli.

"OK, now I know this heffa is on one, freely loving up on us as if she's a white," Keli says.

"I just love y'all. That's it," I say, smiling radiantly.

The Dartmouth Aires, an all-male a cappella group, frame the moment perfectly with their smooth, harmonic voices. They begin their first song, "Can You Feel the Love Tonight," by Elton John, as a crowd gathers. The moment overwhelms me. This is what I've always wanted. To be connected and loved. I have yearned for so long. I don't understand why I had to grow up in a sea of abuse when this was possible all along.

"Harden yourself to stand it," they said. "Obey the rules of society. Save money. Exercise and eat right. Try to achieve something important." They don't tell you that you'll need to be loved. That it's the building block of your very humanity. You can't survive without it. So you come up with clever schemes to get it. Everyone's tactics are different, but if you winnow it down to the root, you'll find the same driving impulse: the need to be loved. Deeper than a need. Woven into the fabric of your DNA.

They don't tell you that yes, you'll use defenses some-times, but everything you need for your soul is on the other side of those walls. How come no one ever told me?

Earnell and I continue our flirting. I know I don't like him romantically but I am enjoying the attention. "Wanna take a walk?" he asks. "Without Ren and Stimpy over there?"

"Sure," I say. "Why not?"

We grab some cotton candy and linger through the sculptures. The Dartmouth Aires continue their melodic crooning in the background. It's the most romantic moment I've ever had and I don't want to leave it, even if this isn't my prince. Earnell grabs my hand and I don't pull away. I know I'm going to have to put a stop to this eventually, but I'm just not ready to release the enchantment yet.

"So, I was thinking."

"Oh boy, what were you thinking in that brilliant mind of yours, Earnell Jackson?" He blushes at my unhidden flirtation.

"Just how we have so much in common. We come from similar environments. Have the same values."

"Yes, very true. Hard to find people with whom you connect so well."

"Exactly! Nearly impossible, I'd say. Out of all the campuses in the world, she had to walk onto mine."

Silence, too much.

He stops and stands in front of me.

Onlookers probably think we are a couple smitten by the magic of the night. They would be justified in their observations. Both of us *are* enthralled, but for different reasons. Him because he thinks he finally got the girl and me as a result of tapping the well of unconditional love inside myself. We are on the same train, but for different reasons.

He leans forward, closes his eyes, and lingers.

The line that divides friends asks if I will cross it further. I consider the invitation. My desire to be intimate with someone in this moment is enormous. So compelling, I consider crossing over and meeting him in the throes of a passion I do not share. Yearning can make you act in such ways. His unkissed lips waiting right there. I stand outside the door of desire, hoping it opens for this caring, intelligent, good-natured human in front of me. I urge it to open, but it doesn't and neither does my heart for him. It would be like kissing my brother. I can't. Attraction is a mysterious force that can't be feigned.

I am devastated. I know what it's like to be rejected. I don't want to be responsible for that.

"Earnell," I say softly, and he sees his interest is not shared.

"Earnell, I need you to listen carefully to what I'm about to say. I want you to understand that it doesn't mean you aren't worthy. The right person will be able to appreciate everything you have to offer. You are one of the best people I've ever met. Anyone would be..."

Earnell's face drops. He steps away from me, bursting the bubble of euphoria I've been living in. My defenses prepare to remount. He storms off before turning around and saying, "Anyone but you, right? Why am I never good enough?"

There is nothing that can be done in this moment. No way to rectify it. It's the nature of relating. I stand forlornly for a few more minutes, hurting for Earnell and myself. I reach down and draw a heart in the snow with an X through it, a warning for others on the cliff of romantic uncertainty. I mill aimlessly, trying to stay out of view of Keli and Gabby, not wanting them to see my fall from grace. I walk, then sit on snow-covered stairs, before beholding the illuminated night sky. Comfort doesn't come. The Dartmouth Aires finish their last song, "Ain't No Sunshine," by Bill Withers, a melancholy number about burning and loss.

CHAPTER TWENTY-THREE

The next four weeks of the semester advance at warp speed. I feel like I traveled astrally from the Winter Carnival to midterms. When the dreaded exams finally arrive, I greet them like a houseguest I don't like but tolerate. *Oh, welcome back. So nice to see you again. Look at that, you brought a fruitcake this time. How lovely.* Not. When I unwrap the other hostess gifts a week later in the form of graded exams, I'm thrilled to see that I've gotten three A's, one B+, and a B-. Luke Skywalker continues to slay with her pencil lightsabers.

Now with two months left in the semester, the pressure to complete everything intensifies.

I feel like a headless chicken running madly in all directions. Before the end of the year, I will have to take final exams, write and memorize my monologue for the final theater performance, attend the end-of-year freshman retreat, and finalize my financial aid paperwork for next year. My never-ending checklist grows daily. As soon as I cross one thing off, something else gets added. It's daunting, but I'm managing.

The people around me also worship the ritual of busyness. I haven't seen Gabby or Keli in over a week, and Earnell is avoiding me. Whenever I see him, he turns and quickly walks the other way. He also wears ridiculous disguises. Ironic. He was right, I still know it's him no matter what he's wearing. I wonder how long he will keep it up.

Tray Tray has canceled two of our recent tutoring sessions. Econ threatens to knock me off the high academic horse I've been riding if I don't reconnect with her soon. I'm definitely not going to let that happen.

Yoda continues teaching me the ways of the other realm. She says bliss is common when making contact with such a deep, profound part of ourselves. "Don't be disappointed when the state fades. Only a master can maintain that energy for the duration of their corporeal lives.

"No, you are not a master."

"Hey! Stop reading my thoughts," I say playfully. I don't actually mind when she peeks into my head since I trust her completely.

"One day," she says. "Just answer one call at a time."

———— • ◆ • ————

"Are you not entertained?!" I shout amusedly at my empty bed, imitating Russell Crowe in *Gladiator*. "Have I not given you my all?"

Except nothing about my rehearsal is outstanding. Mediocre at best. I'm practicing for our final theater performance at the end of the year. Our task is to act out various scenes from scripts with depth and emotion, attempting to project that sensitivity onto an audience. We have finally started rehearsing actual theater seven weeks before the semester ends. I am alone in my room, standing in front of the mirror watching my painful attempts at acting. I beg my higher self to make a reappearance and teach me how to give to others what she gave to me, but she's nowhere to be found. I'm still connected to my heart, but I feel like a robot every time I try to act. There is too much pressure to summon feelings, which are supposed to be private and only shared with people you trust.

Professor Nielson makes it look easy. She performs moving renditions of scenes from plays. I want to cry every time I watch her. "Vulnerability," she says, "is the doorway to transformation. We as artists seek to provide the audience with a transformational experience, which can only come from an open heart."

I look up the meaning of vulnerability. "The quality or state of being exposed to the possibility of being attacked or harmed, either physically or emotionally." If that's what it means, I've rarely been vulnerable in my life. I've seen glimpses of who I can be without all my defenses, but I don't live in that reality yet. Professor Nielson is asking me to perform without my guards. I don't know if I can. I've been behind a shield for so long, it's still difficult for me to take down my protections. "Give your heart," she says, "and you will find your power onstage."

Professor Nielson suggests we read poetry, listen to music, or watch movies that move us in order to facilitate the opening of our hearts for our final monologues. I decide to watch movies. I rent *Cold Mountain* and *Titanic* from the library, two movies that always make me cry my eyes out. I watch the movies when I know Manda Panda won't be home. I don't want her to see me crying.

Titanic offers its timeless, tragic love story to me once again. I shriek, I sob, I hug my pillow for comfort. I wait for the final scene. The one that always knocks down all my walls. It's an imaginary scene after Leo dies. There is an audience of people all standing around the grand staircase. Kate begins to ascend toward Leo, who is waiting at the top. When she finally reaches him they kiss, cementing their love, allowed to blossom if only in a dream. The audience, gracious and supportive, erupts in enamored applause. It will never happen, of course, since Leo freezes to death, but the scene represents what could have been without turmoil and suffering.

I am lying in bed sobbing when Manda Panda comes bouncing through the door. I try to suck in my wails, but she sees me and comes running to my bed. "Oh my God, are you OK?! What happened? Who did this to you?! I will go after them and I will destroy them. Just say the name."

I sit up, heaving in despair. I can't stop crying. "It's just so beautiful," I say through tears. "Their love"—pointing at the movie credits—"so pure and innocent. Why can't I have something like that?"

"Wait. You were watching *Titanic*? Why would you do that to yourself on such a nice day?"

"I had to do it for theater class."

"I just came back to grab my tennis racket, but do you want me to sit with you for a bit? I have some time."

I shake my head no, blowing my nose.

"It's OK. I have to practice this scene now anyways."

"That nutty professor has you acting out scenes from *Titanic*?"

"No, another play. We had to watch sappy movies to open our hearts."

"Did Tina teach you nothing? Keep that sucker closed. If you're all right, I'll catch ya later."

I return *Cold Mountain* to its case. I was going to watch both today, but I'm already eviscerated. My guard is down. I am without my protections. My heart, like the Defiance on its white horses, comes galloping back to me, covering me in a blanket of transcendent energy.

I grab the script and stand in front of the mirror. All the vulnerability I could not summon earlier comes flooding out. I feel my higher self nearby, again gently encouraging me forward. The gladiator rests and the characters come alive with emotion. We are united, the characters and me, meeting at the intersection of the words and my living interpretation. Professor Nielson was right. This is the only way theater can be done. The actor has to leave it all onstage and offer the luminosity of their insides, then pray the audience appreciates the magnificence of what has been given so Russell Crowe never has to ask the question again.

Econ is my least favorite subject this semester, but it's also the class I look forward to most, thanks to Alex Rodriquez from South Central Los Angeles. I've never seen such a beautiful man in person. Even more stunning than Bryce. He is both soft and hard somehow, like he would cry with you during movies but also build a house with his bare hands. It's a combination I rarely see in men that I find really attractive.

Now that winter has released its death-hold on the campus, and spring has announced her arrival with sunshine, chirping birds, and cherry blossoms, I feel especially open to new romantic possibilities. It's late March, so my window for finding a boyfriend is winding down. I've got to be more focused and deliberate. I set my sights clearly on Alex, a bronzed Latino god from the City of Angels.

The first time I saw him, I sat with my mouth open for several seconds until I noticed someone watching and judging me. I pretend to take notes while continuing to glance at him out of the corner of my eyes. *How is such beauty possible? Is the Joker trying to trap me again through this mesmerizing mirage?* I feel like Blanche from *The Golden Girls*, who was always lusting after some guy. I spray myself with imaginary mist and wipe the phantom sweat from my forehead every time he passes.

I don't know what comes over me when I see him sitting alone on a bench three days after my *Titanic* meltdown. I don't really believe I have a chance with him, yet all of my recent inner work has intensified my longing for a connection. I act without thinking. I prance over to him. I have discovered that love makes me prance. I prepare to seduce him with my charms when I feel someone forcefully pull me away. I spin around in shock, dropping my notebook and a six-dollar smoothie I just bought from the cafeteria.

"Yoda! Sorry, Dean Harrison! What are you doing behind me like a creepy crawler? Are you following me?"

"I saw you and was coming to say hi. I see you are spying on that handsome fellow over there. Before you give him your all, make sure he's the right one, OK? Nothing disrupts the call like the wrong man."

"This is not helpful at all, you know."

"I know." She smiles cunningly. "All right, I'll leave you to your spy work."

Her cautioning does not dissuade me. I am determined. I take a deep breath and prance back over to him. I stand behind his bench for several seconds like a serial killer.

"Hey, Alex," I say awkwardly.

He turns, shocked, looking up at me. "How long have you been standing there?"

"I just got here. Saw you sitting and thought I would come over."

I walk around the bench and sit.

"Lovely day today, huh?"

"Beautiful. Almost feels like Cali."

We both stare ahead in silence.

"So interesting how world systems work, isn't it?"

"What do you mean?"

"Oh, I was talking about Econ since we're both in that class. The professor was discussing societal systems the other day."

"Oh." He laughs uneasily. "Yea."

Silence.

"Well, I was thinking, if you aren't busy, maybe we can talk about Econ sometime. Together. At a café."

"Are you asking me out? Oh, that's so nice. You're such a sweetheart. But honey, I'm gay. I'm really flattered, though!"

Rejection and disappointment, my old friends, squeeze in between us. I'm too shocked to speak.

"I'm sorry. I know how hard it is up here to find someone. I've been in a drought all year. You know what, how about we still go out? We'll make it a pretend date. Get dressed up, go to a nice dinner, and take a stroll. No harm in that."

I light up at the invitation. It won't lead me to where I want to go, but I accept anyways. Even a mock date is better than nothing.

"OK," I respond. "When are you free?"

"How about Friday? Tomorrow? I was thinking of going out by myself anyways. Now I'll have good company. We can go to Molly's and eat all their bread."

"I love that place! I can eat two baskets by myself and still have room for dinner."

"I thought I was the only one," he says, laughing. "It's a date, then."

When tomorrow comes, I'm surprised I'm still nervous even though there's nothing at stake. We don't have to figure out if we like each other or if we want the same things. We can just enjoy each other's company. Yet part of me feels like it's the real thing. I search through my closet for what to wear. I've never been on a date before, so I don't know what's appropriate.

Manda Panda, who is approving or disapproving all my options, says, "Wait. I have the perfect outfit for this."

She quickly scans through her own closet and hands me a sleek cream-colored top made of silk.

"It looks so expensive," I say. "What if I spill something on it?"

"Don't worry about that."

She opens her jewelry box and pulls out a pair of diamond earrings.

"Whoa, are those real?! Are you sure it's OK?"

"Of course! You're gonna look so pretty. I can't believe you're going on a date with a gay man, but it'll probably be even better, honestly," she says sarcastically.

I change into the outfit and put on the diamond earrings. I make sure the earring backs are pushed all the way forward. I would never want to lose something so precious and expensive. Manda Panda claps when she sees the finished product.

"You look so gorge," she says. "Gotta take a pic." She snaps a Polaroid and hangs it on her wall. "Be home by ten," she says jokingly.

"Sure, Mom," I respond. "I won't be late."

Conversation with Alex is so easy and effortless. We talk about everything. Liberal politics, what it's like being a student of color on campus, our upbringings. Alex is from a middle-class family in Los Angeles. His family owns a restaurant, where he'll work over the summer. He tells me he's come across all the stereotypes here: people assuming he's in a gang, doesn't speak good English, or is a farmworker, "but I didn't know I would be romantically isolated also."

"I mean I knew dating here would be hard, but I didn't know it would be this bad. I feel like an angsty teenager who's never gonna get laid."

"Well, I'm a virgin."

"Aww, that is precious. You're a real doll. Are you saving yourself for marriage?"

"No. I just can't find someone who's not gay that likes me back. . . . Well, one of my good friends likes me, but I'm not feeling him. I wish I did, but it's just not there for me."

"The way of the world, dear."

I feel like I've known Alex forever. There is no awkward phase of trying to figure each other out, we just click. We eat four baskets of bread between us. I finish mine first, then try to steal some of his, but he playfully smacks my hand. Molly's has white paper table coverings with a cup of crayons in the middle. We draw pictures and play hangman. When Alex tells me Will Smith gave a talk at his high school, we sing the theme song to *Fresh Prince of Bel-Air.* We both know all the words.

I don't want the night to end. I knew it could be like this. That connecting intimately with someone is the best feeling in the world, even if I know it's not intimate for him.

In true date fashion, he pays the bill. I follow him out to grab tea at the Hopkins café across the street.

"I never liked tea before I came here," I say, ordering a chamomile-and-lavender infusion. "Now I can't get enough. You know, some say tea can open a portal to another dimension."

"Oh yea, who?"

"Some."

"OK, weirdo," he says, laughing. "Aww, look, honey," he says, changing the subject, "this is the table where we first met. Remember you had the ganache and I had the cheesecake," he continues, pretending like we're a real couple.

"I'll never forget that night, dumpling."

"Gag. Why do people call each other food? Like are you going to kiss me or eat me?"

"I like it," I say, sipping my tea. "It's endearing."

"I can't believe you never had a boyfriend. How is that possible? I really can't deal with straight men."

"I'm untouchable, that's why. Well, at least that's how I've seen myself until recently."

The untouchables. Those of us that have found ourselves on the opposite end of accepted standards of beauty. We who are too dark, disabled, odd looking, ugly, or short to be desired, especially in a place like this. I didn't know that I would be trapped in this category for so much of my life and that each rejection would burn holes in me. The only thing that has ever drawn people to me is intelligence, but men don't care how smart you are. They want something beautiful that fits nicely on their arm and who their family will accept. They want someone who answers the question "What would people think?" with statements like: "She's perfect for you. She'll fit right in." What they don't want is a Black, too dark Chosen One from the west side of Cleveland. Men don't chase after heroes, they run from them.

"Bryce doesn't deserve you," Alex says.

I smile, embarrassed, finishing the last of my tea. People always say stuff like that when they don't have an answer to your problem.

"But Earnell sounds like a real catch."

"I know. I just wish I were attracted to him."

"Oh, the game of love. Who will win? Who will lose?"

"Stay tuned next week to find out on another episode of the Young, Restless, and Minority at Dartmouth College."

We giggle softly. There are no more words as we both ponder our positions. People walk by. The clanging of pots, pans, and dishes rings out from the kitchen as the café prepares to close. I could have sat there all night, but the next words Alex speaks are of endings.

"You know how we should end our date?" he asks.

"By walking home?" I say sarcastically.

"No," he says. "With a kiss. Like a real date."

"But you're gay."

"So. That doesn't mean we can't kiss."

The moment is right. Yearning takes hold of both of us. I walk around the table and sit on his lap, wrapping my hands around his neck. He kisses me like I am his boyfriend. Passionately. Intensely. It's better than I imagined. It transports me to another place outside of myself. I am here, sitting with him, but I am gone somehow. Elevated again. Astral without leaving the realm.

"Thank you," I say, bashfully staring down at our legs, grateful for the experience even if it can't go on.

"The night is still young," he responds before pulling me up for a starlight stroll.

CHAPTER TWENTY-FOUR

Swimming is the perfect distraction from thinking about Alex. Now that I'm focused on not drowning, I don't have time to obsess about making out with him. Initially, I try everything to forget him. I study constantly to prepare for finals in three weeks. I stay in my room as much as possible to avoid seeing him. I watch more movies than my brain can handle. Action and thrillers like *The Mummy Returns*, *Men in Black*, and *Pearl Harbor* keep me company for days. Until it gets old. All of my antics lose their ability to distract me eventually. Then I'm right back where I started, craving someone I can never have.

After the date, Alex confirms that it was magical, but can't happen again. He's happy to be friends, but he doesn't want me to get romantically attached since he knows I'm attracted to him. He's right. His honesty is a blessing, but I'm already attached. How could I not be? My experience of dating has been distorted. I have known men primarily through the lens of pain, abuse, and rejection.

When a chance is finally given to see the other side, my brain explodes in desire like someone who hasn't eaten in a month devouring the worst food possible. It doesn't matter, at least it's food.

I reflect on my hunger while staring at the amazingly chiseled swim instructor, six-ab Brett. This is my third lesson this week. There are six of us in the class. Everyone else seems to get it, but I keep sinking like a rock. I hate being submerged in water. It's unnatural and dangerous, but Dartmouth is one of three Ivy League schools that still require a stupid swim test to graduate. Something else they never put in those glossy brochures. You have to take it before you graduate, but I decided to start lessons early since I know it's going to be an eternity before I get comfortable in a pool. I only started this week, but I've nearly drowned twice. The lifeguard saved me the first time and another student the second. I freak out when I can't touch the bottom of the pool with my feet and start to pull myself under.

I have always been afraid of drowning. There were no swimming pools in our neighborhood in Cleveland. Moreover, water only brings trouble. In movies, if it's not a comedy or romance, when there is a body of water it's because someone is about to drown or get eaten by a shark. Swimming also has a different significance to many Black folks. I can't forget the pictures of angry white racists pouring acid into pools attempting to integrate. Or dripping wet Black bodies being beaten by segregationists as they emerged from the water. Those images are burned into my psyche, subconsciously convincing me that swimming is not safe for people who look like me.

Brett keeps giving me all these tips, but he doesn't understand the depth of my fear. He's focused on the mechanics of swimming, but I need to overcome the psychological hindrance somehow. "If you don't resist, you'll naturally float. Lie on the water. Don't move your arms or legs. Just relax your body."

"But every time I do that, I feel like I'm being sucked under."

"That's because you're pulling yourself down with panicked movements. Look, let me show you."

He gets in the pool next to me, puts out his arms, and I lie back. While he's supporting the weight of my body, I feel safe. As soon as he lets go, the fear takes over and I thrash wildly.

"Oh my God!" he yells. "Just don't move! Look, watch me."

He lies back and floats effortlessly. The water glazes his finely sculpted torso.

"I can't do it," I say, defeated. "I tried my hardest, but I'm too afraid."

Brett softens. He runs his hand through his wet hair, pushing it back. I stare at his abs.

"Look," he says, "I think it's best if you start off with one-on-one lessons and then rejoin a class. You need focused attention to advance. You'll get the hang of it with enough practice. Don't give up."

Someone weirdly starts clapping. When no one else joins, six-ab Brett shouts, "Yea, let's encourage her." The class claps off beat. I smile awkwardly and climb out of the pool. I walk defeated toward the locker room, despite the lukewarm applause. "Hey," Brett calls from behind me. "You just have to surrender. Don't fight it. Whether the water sinks or saves you depends on that."

"Surrender, like Yoda says. I'll try that next time."

The first-year weekend retreat is the last big event of the year. I'm stoked for more manufactured vulnerability and connecting. I see how these kinds of functions can be addicting. Gabby and Keli are not going, opting instead to focus on the upcoming final exams. I feel confident in my classes, otherwise I would also skip the retreat. I don't know if Earnell is going since he's still not talking to me, or even Gabby and Keli now.

"I walked right up to him," Keli says, "stood in his face, and said, 'Talk to me, Earnell Jackson. This is ridiculous.' He grabbed his tray and went right around me as if I wasn't even there. You broke that boy's heart. More than that, his spirit."

I can't be blamed for Earnell's despair. I know from my own experience: The wound of not feeling good enough was already there. Others can only prick what already lurks inside. Maybe that's why self-love is so important? Then no matter what happens to you, there is an inexhaustible well of contentment inside, like how I felt after meeting my higher self. *The fountain of life is within you.* I remember Professor Nielson's wise message while packing the last of my items into a duffel bag.

Manda Panda says she wouldn't be caught dead doing an activity that is an "obvious attempt to force us to bond." She also didn't go on the hiking trip. I don't know if Alex is going. I hope he isn't.

When I arrive at the meeting spot, I expect to see hundreds of people, but there are only two buses for all of us, which means about sixty (out of one thousand) students are attending. Having it right before finals, which are a week and a half away, is not appealing for most. If they had it after exams, they'd still lose since students start leaving campus right after they finish. I guess there's no optimal time for end-of-year bonding.

I suddenly feel nervous. This is the first time I'm going on a class-wide event without knowing anyone. Freddy is not here to ward off potential murderous racists. Keli, Gabby, and Earnell are not here to keep me laughing. I look around the bus at all the unfamiliar white faces. *I hope they accept me*, I think to myself. I remember my earlier thoughts on self-love and change my mind. *It doesn't matter what they think of me. I accept me. Well, parts of me. Most of me. Close enough, I guess. Progress, not perfection.* The Defiance applauds my growth. *Bitch, you betta werk. Stunt on your haters.*

The road unfolds before us, just like on the hiking trip. Nature and her raw vulnerability come to greet me once more. Out here there are no masks, hiding, or pretending. Just the truth of what a thing is in its natural form. The windows are down since late April has continued to bless us with balmy spring weather. Sunshine and fresh air for miles. I inhale deeply, turning to my neighbor. "Smells good, doesn't it?" He smiles—a wry, *Grapes of Wrath* looking fellow—and says, "It sure does. Nature's intoxicating scent." I understand exactly what he means and realize I've been in New Hampshire for too long. I could never say things like this a year earlier in Cleveland.

The retreat center is an hour away from campus, deep in the woods. I've been through this once and am not afraid to be so far into nature, even without Freddy. I make my way to my assigned room, where four bunk beds await. No one else has arrived yet, so I test each bed to see which one I like the most. I decide on the bottom bunk farthest from the bathroom. I lie on the bed waiting for my bunkmates to arrive. *It doesn't matter whether they accept me or not,* I remind myself.

The first person to walk in is a Black girl from Georgia named Myesha. Even though I've met most Black students on campus—there aren't that many of us—there are still some I don't know. I can tell right away Myesha is sweet and shy but happy to see another Black face. Daniel McCullum walks in next.

"You have got to be kidding me," he says. "Have they really put all the negroes together again?" He begins to unpack while shaking his head in disapproval.

"Sorry about that," he continues. "Where's my manners? How y'all doin'? Echo, what's up, girl? How you been?"

Before I have a chance to respond, Earnell walks in, sees me, turns around, and says, "Oh no. They gon' have to change my room. No. Definitely not."

I run after him.

"Earnell! Earnell, come on. You can't avoid me forever. I'm sorry."

He ignores me and races to one of the chaperones to request a change. The chaperone spins around, dropping his clipboard. As soon as he exclaims "Goddamnit," I know who it is.

"Connor! Come on, this is ridiculous, don't let him bully you into moving him for no reason."

Earnell and I both talk at the same time.

"I demand to be relocated immediately. I have a right to free speech and the power of choice, I learned that at the *Dartmouth Beacon* meeting. I cannot be bunkmates with this woman."

Connor stands in stunned silence watching us argue back and forth.

"But aren't you guys best friends?"

"Yea, well, things change," Earnell remarks snidely.

"Look, I have a ton to do. I don't have time for this. We had someone drop out in room 323. You can move there."

"Thank you," Earnell barks before storming off.

"What's gotten into him?" asks Connor.

"You don't want to know."

"How've you been, buddy? I haven't seen you since last semester when you were standing on those stairs like a warrior princess. I wish I had taken a picture."

Just as I'm about to answer, out of the corner of my eye, I catch something that my mind refuses to accept. *Couldn't be,* I think to myself. *There's no way he's a chaperone here also.* I'm afraid to look. I stand in the lobby as students file in and head to their rooms. *It can't be. I'm just being paranoid.* I relax and turn to look toward the door. *It is.*

"Oh my God. I have to run, Connor. Nice to see you! Bye!"

I race back to my room and sit on the bed. *Is this purgatory? Have I died and gone to hell? Earnell AND Bryce are here. Darth is definitely riding again. Why didn't the portal warn me about this oncoming malarkey!* I'm sweating, breathing hard, clutching my imaginary pearls, saying aloud repeatedly, "Oh my God."

"Are you OK, girl?" Myesha asks.

"What if your worst nightmare walked through the door and you can't leave for two days! I'm going to die. Are there drugs anywhere? Do either of you have any drugs?!"

"This is not that kind of trip," Daniel responds. "I mean that could be nice, but imagine the lawsuits. Dartmouth would be bankrupt in a year."

The name of this retreat is Building Community: Enriching the First-Year Experience. The workshop leader, Kurt Rushbrook, is a renowned connection coach who travels the world leading these kinds of events. He's a tall, gray-haired white man, with big hands and boots. He looks more like a park ranger than a guru. I can tell by the look in his eyes he's going to make us do all sorts of things we are resistant to. I prepare myself for more discomfort.

After we've all checked in, we gather in the main hall, which is big enough to hold two hundred people. Mats, cushions, and blankets have been set up around the room. I wait for everyone to wander in before peeking to see if Bryce is here. I don't see him (or Earnell) and choose a cushion in the back of the room. I'm relieved at how easy it is to avoid them in a group of sixty.

Kurt Rushbrook is giving an opening talk tonight, then we'll have dinner, but most of our activities will happen tomorrow. I scan the room in paranoia. Still no sign of Bryce, who is probably here as a chaperone. I sit with my arms wrapped around my legs, rocking back and forth, scanning. I must look ridiculous, but I don't care. I can't risk accidentally sitting next to him. Someone suddenly bumps my shoulder. I shriek in shock. Kurt stops his talk to ask if everything is all right in the back of the room, prompting everyone to turn around and look at me. "There's more space up here," he says.

"It's fine. Nothing wrong back here. Carry on," I say in almost a whisper, putting my hands up to shield my blushing face. *The Joker is definitely playing tricks again*, I think to myself.

"This weekend will reveal the power of human

281

connection in ways many of you haven't experienced," Kurt says. "We are taught as children to run from each other. Keep out the bad strangers. So we build walls, but those barriers also trap us. Over the next two days, we'll see what's behind those walls. You will be shocked at the beauty of each other's humanity."

I know all about barriers and walls, but I will never be able to unmask myself here. If anything, I reinforce my protections, preparing to stay hidden as long as possible. After Kurt finishes his talk, I race back to my room, the safe zone free from both Earnell and Bryce. I sit on the bed pondering my situation. What good is it being a Chosen One if supernatural forces can't prevent this drama? I shake my head.

Everyone is in the dining hall. I'm starving but consider skipping dinner altogether. I've never been able to deny my hunger, so this won't be easy. My stomach growls. I try to give myself a pep talk. The Defiance fills my head with courage. *He's just a regular person, you feel me? Bitch, don't give him your power. Forget that undeserving lost sheep, hah, you are the prize.*

"Yea, that's right!" I say, rising from my bed. "I'm the prize!" I leap toward the cafeteria with newfound determination.

I peek in, still no sign. I breathe a sigh of relief. Then, like a Shakespearean tragedy, he appears right in front of me, holding a clipboard. He's checking people in and sending them to their assigned tables. "Echo!" he yells in glee. "It's so great to see you! I didn't know if you were gonna come or not. Really killer you're here. I hope to see you tomorrow during some of the activities."

There is no hint that he has been carrying the same burden as me. He has moved on with his life, the situation between us an afterthought. I alone am carrying it. Is this how Earnell feels? I smile uneasily. "Yea, see you around," I say before awkwardly walking to my table, which is full of unfamiliar faces, luckily. We smile, we eat, we give a summary of our background. All while feasting on baked chicken breast, mashed potatoes, and string beans. It's so delicious, I forget the higher-class codes of conduct and lick my fingers. I look down at my protruding belly, proud of the haul.

I scram back to my room while everyone makes polite conversation over dessert. Tonight, they are serving apple pie and vanilla ice cream. I don't love most sweets, so I don't feel like I'm missing out.

When I return to the comfort of my room, I exhale, finally. Shakespeare was right. The gods or the Keepers or whoever's in charge love playing with us. "All the world's a stage." I'm the fool trapped in the spotlight right now. I turn off the lights and pull the covers up to my neck. For the first time in my life, the darkness is my friend, shielding me from the reality of my current situation. I try to force myself to sleep and find refuge in the limitless dreamworld. Any dream will be better than this. Even a nightmare, since I know it'll be over by morning. When do you wake up from life, though?

———— •◆• ————

The retreat has turned into a game of hide with no seek. Any time I catch a glimpse of Bryce or Earnell, I duck behind the nearest object.

"What on earth are you doing?" Connor says, catching me standing behind a large, broad-leaved plant. "You've been jittery since yesterday. Is everything OK? Do you think you might have a problem with alcohol? I mean after that night at Professor Alexander-Grant's, I wondered if that might have been a red flag or something."

"What? No. That was just a mistake. I was going through something. Now leave me alone, Connor. I'm trying to be one with this plant. I'll clap. I'll do it. Don't force my hands."

"Whoa, whoa. No need to be cruel. I just wanted to ask one more thing, then I promise I won't bother you for the rest of the weekend. I was wondering if you might be interested in leading one of the first-year hiking trips next year. I think you'd be great. You're so thoughtful and would really look after people."

"Me taking an entire group of students into the woods alone? I'll pass," I say while peeking anxiously through the leaves of the plant.

"Just think about it, OK? You might be surprised at how much you have to give."

———◆———

The rest of the day is full of icebreaker activities designed for us to get to know each other. I feel closer to everyone I've met, even though we've only exchanged superficial information about ourselves so far. The mood shifts when we get to the final activity of the evening.

"Now we've come to the main event," Kurt says. "Eye gazing."

"What the fuck?" I say out loud before covering my mouth with both my hands.

"This is a powerful activity," he continues. "We so rarely stop and take the time to see each other's humanity. Really witness. If we did, we wouldn't create this kind of world of competition, strife, and turmoil. It's because we don't see that we abuse and harm one another. That ends tonight. In a moment, I'm going to ask you to close your eyes. Some of the chaperones will make their way around the room and mix you up a bit. The goal is to sit with a stranger, but if you end up in front of someone you do know, that's OK. Maybe you have unfinished business. The more open you are, the more impactful this exercise will be. All weekend we've been slowly unmasking to get to this point."

The fear in the room is palpable. None of us wants to look at each other. We are afraid not of witnessing but of being seen. Fearful the other might see the parts of ourselves we don't like. Seeing myself for the first time in theater class was hard enough—this is excruciating.

I prepare for a battle. *Put up all the shields! Man the oars! Prepare for incoming!* I tell my defenses, but something in me shifts. *Am I going to hide my entire life?* The thought pounces on me like a hyena on prey. I am not the same as I was before I got here. I stood on the brink of defeat and returned. I have traveled to the other realm and healed my family lineage. I have met the highest version of myself and still carry her wisdom within. I am magic, supernatural, and unstoppable. Maybe I deserve to be seen. Maybe you can't let people love you if they never really see you. The real you. Until then, they just love what you are projecting. The realization floors me. Have I ever *not* projected a false self in the presence of others? Have I gone unseen my entire life?

A sadness washes over me. I didn't intend for things to be like this. I don't want to spend my life hiding. I submit to the vulnerability of the task. No more resistance. I am what I am and that will always be true, no matter how many masks I wear. I take a deep breath and close my eyes. "Do your worst," I say to the gods.

The chaperones begin mixing us. Moving some here and others there. Unless you are peeking, no one knows who will land in front of them. I am in total acceptance of every outcome. Is this what Dean Harrison experiences all the time? I know this peace will not last so I try to revel in it, roll around in the gardens of inner contentment.

Then the shuffle is done and the moment of truth arrives. Who will I see when I open my eyes? I'm unsure, but I know what they will find. The real me. The curtain drops. The barking guard dogs yield. I am revealed. I open my eyes, and of course, the gods have given the absolute worst possibility, Bryce.

"So there you are," I say.

"Here I am."

Attraction compels us like magnets. I try to turn it off, but just like I couldn't turn it on for Earnell, I can't shut it down in this moment. It aches. He is so beautiful. His curly blond hair pulled up into a bun again. The softness of his spirit shining so bright. I can't stop smiling.

Our task is to sit in silence for five minutes doing nothing but looking into this person's eyes. "Much more can be seen without the words," Kurt says.

At first, they are just eyes. Light green and soft. He smiles. He knows I am seeing. Then, a force takes over us both. An opening. A doorway into the being of another living creature. An exquisite feast of emotion. Maybe all of them. Sorrow, joy, and so much vulnerability. The inside of him exposed. Pleading with me to come and save him. At the core, the desire for love. He wants it too.

Tears roll down both our cheeks. When the moment is too much, we look away, but return again to soak in more of the living presence in front of us. Then it's over, but I don't want to leave. I don't want another partner. I want him. Like the sun in the east, she rises, my hope. Any signs of new life set it on fire. I am burning.

He leans over and gives me a hug, holding on even after it's time to let go. Something about it feels final, despite the beauty of our previous moment. "I'm sorry," he says. "That I can't be brave." Then he is gone, on to his next partner. Me: left sitting in a pile of my own ashes, again.

When I open my eyes for round two, I am not surprised to see Earnell. The gods really want chaos. I expect him to dart again, but he remains, also a pile of ashes in my presence, having been softened by his previous partner.

"I've missed you," he says.

"I missed you too. I'm sorry. I don't know why it's like this."

We begin the exercise. I've known Earnell since the beginning of the school year, but I've never seen him like this. In raw form. Behind all the humor and antics, a tender soul. The jokes just a mask to keep it protected.

His eyes drop. He knows he's been seen. When they return, tearful at the gift of being witnessed, finally. A weight lifted. He can stop hiding, at least for a little while.

There are no words, but some part of him asks for something I don't know I can give yet, until it happens. The light comes on in my own heart center. It moves up to the middle of my forehead and spins. A presence—not my own—inside with words to deliver to Earnell.

"It's not your fault, lil bro," it says through me. "Let it go. We'll always have Tybee."

The light moves on. Earnell looks just as perplexed as me.

"How do you know about Tybee?" he asks confusedly.

"I don't know."

He swims deep down to the bottom of his thoughts.

"That was the last time we had together before it happened. We stayed out there talking all day. About life, the future. It took us almost four hours to get to Tybee Beach from Atlanta, but we didn't care. We just wanted to sit in front of the ocean. We buried it, our time capsule, just as the sun was setting. I put in a letter to my future self and my favorite Power Ranger action figure, the red one. I don't know what he wrote in his letter, but he put in the black Power Ranger. We used to play fight with them when we were kids. We buried our treasures and said we would dig it up in twenty-five years. Sixteen more before I can go back, without him."

Earnell breaks. He sobs. Kurt likes the wailing.

"You'll notice that as we go on, this exercise becomes deeper. That's OK. Allow it. Tears are an indication of healing, contrary to what you've been taught."

Others are crying also, all around the room. It's an unbelievable sight that would never happen in the "real world." Is this the answer to world peace? Have political leaders sit and look at each other in silence until the truth is revealed? All is unmasked here.

"I'm sorry about your brother, Earnell. From the bottom of my heart. I can go with you if you want, in sixteen years, to dig it up."

Earnell is moved by the offer. He leans in, hugs me, lays his head on my shoulder, and lets go. The first time in a long time he has had any rest.

We smile at each other. I extend my hand, the olive branch.

"Friends?" I say.

He reaches back and says, "Welcome home, Negro Brown."

CHAPTER TWENTY-FIVE

After the retreat, there's nothing left in the semester but final exams and bonfires. Unlike the first semester, the end of this term feels different. Seniors will be graduating, moving on to lives in the real world. Some staff and professors will not be returning. The temporary bubble of safety we all created together bursts before our eyes. Just when we thought it could go on like this forever, we are all tasked with letting go whether we're ready or not.

I attend three bonfires by the river with various groups of friends. It's tradition to end the year getting drunk and singing by the river. The last one happens on the eve before my final performance. Keli, Gabby, Earnell, Alex, Manda Panda, a few of her friends, and I stare into the flames like psychics into a crystal ball, waiting for our fortune to be revealed. What does the lady of fate have in store for us next?

There are no streetlights. It's pitch black except for the fire and the moon, which sits in the middle of the sky like a luminescent orb. The light dances across the gentle waves of the water. The evening has been filled with reflection, memories, and laughter. Earnell laughs the loudest, of course.

We sit in a circle contemplating the time behind us and the journey ahead. Whatever comes, we know it can be survived now. That every reckoning is an invitation for renewal. Every fall an opportunity to rise. Thankfully the Joker's reign doesn't last forever.

Someone poses a question: What would you say to your first-week-of-Dartmouth self? Wisdom drizzles down into the fire:

Trust your instincts.

Ask for help.

Relax.

This journey will change you.

When it happens, it won't be your fault.

Self-love is your only salvation.

Let go.

We marinate in silence on the lessons learned and the obstacles defeated. Jimmy, one of Manda Panda's friends, picks up his guitar and starts playing "What a Wonderful World," by Louis Armstrong. We hum along gently at first, still reflecting. Eventually, we all sing loudly to each other. "And I think to myself, what a wonderful world!" we shout into the jet-black sky. Manda Panda and her friends begin dancing wildly and singing while me and the rest of the negroes hold waists and sway. This is not a dancing song.

"Fuck yea!" someone shouts. "We did it!"

"Be careful," Earnell whispers in my ear. "When drunk white people start cursing and dancing, mayhem may follow. Don't worry, Freddy is near."

When the song reaches the final crescendo, we all chant, "WHAT A WONDERFUL WORLD!"

A volcanic eruption of applause and cheers. Excitement that ripples out in all directions. A surge of adrenaline and then the white people get naked, jumping into the river. Earnell, Keli, Gabby, and I watch in shock and disdain from a safe distance.

"I told you mayhem would follow," Earnell says, shaking his head.

Three of the naked swimmers emerge from the water. "Aww, come on! You guys have to get in!" They pull two of Manda Panda's sitting friends in and shout, "Woo-hoo!" at the top of their lungs. When one of them starts to approach the rest of us, Earnell, Gabby, and Keli immediately shuffle away from the dripping wet assailant.

"Come on, Echo!" Keli calls out from behind me. "It's time to go."

I'm not ready to leave this beautiful night by the fire. I assume politely saying "No, please don't," will be enough to curtail his actions. I am wrong. He is pumped, drunk with energy and booze. He grabs me, lifts me over his shoulder, and starts running toward the river. I beat his back in fear. "No! I can't swim!" I shout. "Put me down! Stop it! No!" Earnell, Gabby, and Keli run after us, but they will never be able to catch a drunken white boy pumped on life. He escapes their efforts and launches me up into the air. For a moment, I am weightless, floating and glowing under the moonlight. A Black phoenix at last. I imagine this is what it must be like to be a bird, forever soaring. I do not have the anatomical structure to stay up in the air so I come plunging back down into the water.

It's not the river's fault I still don't really know how to swim, definitely not in water like this. She didn't pull me in. He did. She opens her jaws and swallows me whole, against her will, into a cold, ominous underbelly. I am submerged totally in a dark, uncontained space. My body panics. I flail. My head bobs above water for a brief second before I'm sucked back down.

I try to surrender like six-ab Brett recommended. I stop moving, but I sink deeper. Yielding has never delivered favorable results. Only the struggle has saved my life over and over. I defy his advice and flail more. What does he know about fighting to survive? Nothing. I force my will upon the river, but she is much stronger than me, effortlessly pulling me farther below the surface. Willpower, for the first time in my life, is not enough. Resistance is futile, just like Yoda said. My clothes feel like they weigh a hundred pounds and cling to me like a weighted blanket. I try to take off my sweater, but the sensation of sinking quicker causes me to panic again. It's been too long without oxygen.

I convulse. My lungs search desperately for the air. My throat burns. My mouth opens, trying to breathe. I swallow water. The convulsions intensify, violently shaking my body. I stop moving. Finally, I'm floating, beneath the water. The melee that has been my life halts abruptly. Maybe the warrior can rest now. My mother flashes before my eyes. Not her regular self—an ethereal version, surrounded in light. Her higher self. She looks like an angel. *I love you, Momma*, I say, preparing to accept the end. *I almost made it. Thank you for . . . everything.*

A tingling in my chest spreads out to my whole body. Then, euphoria. A deep peace settles all over. I smile. A Buddha at last. I glance up at the moonlight one last time. Shimmering, and still dancing on the surface above. An enchanting waltz of luminosity. Beautiful. A fitting final sight.

One more convulsion. The last attempt to search for air. Then gone.

A tunnel. *The same tunnel?*

Moving so fast. Much faster than last time.

Gone. A break from the body again.

The speed intensifies even more. It's too much for me to comprehend. Sleep. Rest. A blankness

⬥

with no end. Eternity spins in a circle around me. The clock holds no power here. One moment feels like hours, the next like years. Timeless and thoughtless empty space. Then a string of familiar words. The same ones every cycle: *And what if I can rise?* The call. A momentum of ancestral forces, the Keepers

⬥

galvanizing a stunned Earnell into action, pressing down upon him, his brother's voice the clearest, "Try again! Keep trying!"

"Move!" Earnell says, falling to his knees to begin CPR again. He presses and pumps his hands desperately against my chest.

"She's gone," someone says in the crowd, but Earnell continues. He blows air into my lungs, then cries out in anguish, "No, not like this! Come back," he demands to a God he thinks isn't listening

⬥

to the prayers of the living. They all come here, to the realm of the infinite. I hear them echoing throughout the space. So many voices all at once. *Dear God, please save my mother. I pray to you for guidance and hope. Help me, Father, I need your grace.* Prayers rising against the backdrop of an ethereal hum.

An unimaginable, incomprehensible power reveals itself. I have never felt such love and healing, all around, vibrating in every particle. A blanket of peace envelops me. A tunnel of white light, a brilliant luminosity, so bright and mysterious, moving toward me. I hear their voices before I see them:

Nitori awa li OLUWA Ọlọrun rẹ
Eniti o di ọwọ rẹ mu
O si wi fun ọ pe, Má bẹru
A yoo ran ọ lọwọ

A procession of ancestors walking slowly, dressed in white and each carrying a white rose. An ancient song infused with the first sounds ever to emerge from the ether:

Nitori awa li OLUWA Ọlọrun rẹ
Eniti o di ọwọ rẹ mu
O si wi fun ọ pe, Má bẹru
A yoo ran ọ lọwọ

They each drop their roses near me and form circles around me. They continue their song:

Nitori awa li OLUWA Ọlọrun rẹ
Eniti o di ọwọ rẹ mu
O si wi fun ọ pe, Má bẹru
A yoo ran ọ lọwọ

Their voices grow in power. They sing as if this is the last song that will ever leave their lips, as if their words can reanimate the dead. I start to comprehend what they are singing even though it's in Yoruba. I have never heard that language before, but here in this eternal place there are no limitations or barriers. All my questions are subliminally answered. They are chanting an amended Bible verse: "For I am the LORD your God who takes hold of your right hand and says to you, do not fear; I will help you." Only instead of *I*, they sing *We*. Finally, I have met "God," the ones who called me forth. My omnipotent creator. He's not a man at all, but a collective consciousness.

The procession continues until they form five rings around me with intermittent gaps, like an elaborate crop circle. White roses cover my body. An ocean of energy toils forcefully nearby. Not a body of water, but a vast amount of multicolored energy crashing into itself, turning and rolling, a primordial cosmic soup.

"Allow us to meet again outside of the space-time continuum. We are the Keepers in astral form. We have known you since the beginning. Now we must know: Do you want to return as Echo Brown?" They do not speak clear words, but send direct transmissions through electrical pulses.

I ponder the question. I feel so joyous and serene. Why would I go back to the pain and suffering of the living world? This place feels so much more real than Earth. The truth of all there is permeates my being. I bask in the solace of being home at last.

"I don't want to return," I say finally, also through transmission.

"Are you sure?" they ask. "The call is not completed. You will have to start again."

The call comes rushing back again. *And what if I can rise? And what if I can help?* An intense magnetism draws me toward the world of the living.

I don't want to go, but a much bigger force compels me to return. The life of Echo Brown fills my consciousness. I remember. Cleveland. Dartmouth. My mother. The forgiveness. My father. My sweet brothers, whose prayers for me I heard before the tunnel of light. *Dear God, please watch afta my sister up dere wit all dem white people. Please make sure she stay safe and bring her back to us eventually.* Not just their prayers, but my mother's and father's and friends' and teachers' and strangers I encountered only once in a grocery store, praying for me:

> *Keep her in grace, Lord, that's my baby girl.*
> *There's a little girl in my class this year.*
> *I want her to make it, God. Let me do my*
> *part to ensure that she does.*
> *What a sweet woman, I hope she has*
> *a good life, a fulfilling one.*

And Earnell's, Gabby's, and Keli's prayers from the banks of the river:

No, please, no, God. Please don't take her
from us. Not like this.
Bring her back! Bring her back to us

Earnell begs
while pumping his palms against my chest. He is crying
now, weeping, and shouting, "Echo! Please!" Someone tries
to pull him away, but he overpowers them and starts once
again. Ambulances blare in the distance. The river churns,
lapping at the shore, as if she too is pleading to be forgiven
for actions she didn't intend.

Their testimonies would all be different, but many would
swear that some entity leaped up out of the water. A supernatural force. As soon as it hit my body, I heaved dramatically, coughing up water. "It was a fucking miracle," one
would exclaim. "She was dead," another would report, "for
at least five minutes. How is any of this possible?"

Earnell, Gabby, and Keli would not ask any questions.
They would just sit, sobbing, their heads in their hands,
taking turns hugging me and welcoming me back. They
would carry this moment forever and understand deep
down, from the wade-in-the-water place, the tremendous
power of the beyond.

CHAPTER TWENTY-SIX

Everyone is watching me. The air buzzes with electricity as unblinking eyes wait in anticipation of my first words. The final theater performance. An original monologue.

———— • ◆ • ————

After nearly drowning, it was hard to finish preparing for the final theater performance. I was caught between worlds, both of which seemed stunningly real to me. I could not shake the serene memories of the ancestral realm. I yearn, even now, for the peace of that supernatural place. Jennifer says I had a "near-death experience." I raced to her office when I got out of the hospital to tell her all about it. "I've always believed some things transcend science," she says. "I am so happy you are still here."

Mine is the last monologue. We each had to write a performance piece that best "captured our essence" while also trying to connect to the audience. "Let them see who you really are," Professor Nielson urges.

I decide to dress like my higher self since I believe she is my true essence. I feel radiant and empowered. I can hear the audience still humming from the last performance, which got a standing ovation. Earnell, Gabby, and Keli watch from the front row. I have heard Earnell's larger-than-life laughter throughout the show. I imagine Gabby and Keli have been trying to quiet him down.

I can't see them, but I know Manda Panda, Alex, Bryce, Dean Yoda, and Jennifer are also somewhere in the crowd. Even Connor came to support my artistic expression. "Wouldn't miss it," he says, "and will keep following you like a creep until you agree to my proposal." Professor Alexander-Grant also comes after I bump into her on the Green. "Really great to hear you're doing well," she gleams. "I prayed for you."

"I know," I respond. "I know."

The stage manager gives me the final cue, dropping the curtains, as the Defiance huddles around me like a football team before a big game. *We're gonna raise the roof on this one, you feel me?* He pumps his palms toward the ceiling, remarkably offbeat imitating Manda Panda. *Bitch, you betta go out there and snatch they wigs, OK? Thine eyes hath seen the glory, hah. Deliver them to the promised land, sister.*

———•◆•———

I mail a copy of my first-year transcript to Mr. Walsh and sign it, "Here's me NOT flunking out of an Ivy League school." Luke triumphs again over Darth and his dark forces, false prophets, and nonbelievers. Long may she reign.

I manage three A's, an A-, and a B-, in Econ, of course. Keli, Earnell, Gabby, and I go back to Denny's for our final Grand Slams. The windows, open for real this time, welcome the gentle breezes of spring and now plausibly trigger Earnell's continued stream of tears. *I just can't believe we did it*, he wails.

———•◆•———

The curtain lifts. Showtime.

For the Keepers so loved the world

They gave all of their begotten daughters

To the realms of the living

But ain't I a woman?

Someone told me I had to save the world

They said I had to be strong, unbreakable,
superhuman to survive the madness

But who's gonna save the girl, after
she saves the world?

The Keepers permeate the room with their presence. I start to levitate from the stage, harnessed and hoisted by our stagehand. A risen Black phoenix at last. A halo of light surrounds me. It is so bright, like the tunnel, it submerges the entire audience.

My consciousness travels back to defining moments in my life to honor what has already been overcome: my first steps in the living room of that one-bedroom apartment, the whiskey man, all those sleepless nights studying until dawn, the inexplicable occurrences, and the final triumph of successfully completing finals. Standing on the other side of a year— of a life—I thought I would not survive, gratitude washes over me. I float higher into the air above the audience and the stage lights brighten intensely. I am glowing like an angel.

I curl the fingers of my left hand into Gyan Mudra, like my higher self from the mirror. Now I can't tell where she ends and I begin.

I answered the call and defeated the
God of Opposition

And it cost me everything I thought I knew.

I followed my heart to the depths of despair

And then to the peaks of bliss

Only to discover I was a woman,
human and vulnerable.

I come crashing down to the stage. A loud, sickening thud. The watchers gasp in fear. The rope attached to a hook above the stage released too soon. I struggle to climb to my feet, instead finishing the monologue from a cross-legged position, pressing my dress down between my legs. My knee bleeds from scraping roughly across the floor. Blood drips onto the black stage.

See, ain't I a woman?

If I bleed every time a stone is cast, ain't I a woman?

If the Joker can ride against me until insanity
prevails, ain't I a woman?

And if I can die, like every living soul that's
walked this earth, then ain't I a woman?

But this monologue is not about me.

My voice grows quiet, pregnant with vision and ambition.

It's for the ones who come next

A prayer for girls not yet born.

Please bow your heads and pray she finds mercy
in this unforgiving world.

Dear God

If there is a puddle, let her be helped over it.

If there are seeds to plant and earth to plough,
let every knee bend to help her.

If there is trouble in the water, let a
boat be built for her.

If her load is heavy, let her not have
to carry it alone.

For once, let her body not be stolen by evil intent.

If Christ returns, let him be a woman

For only the divine feminine grants life eternal,
birthing form from the infinite over and over.

A mercy She gives

A miracle She grants

Honor her

The Great Mother

The original Chosen One

But remember her humanity first and foremost

'Cause ain't I a woman, too?

The audience sits in stunned silence. Understanding takes several moments to arrive. When it does, an eruption of applause, hoots, and hollers.

And then, she rose.

CHAPTER TWENTY-SEVEN

Baker Library, empty and dark, looks eerie under the milky moonlight. I can't go home tomorrow without saying goodbye, for now, to Matthew. I stand on the Green in a kind of nostalgic shock. *How did the year pass so fast?* Flashes of final moments rain down over me.

Keli and I walk Gabby and Earnell to the bus, the Hanover Coach. They leave a day before us. We load all their luggage in the storage compartment and then stand in a circle trying to joke around.

"Ooo, let's sing 'Makidada' from *The Color Purple!*" Earnell blurts out. He is referring to the hand clapping and song Celie and Nettie sing to each other during the movie to strengthen their bond. It's especially important when they are forced to part since it's the last thing they say to each other.

"You are insane," Keli responds, "but let's do it."

We all start clapping hands and singing the song. "Me and you us never part, Makidada." It probably looks ridiculous from the outside, but it lightens the heaviness of the moment.

When it's finally time and the bus driver yells "All aboard!" we do a group huddle trying to soak in the essence of the spirits who have helped us survive this place. Gabby rushes onboard, overwhelmed by the moment. Of course we all understand her haste. Earnell walks slowly toward the stairs before turning around and saying, "Thanks for coming back." The doors close and as the bus drives off, Earnell flings himself against his window while launching into a final rendition of "Makidada" while clapping at the air. I have never witnessed a more "Earnell" moment, equal parts hilarious and thoughtful.

Jennifer prays for me in our final session. She asks permission first. "Are you comfortable with me saying a few blessings on your behalf?"

"I never turn down prayers," I say gleefully. "Especially not after hearing so many in the above plane. There was so much power up there."

She smiles her warm, white-lady smile one more time and begins: "Beloved, I pray that in all respect you may prosper. May she be in good health. May she know peace. May she find healing. May she summon the courage to face it. Ashe." I feel the love of her Lord coursing through my veins. The Holy Spirit ignites me. I stand and launch into a series of silly dances like the running man. I end by raising the roof, intentionally off beat, which is challenging for me, as an homage to Manda Panda.

"Oh, well, that was an interesting little display," she says, laughing uncomfortably, not sure how else to respond. "You seem so free and unburdened. A beautiful sight."

"I can't wait to come back next year and continue our work. Who knew I'd actually end up excited about therapy? Life comes at you fast." Jennifer suddenly grows weary, glances up at the clock, and looks directly into my eyes.

"You know, they tell you not to get attached when you do this kind of work. I am here to fill a role and you are my patient. It never works like that for me, though. I carry you all in my heart like a mother hen afraid to release her young before they are ready. I just want you to know it has been a tremendous joy to work with you, to witness your progress. I have no doubt you will continue to blossom in extraordinary ways."

"Why does it sound like you're saying goodbye? Won't you be here next year?"

"I only work with first-year students."

"But how am I supposed to

find my way without you? Where will you go?"

"Wherever I'm needed next," Yoda says. "I'm not sure yet."

"I haven't learned everything!"

"You've learned enough for this leg of the journey."

"You can't go," I say, dropping my head in sadness.

"Nothing can be held forever here. Where you end is not where you start. That's what matters. The space between. We had a good in-between space, you and I. Maybe we'll see each other again sometime. In another life, another reality. I would very much like that."

Dean Harrison smiles the way you do when you know you won't see someone again. It's a particular expression that sears the heart and pains the soul. We were together for a little while, but our time has passed. It happens so quickly, coming to love another person. One day you are strangers, the next they are part of you. Everyone you meet becomes part of you in some way, big or small. All those people define the tapestry of your experience in this world.

I lunge around the desk and hug Dean Harrison. I hold on for too long, but she doesn't force me to let go. She wraps her arms back around me this time. I walk silently toward the door, my body heavy with grief. I fight the tears, but they fall anyways. *I am alone again,* I think to myself.

"You are never alone," Dean Harrison says. "One more thing." Her voice cracks. "May the Force be with you, always."

Manda Panda wears black sunglasses during our final moments together to hide the sadness in her eyes. But her voice, which keeps cracking, gives it away.

"Let's take one last picture," she says. She angles the camera high above. Our young, still innocent but matured faces find the lens once more.

"You know you're never gonna be this young again," she says jokingly. "I'm getting Botox as soon as I see one crease. I'll fight the goddess of aging for as long as I can."

"I'm OK with getting older, I think," I tell her. "I don't wanna go backward. I like the new me."

"Cool, that's like super thoughtful and wise. Good for you."

"Aren't you going to take off your sunglasses?"

"No, bitch. I refuse to shed one more tear in this room."

She grabs the rest of her stuff and walks toward the door. "I wasn't kidding, you know. I love you." Her voice, infused with emotion, carries the bond of sisterhood. "I hope we can hang out next year."

She tries to rush out the door, but I propel myself forward and give her a hug. "I love you too," I respond, dissolving myself into the tenderness of the moment, without a shield, maybe for the first time in my life.

I assume Manda Panda is my last major goodbye, until Yoda finds me in Hollis Café earlier today. I hadn't seen her since parting ways in her office the day after my performance. I'm eating dinner alone, reflecting on what has passed and what is to come. I get up to return my tray and suddenly she is standing there behind me in silence with her strange Mr. Spock face. "Yoda!" I yell enthusiastically. "You really need to stop sneaking up on people. It's alarming.... I thought we'd already said goodbye."

"I know," she responds. "I was supposed to leave early this morning, but I couldn't leave without telling you that no matter what happens in your life, keep going, OK? Promise me you will?" I nod faithfully. "If you should lose your way, call on me. I will find you wherever you are. It's against protocol, but I can't seem to extract you from the corridors of my soul."

"Corridors of your soul! Who says that?"

She smiles, pats me on the shoulder as lovingly as she can muster, and turns to leave. She looks back and says, "Always." Then, like a leaf in the wind, she is gone. Even after all those lives, she still has trouble saying goodbye. Another testament to the interconnectedness of all living beings.

Now it's just me and Matthew sitting under the stars like it's our anniversary. This tower was one of the first reasons I decided to come here. When I saw it in the brochure in all its majesty and glory, I just knew Dartmouth was the place for me. It was a symbol of hope despite the obstacles. I think of all the other students Matthew will call from different creeds, races, religions, sexual orientations, and backgrounds around the country. *May they find the courage to listen to their hearts and choose the impossible journey*, I say quietly to myself.

I rename Matthew Obi-Wan Kenobi, which clearly conveys his role as the keeper of possibility for generations to come. "Until next year, Obi." I turn and make my way back to my room. "Wait!" I hear Obi call out behind me. "The road lies before you, Jedi, will you walk it alone?"

Before I can answer, the Defiance races toward me like ghetto superheroes. They are not alone—ancestors from far and wide make their presence known by whispering in the wind. Warriors of the fight that made all this possible for me in the first place: Dr. King, Malcolm, Dr. Angelou, Toni, Sojourner, and so many more. Earnell, Keli, and Gabby emerge next from my consciousness. I picture our gleeful reunion in the fall, ready to find new tutors and face the next round of not-so-insurmountable obstacles together. Jennifer and her prayers infuse my spirit once more. Yoda and her promise ring through me like one of Obi's bells. Lastly, I imagine my mother, brothers, and father rooting for me by imploring me to break every barrier they couldn't. *Challenge accepted*, I think to myself.

I glance up at Obi one last time and say, "Will I walk alone? Not with this many people behind me. A Chosen One never walks alone." His hourly bells ring, celebrating the growth of another Jedi master in training.

AFTERWORD

When I was ten or eleven, my father found an old type-writer on the street and brought it home. I became obsessed, spending hours writing short stories and poems. I was living in a one-bedroom apartment in one of the worst neighborhoods in Cleveland. But through writing, I learned to create different worlds and escaped into the frontiers of my imagination. This marked the awakening of the artist within me.

She didn't thrive for long, however. Soon, the pressure to focus on intellectual pursuits would smother the bur-geoning artist in my soul. I was accepted into the Cleve-land School of the Arts, but at the behest of my mother, I ended up going to a school that had honors classes instead. I believed the voices around me that warned studying art would never pay off. This sacrifice was the great turning point in my life, leading in a direction that would catapult me out of poverty, but it would not be my true calling. I would remain on that path for a decade.

My intellect sharpened. I reimagined myself as a social justice warrior. When I got to Dartmouth, I studied politi-cal science. I hated every class, but I pressed on. I interned for a Cleveland congresswoman in Washington, DC. I met Barack Obama when he was a junior senator. I believed I was on the right path, even as I grew more unhappy with my pursuits.

Quietly, in the shadows, my creative self rang bells from the grave. She whispered to me constantly, "Why don't you take a photography or drawing class?" I listened and became alive in those classes, yet I still didn't think art was for me.

When I graduated from Dartmouth, I became an investigator, looking into misconduct allegations against members of the New York City Police Department. It was intense and draining, but I felt like my work made a difference in the world. I then took another misstep into the field of journalism, which also proved to be the wrong fit.

I kept trying to figure out what might be wrong with me. It didn't help that I was also battling intense depression. The childhood trauma I had buried for so long finally came home to roost. I battled suicidal thoughts. *Why don't you just end it?* I felt lost and alone in the world.

In that moment, I had a choice to make. Give in to the pain—which was loud, thunderous, overwhelming—or try to see beyond it. I began taking spiritual development classes, searching for a wisdom that could help me transcend the heaviness of my situation.

What I discovered was that I was on the wrong path. I had forgotten that typewriter. I had forgotten how freeing it was to live animated by creative fire. I knew then: I had to answer the call. I abruptly changed my whole life and became an artist, writing and acting in a one-woman show to tremendous results. I had never done anything onstage before, but I got a standing ovation almost every single night for three years.

Suddenly, unexpected opportunities began emerging throughout the entertainment industry. But the momentum dissolved as quickly as it first came. I was left shaken, disoriented. How had I failed after such early success? It was in that space of confusion and despair I received a call from a young editor at Macmillan. She had read an article about me in the *Dartmouth Alumni Magazine* and thought I had something special to say. "You'd be such an inspiration to young people," she said.

Not once had I ever imagined writing books for young adults, and yet I was propelled forward by forces much bigger than me. I accepted her invitation to write my first book, *Black Girl Unlimited: The Remarkable Story of a Teenage Wizard*. In doing so, I made the biggest discovery of my life: my sense of purpose. It was now my job to mine the experiences of my life for nuggets of truth to inspire younger readers. It was my job to make sense of so much pain and strife, but also to recognize the many lessons, wisdom, and strength.

This is how my words have found their way to you. Through a combination of faith, honoring my inner voice, and bowing to forces beyond my control, I have reached the right path. I am doing exactly what I was called to do. My gratitude for this work is immeasurable. My connection to you, the reader, is prophetic and profound. I hope this book—the gift of my soul—inspires awakening in you also.

DISCUSSION GUIDE QUESTIONS

1. As one of the few Black students, Echo goes into her freshman year at Dartmouth feeling watched and judged by her peers. How does Echo try to combat the constant staring? How effective is her way of doing things?

2. Who are the Defiance to Echo, and why do you think they are portrayed as archetypes of people in the Black community?

3. Why is Echo so adamant about finding her white Prince Charming? What does her desperation to be romantically accepted by a white person mean for her own perceptions of her self-worth?

4. Echo constantly struggles with the belief that she doesn't belong anywhere and can never really be herself. In what aspects of her life do you see her using performance as a form of survival? What is the emotional toll on Echo of always portraying the opposite of what she's feeling or thinking?

5. Discuss Echo's relationship with Christianity. In what ways does she distance herself from religious belief? Do you think her standpoint on it changes by the end of the book?

6. What sorts of pressures does Echo feel as a first-generation college student? Why does she feel she cannot share what she has been going through at Dartmouth with her family back in Cleveland?

7. How does Echo's attitude toward seeking help shift? How does asking for help make you stronger? In what ways does Echo change when she opens herself up to accept support from others?

8. "So much sorrow and despair, with roots that go all the way down to the bottom of time. A line, a matrix of generational pain. A legacy of suffering. Inescapable" (p.186). This passage is speaking to generational trauma, meaning the pain inflicted on Echo's family in previous generations can have lasting impacts on current ones. View the outline on page 187 and discuss how the tragedies of those that came before Echo have manifested in Echo's own life.

9. Echo's story emphasizes the importance of growth and healing, whether through professional therapy or portal travel to alternate universes. How do these practices spark change within Echo, and what other examples of healing practices does she attempt throughout the book?

10. How would you define Echo's character development throughout the story? Do you believe she has unlocked her fully authentic self?

A NOTE FROM THE AUTHOR

To First-Generation College Students:

Like you, I was bright-eyed and hopeful on the eve of my ascent to higher education. Few in my family graduated high school. Then I came along with dreams and ambition way up in the stars.

Dartmouth in all her Ivy League glory promised there was a place for someone like me regardless of my background. It didn't matter that I had climbed up out of the dark underbelly of American society. In fact, it made me a more appealing candidate. Who was this girl that came from the shadows, where opportunity is scarce and potential is smothered by a succession of seemingly insurmountable obstacles?

There were those who believed in me all along, including the outstanding high school honors teachers who understood my gifts and spoke possibility into my fragile, uncertain mind. Their belief in me relieved some of the despair I felt growing up in poverty and convinced me I could rise above.

There were also nonbelievers and false prophets, like

the college counselor who told me it was better to do well at a third- or fourth-tier school than risk flunking out of the Ivy League. He was certain I wouldn't make it past my first quarter at Dartmouth. One of the biggest challenges first-generation students face is overcoming the false prophecies of nonbelievers. His was the loudest voice in my head, especially when I met a challenge I thought I couldn't transcend.

And there was God. The creator. The infinite. The beginning and the end, as it says in the Bible. My eyes were watching. Waiting. Wondering if he/she/they was going to grant the miracle or not. If I was going to be a Chosen One. Those mythical Horatio Alger people who rise from the dust and conquer unimaginable circumstances because they have no other choice.

"Steady," God would reply. "Forward. Many fields brimming with possibility lie ahead."

When I finally arrived at Dartmouth, I understood viscerally what I was up against. The energy of my spirit collapsed to a singular point of focus, which is what I've done my entire life. Focus. Not on all the privilege, wealth, racism, and sexism around me, but on the resources available at my disposal. Dartmouth was rich in opportunity and resources.

I leaned into professors and mentors who could see inside me and knew I couldn't fail. Professor Edlin, who told me I was lit from within. I didn't understand then. I do now. Professor Lenhart, who taught me to revere the written word. Were it not for his introductory English class, I may never have thought to become a writer. Professor Hamlin, a consummate artist, who taught me how to cultivate my own burgeoning artistic impulses. I did not think it was possible to be an artist before meeting her. President Wright, who spoke so passionately at my convocation about pushing Dartmouth in a direction that was more inclusive of minority students. I will never forget how welcomed his words made me feel. When I heard his speech, I knew I had made the right decision. Tommy Woon, who sheltered me with his calm, knowing spirit and introduced me to life-changing diversity workshops and programs along with Dawn Hemphill. Sadhana Hall, whose grace, wisdom, and brilliance showed me how to cultivate true internal power and stay lifted as a woman of color in a world stacked against you. The high school English teacher and her husband who drove me to Dartmouth, paid for my flights home on holidays, financially supported me when I studied abroad, and drove my mom to my graduation.

Casque and Gauntlet, the senior society I was inducted into my senior year, who became my community after three years of feeling out of place. I met some of the most amazing people I've ever known there. Skywalkers, like me, wanting a better world for all.

I would not have survived Dartmouth without these people.

My message to you is this: Your destiny is yours for the

taking, but you have to find the people that can help you survive it. Remember, a Chosen One never walks alone.

This journey was never meant for people like us. The proof is in the long lineage of ancestors in our families who have been beaten down and denied. Yet, here we are reaping the fruits of their sacrifice and efforts. Here we are standing on the other side of an oppression that can never murder our spirits.

Let no one tell you that you are not worthy. Let no one belittle or undervalue the enormity of your spirit. Let this be a reminder of the magnitude of what you have already overcome. May you decide to join the ranks of the Jedi and shine your light into the world. I hope you answer the call of your soul. I hope you do what you came here to do. I pray you never forget who you are, on the inside, and if you do, I pray you remember the way home.

May the Force be with you, always.

Love,
Echo

ACKNOWLEDGMENTS

There is no greater supporter of my work than my editor, Jessica Anderson. From the beginning, she knew my voice and experiences were uniquely suited for young readers. While I never imagined this path for myself, I can't think of a more noble and profound calling. Thank you, Jessica, for helping me realize such an important mission in my life. May the words continue to flow like water until the purpose is fully realized.

Macmillan was the home of my first book, *Black Girl Unlimited: The Remarkable Story of a Teenage Wizard*. I am deeply appreciative of the advocacy, commitment, and efforts their team put into launching *Black Girl Unlimited*. I could not have asked for a better introduction to the book community.

I am so grateful to have the constant support of Christy Ottaviano Books in publishing my work. Thank you to my publisher, Christy Ottaviano; my jacket artist, Noa Denmon; and the many gracious, passionate advocates I am lucky to have at Little, Brown Books for Young Readers: Megan Tingley, Jackie Engel, Emilie Polster, Stefanie Hoffman, Shanese Mullins, Jéla Lewter, Savannah Kennelly,

Marisa Russell, Sasha Illingworth, Victoria Stapleton, and Annie McDonnell.

Janine Kamouh, Sanjana Seelam, and Olivia Burgher at WME: Thank you for championing my work and preserving the creative soul of my words in our journey toward converting my books to the screen. I'm confident we will strike gold eventually.

Like so many others, I will remember 2020 as a year of loss. I lost my baby brother to a fentanyl overdose. He was thirty years old. The pulse of his spirit will forever beat inside of me and the stories I tell. I hope you are at peace, Demetrius Dante Brown. I hope you know now how much we love and adore you. I hope I see you at the crossroads so you won't be lonely.

My kidneys also failed that year due to lupus. At the time I was living in Paris, and a team of French doctors and nurses, few of whom spoke English, saved my life. My gratitude cannot be captured in words. May karma find you and weave an abundance of blessings into the fabric of your lives.

When it became clear that I would need a transplant, I returned to Cleveland. It was the only place where I knew love was waiting for me, which is what I needed most. I'll never forget the look in my parents' eyes when I returned from my travels, battered but not defeated. "Ecka back," they said. No other words were needed. My mother and father remain the only true home I have ever had in this world. Spending this precious time with them has given me so much joy through the strife. To my parents: may your forthcoming days be long and full for my and Lee's sake.

I will be thirty-seven by the time this book is released. The most important lesson I have learned so far is to give it your all, but be prepared to surrender to the great mystery of life. It cannot be controlled no matter how hard you try. Trust me, I tried really hard.

To my sweet kitty, Baba Baby, whose gentle and steady spirit has anchored me through the chaos, suit up: the next mission awaits.

ECHO BROWN

ECHO BROWN

is the award-winning author of *Black Girl Unlimited: The Remarkable Story of a Teenage Wizard*, which was named a William C. Morris Award Finalist, an *SLJ* Best Book of the Year, a New York Public Library Best Book of the Year, and a Rise: A Feminist Book Project Selection, among other honors. A performer and playwright, Echo created the acclaimed one-woman show *Black Virgins Are Not for Hipsters*. She is a Dartmouth alumna and the first female college graduate in her family. She invites you to visit her at echobrown.com.